diplomatic IMMUNITY

diplomatic IMMUNITY

BRODI ASHTON

BALZER + BRAY

An Imprint of HarperCollinsPublishers

Balzer + Bray is an imprint of HarperCollins Publishers.

Diplomatic Immunity

www.epicreads.com

Library of Congress Control Number: 2015051497

ISBN 978-0-06-236856-0 (hardcover)

Typography by Brad Mead

16 17 18 19 20   PC/RRDH   10 9 8 7 6 5 4 3 2 1

❖

First Edition

Dedicated to: My boys. Hi Carter! Hi Becks! *waves*
blows kisses *Carter gets embarrassed*
Becks yawns, unimpressed

diplomatic IMMUNITY

1

In seeking truth, you have to get both sides of a story. At least, that's what Walter Cronkite says.

He was the anchor who announced, on live national television, that President Kennedy had been assassinated. My gramma Weeza remembers exactly where she was when Cronkite made the announcement. She was in her kitchen, chopping onions. To this day, onions make her think of presidential assassinations. Sometimes, if I'm helping my mom cook, and Gramma Weeza is invited over, I'll purposely leave out the onions.

They have too much baggage for her.

Gramma Weeza says we all have those *Where were you when* blank *happened?* moments, and then the *blank* is usually something about when Pearl Harbor was bombed or when 9/11 happened or when the Beatles appeared on *The Ed Sullivan Show*.

Now I had one of those moments of my very own.

I was sitting in the living room, balancing a paper plate with a leftover taco on my lap, watching the nightly news. My mom had a talent for stretching leftovers into five-day territory. Even on day five, I still usually chose to eat the leftovers, because the other option was always instant ramen.

On the television, there was a press conference about a senator who had died in the arms of his mistress. It was a typical headline inside the Beltway of Washington, DC. My nine-year-old brother, Michael, wandered back and forth in front of the television, spinning a plastic hanger around his fingers, his gaze distant because he was in his own world. He was often in his own world.

My mom sat next to me, half watching the news and half folding laundry. She used to have a separate laundry room, with plenty of space for folding clothes, and even a midsize flat-screen TV on the wall for entertainment, but that was before the economy crashed and my dad's start-up folded, leaving him with massive debt. Now the "laundry room" is behind a plastic beveled folding door in the kitchen, and the "folding area" is on the couch in the living room. My mom called us a typical middle-class family, but I think she did that to make us feel better about our situation. We were barely clinging to the lower half of the middle class.

"Pipe, why don't you change the channel?" she said, using

her hand to flatten a collar on one of Michael's shirts. "This is so depressing."

"But it's news and it's the truth. We shouldn't be scared of the truth."

I turned back toward the television. The monitor showed the questionable woman who had been with the senator when he had taken his final gasps. (When I become a reporter, I will never shove a camera in the face of a mistress. That is so tabloid.) As the woman shook her head in front of the press corps, mascara tears streamed down her face, making her look even more like a prostitute. Is that uncharitable? Maybe so. I'd have to cut that out if I wanted to be unbiased.

The next video showed the press hounding the senator's wife, who insisted she'd had no idea of her soul mate's infidelity.

I shook my head. "Everyone in politics has something to hide, and if a senator hasn't been involved in a scandal, that's just because the skeletons in his closet haven't been discovered yet. The privileged always get into trouble. Rich people are bored people. And that equals trouble."

My mom sighed through her nose. "You're so cynical."

"Reporters are supposed to be cynical," I said. "That's how we get the dirt." I shoved another bite of leftovers into my mouth as I looked at my watch. I still had a half hour before my shift at the Yogurt Shop started.

The kitchen door opened and my dad walked in, looking war torn from his latest day at the Virginia Power and Light Company.

He used to be an investor in a company with a big contract to provide glass for smartphones. The problem was, most of his savings were tied up in stock, and he borrowed against it, so when the economy crashed, he lost everything. After that, he took what he could get: shift work at VP&L. He always said he felt safer with shift work.

I never understood how someone could start the day looking fine and end it looking as if he'd just been released by the Mexican drug cartel. He used to wear Armani and smell of Clive Christian cologne. Now he wore secondhand Men's Wearhouse and smelled of quiet resignation. But he still always managed a wide smile when he walked in the door.

"How are my people?" he asked.

My mom smiled even wider than he did. "Piper was just telling me how every politician is dirty."

He raised an eyebrow. "So, the usual?"

"Yep."

"It's not me saying it," I said. "It's the news."

My dad plopped the mail down on the kitchen table, and that's when I saw it. The large white envelope with the red Chiswick Academy insignia in the corner.

I drew in a breath as my stomach fluttered. "That's it," I said.

"That's what?" my mom asked.

I nodded toward the table. The rest of my body was frozen in anticipation. "Large envelope. Third from the top. Under the *Economist*."

My dad made a move to reach for it.

"Don't touch it!" I blurted out. "Sorry. I'm just nervous. Go ahead and touch it. But don't open it." I sighed. "Never mind. Open it. Not yet, though."

I realized I had stopped eating my taco midchew. I didn't mean to be so dramatic. It was just that senior year had started a month ago and I'd given up hope.

My dad picked up the letter delicately with two fingers, as if it were a bomb. "Is this okay?" he said, one corner of his mouth turned up.

I nodded.

My mom set down the shirt she'd been folding. "Odds are the school wouldn't waste time writing you a letter if you *didn't* get the scholarship."

"Who knows what a school like that does?" I said, my voice noticeably higher than usual. "It's Chiswick Academy. Seven-to-one student-to-teacher ratio. Forty-one countries represented in the student body. A faculty full of doctorates. And home to the Bennington Journalism Scholarship." I said the last part with reverence, resisting the urge to put my hand over my heart. Winning the Bennington would mean a free ride to the school of my choice. No more hand-me-downs. No more leftovers.

My mom raised an eyebrow.

"I memorized the brochure," I explained.

"If you're not going to open it, I will," my dad said.

I nodded. "And while you do, I'm going to eat my taco and

act like I don't care."

"Well, then we have a plan." My dad ripped the end of the envelope as I swallowed my bite of taco. He smiled as he read the first sentence. "You're in," he said.

And that's why I will forever associate tacos with the end of life as I knew it.

I felt the bite of ground beef make its way down my esophagus and toward my stomach, and I wondered if the tacos at Chiswick would taste the same as the ones at my current school or if they would taste unfamiliar and elite. Or maybe Chiswick Academy didn't even serve plain old tacos. Maybe they served something hoity-toity like tofu tacos. And maybe they called them "tofacos."

I couldn't wait to find out.

That night, I worked my usual shift at the Yogurt Shop with my best friend, Charlotte. We were also coeditors in chief at the school paper. When I got the job at the Yogurt Shop, she applied too, I think for fun. I thought of telling her about the Chiswick scholarship, but as I opened my mouth to do so, she raised a cup of frozen yogurt and said, "To the best coeditors Clarendon High has ever seen! Together forever!"

She always made toasts like that as an excuse to eat free yogurt. Nevertheless, I filled a cup and clinked with her, and decided to keep the news that we might not be together forever to myself, at least for the weekend.

The front doorbell rang, and we put down our cups as a man walked in.

"Chocolate milk shake," he said.

Charlotte nodded and made the order, and when he put a dollar bill into the tip jar, I groaned. The label on the jar said, "Will sing for tips," so any time we got a tip, we had to sing a song.

"Your turn," Charlotte said.

I sighed and proceeded to sing "There's No Yogurt Like Our Yogurt" to the tune of "There's No Business Like Show Business," and dreamed of the day I would win the Bennington and never have to sing for tips again.

2

The following Monday morning, Charlotte and I were hunched over the layout for the front page of our school paper, the *Clarendon Community Gazette*. We were arranging the placement of the cover story, an exposé about nonrefrigerated times for the lunchroom mayonnaise. But I wasn't focusing as I should have been. I was working up the nerve to tell Charlotte about the scholarship.

When I left for Chiswick next week, Charlotte would have the editor in chief job to herself, but I knew she would rather share the job and work as a team. I took a deep breath.

"So, Char, I've got some news."

"Perfect." She smiled. "We just so happen to be in a newsroom."

"I got the scholarship to Chiswick." I took in a breath.

"What?" Charlotte looked up from the layout.

I nodded, feeling a little pit in my stomach that I was abandoning her. "I got the scholarship."

"But it's October."

"One of the scholarship students must have dropped out or something. The point is, I'm starting there Monday."

"Wow," Charlotte said, her hands gripping the stylus as if this news might throw her off balance. "Top story, team coverage. But what about the paper? What about school? What about . . ." Charlotte gasped in dismay, as if Barry Manilow had just canceled a concert. She loved him more than anything. It was the weirdest thing about her. "The Schmulitzer?"

The "Schmulitzer" was Mr. Peters's version of the Pulitzer. The student with the best-reported story of the year would win a cheap plastic trophy, and also a letter of recommendation and résumé packet assembled by Mr. Peters himself.

"Well, now you have a clear path to the most prestigious award in the entire boundaries of Clarendon High." I bowed toward her and made a circular gesture with my hand.

"Nobody likes to win by default," Charlotte said. She frowned.

"Are you all right?" I asked.

"It's okay," she said. "I'll be fine." She studied the layout so closely, I was afraid she'd impale her eye on the stylus.

Right then, Jorgé Robles came over to our desk. "Hey, Piper, do you have any contacts at the dog pound? I'm doing a story on—"

"Paul Jensen," I said, cutting him off. I pulled out my phone and sent the contact info to Jorgé. "Ask him about his eclectus parrot. That always gets him talking."

I turned back to Charlotte, who seemed to be blinking back tears. The sight pricked at my eyes. So I resorted to the only surefire way to coax her out of her funk. I switched my phone to camera mode and then to film, and turned the lens on her.

"Charlotte Giovanni, you've won the Schmulitzer Prize, despite what some might call insurmountable odds."

It was a game we liked to play, the Joyce Latroy Game. Joyce Latroy was a talk show host notorious for making everyone who came on her show cry. She even made the ousted dictator of Libya tear up when she mentioned his boyhood dog, Giaque.

The rules of the game were simple: first person to laugh was the loser.

"Your father was an alcoholic," I said in a low, grave voice. "Your mother lost one of her legs in the war and the other in a freak toaster oven incident. The money your family received in the toaster settlement was stolen by your mailman."

Charlotte nodded solemnly. "That bastard. We never should've hidden the money in our mailbox in the first place, but still, that bastard."

I felt my lips twitch.

"But the tragedy didn't end there," I said. "You wrote in your memoir about a humiliating incident with a kebab stick . . ."

Charlotte pressed her lips together.

I continued. "Your uncle made you chicken kebabs for your fourteenth birthday. But when you went to raise the kebab to your mouth, you missed your lips completely and impaled your left eye."

Charlotte nodded, her lips trembling. "The other kids made so much fun of me. They would stand behind me and tap my back and then move to my left."

I knew I almost had her. "To add insult to injury, your father then gambled away your other eye."

That was it. She spit-laughed. But it didn't count as a win, because I laughed too.

Out of the corner of my eye, I saw a freshman, Scott Summerdorf, hovering.

I kept my eyes on the layout. "Scott! Stop loitering. What do you need?" I frowned deeply and caught Charlotte's lips twitching out of my side view. Mr. Peters had warned Charlotte and me that we could be intimidating to the younger reporters. But his news hadn't had the effect he'd intended. It just made us torture them a little bit more.

Scott stared at his feet. "Um, I'm supposed to interview the janitor, but he's, like, playing deaf."

I sighed. "Start the conversation by telling him how annoyed you get when the students don't dump their own trays. His temporary deafness will subside."

Scott stood there for a moment more, probably wondering if it was safer to thank me or to just stop talking. I decided to put him out of his misery.

"You're excused."

He all but ran out of the room.

"You're terrible," Charlotte said with a smile.

"I know." I raised the camera again.

"My turn." Charlotte tried to reach for the camera, but I shook my head. If there was one thing I was really bad at, it was being on camera. I had this stupid nervous tic where my mind would go blank and my mouth would stammer. I also had this overblinking problem.

"Please? Just once?" Charlotte said. "Our last days together must be documented."

"You're the one who wants to be on camera. This is good practice." Print reporters are rarely seen, except for a favorable head shot next to the byline.

Charlotte sighed. "Fine. Piper Baird. You've just found out you've been awarded a scholarship to the prestigious Chiswick Academy."

I let the camera sink. "Wait. We don't address real subjects."

"Don't interrupt Joyce Latroy!"

I frowned and raised the camera back up to my eye. Joyce could be so demanding.

"Yes, you'll miss out on the Schmulitzer, but you gain the chance to win the Bennington Scholarship, an opportunity many of us would give Mr. Peters's right arm for."

"I heard that, Miss Giovanni," Mr. Peters said from his desk at the front of the room.

It was quiet for a few long moments, save for the clicking and clacking of students finishing up their edits. Charlotte had an uncle who worked at *People* magazine. She wanted to be just like him, except the television version. I knew Charlotte would've killed for the chance I was being given.

"What if I fall flat on my face?" I said softly.

"What if you do?" Charlotte said.

I closed my eyes and took a deep breath. "Well, Joyce," I said. "You know what my father used to say every time I fell down. . . ."

"What's that?" Charlotte said.

"He'd say, 'Son, why do we fall down?'"

"I think that was Batman's father," Charlotte said.

"Oh. Right. Well *my* father always said, "With great power comes great—"

"That's Spider-Man's uncle," Charlotte said.

"Hmmm . . ." I put my finger on my lips like I was thinking really hard. "What *did* my father ever say?" I thought about my real father, and what he had told me when he was facing a difficult raise negotiation at VP&L. "Oh, yeah. He said, 'Don't be afraid to live on your edges. That's where you'll find the truth.'" My dad was always saying stuff like that. He was like a walking platitude.

"I have just one more question for you."

"Shoot."

"What is your best friend going to do without her most kin-dred soul?"

I frowned and reached over to pat her leg. I would miss see-ing her every day. I shook my head and pushed the sadness back to the special compartment in my brain labeled "Painful stuff that I'm not ready to deal with now. Or maybe ever." It was a large section of my mind—probably because I was always put-ting stuff in and never taking stuff out.

"Just promise me you won't become one of *them*," Charlotte said.

I knew the "them" Charlotte was referring to. The privileged elite, who made up the other 95 percent of the student body at Chiswick. The nonscholarship part. The part that came with chauffeurs and nannies and silver platters and no side jobs.

I'd had a job ever since my first paper route at age twelve. By the time I was sixteen, I'd earned just enough to buy a ten-year-old Toyota Corolla.

"I promise," I said. "I won't change one bit."

We stood there awkwardly for a moment. I wasn't sure where to go next, but Charlotte pulled me over to a laptop in the corner.

"I think we need a little bit of Post-Anon," she said.

Post-Anon was our guilty pleasure. It was a website full of postcards that people sent in anonymously, revealing their deep-est, darkest secrets. Things they would never dare tell anyone else but had to say somewhere.

Light things like:

I rationalize my Fig Newton binges because they are vegetarian.

And darker things like:

I fear something horrible happened to me as a child that I've blocked out and that my parents keep from me.

And:

I love you more than anyone I've ever known, but I still wish I'd never met you.

We always said someday we would send in a secret, but not until we had a really good one. Maybe I'd find one at Chiswick.

That Saturday, my gramma Weeza invited me over for coffee to celebrate. We sat in her tiny kitchen as she poured fresh brew into a mug in front of me and another one for her. She put a few drops of cream in the coffee, then added one . . . two . . . three spoonfuls of sugar.

"When," I said, putting my hand out.

"Sorry, is that too much sugar? That's the Danish in me."

She always said that. Her own grandma came to America from Denmark in the late 1800s, and if there's one thing those Danes like, it's their sugar. Either that or Gramma Weeza just liked it and wanted to blame her addiction on an entire nation.

"How's the plumber?" I said. Grandma had been seeing a plumber for a few months now, and by "seeing," I mean they bowled in the same league two nights a week.

"Oh, he's seasoned but sturdy," she said. "And if my pipes

ever get clogged . . . Know what I mean?" She did this exaggerated wink.

"Ugh, Gramma."

"Well, dear, just because we're old doesn't mean we don't have pipes."

"Gramma!" I said, squeezing my eyes shut. "I prefer to picture you bowling. Not . . . cleaning each other's pipes."

"All right, have it your way. We'll talk about bowling." She grinned mischievously. "And I'll tell you, he can sure knock down my pins."

"Gram! How do you make even bowling sound dirty?"

"It's a talent, dear." Gramma refreshed my coffee and added another spoonful of sugar. "Now tell me, what have you been up to?"

I shrugged. "The usual. Reporting on stuff. Uncovering truths. You would not believe how the lunch ladies handle mayonnaise."

"I'm referring to life outside the paper."

"Is there . . . ? Life . . . outside . . . ," I joked.

She laughed.

"I'm all for fun, but I'm not going to do anything to mess up my chance at college."

"I know, dear. I've heard."

That night, as I was watching the evening news, I made a chart documenting every time the anchors dropped the "to be" verb.

It happens when they try to sensationalize a headline, like "DC Residents Waking Up to Icy Roads Today," or "Government Employees Feeling the Pinch." They said them as if they were complete sentences. But they weren't, because there was no "are."

It was a new trend in reporting, and I didn't like what it was doing to the English language and the rules of basic grammar.

When the news was over, I got a text from Charlotte.

Charlotte: Male anchor, 22 drops. Female anchor, 17. Because girls are awesome.

Me: Much awesomer than boys.

Monday morning, I reached into my closet and took out my blue cardigan, then threw it on the floor. Too dowdy. I flung out the floral shirt I'd modified from the Salvation Army. Too obvious. I appraised the green skirt that I'd updated from a donation from Gramma Weeza. . . . I threw it over my shoulder.

"Hey!" Michael's voice came from behind me.

I turned to see the green skirt on top of Michael's head.

"Sorry, bud."

"Why are you throwing green clothes?" Michael asked, as if he was personally offended for the color green.

"I'm just trying to go through my closet." I settled on a red sweater and a gray T-shirt. I assessed the look in my mirror.

"This'll have to do," I muttered.

"It will have to do what?" Michael said.

"My outfit, bud."

"What will it have to do?"

"It will have to do . . . fine."

He shrugged and walked away.

Chiswick Academy wasn't a very far drive. I lived in Arlington, Virginia, and Chiswick was in DC, which basically meant it was across the Potomac River. But when the school came into view, I thought I'd entered the nineteenth century. It looked like a Southern plantation out of *Gone with the Wind*. I followed the other cars up Cathedral Avenue and pulled into a cement roundabout, my Toyota sticking out among the dozens of long black sedans. Several of them were limousines with colorful flags sticking upright above the headlights.

The parking lot was only about a quarter full. At my old school, I had to arrive early to get a good spot, but at Chiswick, most students clearly had drivers. I was probably parked by the faculty and any other scholarship students who'd bought their own junky cars.

I stared at the students milling about in front of the main doors. They looked . . . different. I couldn't exactly explain why; but something I couldn't pinpoint made them seem more sophisticated. Their clothes were sleek. Their hairstyles seemed about two trends ahead of those at Clarendon. It all made them seem exotic. Older.

I glanced down at my red cowboy boots, and really noticed for the first time the cracks showing near the toes and around the ankles. Tiny flecks of red dye were peeling off the sides. I might as well have been wearing a billboard that said, *Outsider here. Do not engage.*

But really, what was the point of dressing nicely? My clothing choices wouldn't affect my scholarship.

I cut the engine just as the gas light came on. I wasn't sure where the money for the next fill-up would come from. I'd have to focus on the tip jar at the Yogurt Shop.

Right at that moment, the dark clouds that had earlier seemed so far off now blotted out the sun. As the first raindrops splashed on my windshield, I pulled my hood up and opened the door, acutely aware that I was taking my first official step toward the Bennington Scholarship. My ticket. My free ride. I tried not to think about it for my second and third and fourth steps, because that would seem obsessive, but I couldn't help it. My breath made cloudy puffs in the air, which should've been a sign of what was about to happen, but I had scholarship on the brain.

I was almost to the steps in front of the doors when the smooth bottoms of my cowboy boots slipped and I careened sideways into the rosebushes, ass first.

"Owwwww," I said. "Effing freezing rain!"

A dark hand shot into the bushes. *"¿Estás bien?"*

"Qué?" I said in response, using the one word I remembered from seventh-grade Spanish. "Um . . . *oui.*"

A chuckle came from somewhere above. "It's okay. I speak French, too."

"That makes one of us," I said. I grabbed the hand, and whoever it belonged to pulled me out of the bushes. When I was once again upright, I looked at the hand's owner.

And tried to keep my mouth from dropping open.

3

Standing before me was the most exotic, rugged, beautiful piece of personhood (of the male variety) I'd ever seen. I always got wordy in my head when I was caught by surprise, and the guy in front of me looked like the type who constantly caught girls by surprise. He must walk around thinking it was normal for people to pant. Tall, brown hair, gorgeous skin that covered his whole body, top to bottom . . . Ah, crap, was I panting?

It took me a while to realize I was having this whole inner monologue right in front of him, but I had yet to say anything out loud.

"Uh, thank you." I tore my eyes away and brushed some leaves off my shirt.

"Are you okay?" he asked, his voice rich and layered, with a Spanish accent.

I took a mental assessment of my body. "Yes, only my pride is wounded."

He tilted his head and scratched his chin. "Hmmmm. That being the case, I hesitate to share some news with you regarding your appearance."

My hands flew to my face. "What's wrong? Do I have dirt on my cheeks? Are there rose petals in my hair? Oh my gosh, is it a booger?"

At the sudden movement of my hands, a man in a dark suit, with sunglasses and a coiled wire hanging from his ear, shuffled closer to the guy in front of me, like a Secret Service agent. Wait, this was Chiswick. He probably *was* Secret Service. So who was this boy in front of me? Why did he need protection? Was it from the likes of me?

The boy put his hands out, palms down. "Calm yourself, it's not a . . . *booger.*" He said it as though it was a foreign word to him, which it probably was.

"A booger is in this region," I said, circling my finger around my nose.

He suppressed a laugh. "No, the problem is more . . . in the Southern Hemisphere."

He seemed to be working hard to keep his eyes on mine. I looked down and caught a glimpse of familiar pink satin peeking through a fresh tear in my blue jeans right next to the front zipper.

I was wearing pink underwear.

"Ohmygosh," I said. My hands flew to my crotch, but which would be worse? The new girl with the tear in her crotch? Or the new girl who couldn't stop touching herself?

Other students filed past as if this were something they saw every day. "Desperate," one of them said. I couldn't see which one. My face burned.

The guy reached out for my hand. "Here. Follow me." He paused. "Closely."

I didn't have much choice. First off, he was very strong. Second, he was blocking the view to my nether regions. Maybe I did look like a desperate scholarship student, but it was worth hiding the view. He dragged me behind him and kept me close.

"Just act normal," he said.

"Sure. Normal. Because whenever I walk anywhere, I always spoon the person in front of me."

He chuckled, a rich, smooth sound that didn't resemble the word "chuckle"—it sounded more like "*chocolat*," pronounced as the French do.

Thank goodness he couldn't hear thoughts. At least, he *probably* couldn't, unless he had superpowers. The man in the dark suit followed, about ten feet away.

"Since we're basically twerking, shouldn't we at least know each other's names?" I said, gasping a little for breath. "I'm Piper."

"Pipper?" he said as he darted around a group of students. "Nice to meet you. I'm Raf."

"It's not 'Pipper'—"

"You prefer just 'Pip'?"

I sighed. Maybe we should wait to discuss personal details until we had only the language barrier and not the wardrobe malfunction to deal with. Raf led us through the main entrance, down one hallway and then another, and finally to a darker corridor that looked as if it hadn't been used since the Civil War.

"This is the least crowded toilet," he said.

I raised my eyebrows. "This is a horror movie waiting to happen."

He cracked a smile and pulled me toward one of the swinging doors. I could barely make out the remnants of a blue stick figure with a skirt painted on it.

Raf pushed through it and motioned me inside. "After you."

"Wait, *you're* coming in too?"

The man in the dark suit stepped closer. Raf held up his hand.

"Fritz, you cannot come in the girls' bathroom. Remember what Papa said about not embarrassing me?"

I raised my hand. "What about embarrassing *me*?"

Raf pointed to his backpack. "I have the answer to your problem in here. Trust me."

Before I could ask why in the world I would trust him, he pulled me inside and let the door swing shut behind us.

I thought about my recent decisions. In the course of ten minutes, I'd fallen into a thorny bush, torn my pants in an unmentionable spot, and then allowed a complete stranger to drag me to . . . What was this place? The Restroom of Getting Shivved?

"You look scared," Raf said. "I told you I have something that can help." He swung his backpack up onto the counter and opened the zipper.

Please don't be rope. Or a gag. Or chloroform. Or a drink laced with a roofie.

He dug around and produced a roll of duct tape.

Or duct tape, I thought.

"Duct tape fixes everything," he said.

"What?"

"Duct tape. It fixes everything. That's what my grandmama always told me."

I smiled. "My gramma Weeza says the same thing. Whenever I get a hole in the heel of my socks, she puts duct tape over it. She says it buys you an extra month of wear." I had a drawer full of duct-taped socks to prove it.

"Your grandma is a smart woman," Raf said.

I doubted someone like Raf had ever had to duct-tape socks in his life. He probably had a new pair each morning.

He peeled off a strip of the tape and ripped it, then handed it to me. "Overlap the two sides of the tear. Then put the duct tape on the inside. It will give you a little bit of time until you can get a needle and thread."

I held up the tape on my finger. "That's what all this superspy stuff was for? A square of duct tape?"

He raised his eyebrows. "You have something in *your* back-pack that will hold it together?"

He had a point there. I ducked behind the door of one of the stalls and did as instructed.

"So, you seriously walk around with a roll of duct tape in your backpack?" I said from the safety of the stall.

"Well, it was left over from an experiment last week."

"What kind of experiment?" Zipping up my jeans, I emerged from the stall and checked out my repair job in the mirror. No pink underwear to be seen, and the tear was barely noticeable.

"The very important experiment of seeing if we could duct-tape Chiswick Academy's smallest cheerleader to the wall."

I stared at him for a long moment.

"It turns out you can," he said. "But the amount of duct tape used is proportionate to the weight of the subject you would like to attach to the wall." He explained this as if he were debriefing a room full of scientists.

"You duct-taped a cheerleader to a wall?" I asked.

"Yes. But it wasn't without her permission, if that's what you're worried about."

At this point, I wasn't sure what I was worried about. There were so many things.

"And now, Pip, since I have helped you," he said, "I was wondering if you might be so kind as to return the favor." His expression was super innocent, which made me super skeptical.

"How? You . . . person who tapes random cheerleaders to walls. How can I help you?"

"One cheerleader, and she was by no means randomly chosen." Raf glanced at the door. "I'm a little parched, and I'd like to procure some libations, but I have this . . . constant companion."

My mouth dropped open. "You want me to help you ditch your security detail so you can get booze?"

He scoffed. "You make it sound so pedestrian."

I sighed and then thought about it for a moment. He *had* helped me. And it was just booze. For him, not me. "What would I need to do?" I asked.

"One of two things," Raf said. "The first, less fun, way is to provide a distraction while I climb out the window."

I glanced at the window near the top of the ceiling. It looked like it hadn't been opened in centuries.

"A distraction? Like you want me to blow something up?"

"I was thinking more like you could run down the hall screaming, 'Fire.'"

I frowned. "That doesn't sound fun at all. What's the 'more fun' way?"

This time his expression was decidedly mischievous. "Well, Fritz out there gets ruffled when in the presence of romantic liaisons. He is new to my security detail, you see. If we were to exit the toilets while kissing—"

I smacked my forehead. "Oh. My. God."

"He would probably turn away, which would give me time

to run out the side door. Provided, of course, that you can still make the kissing sounds and perhaps a soft moan here and there to throw him off."

I pointed my finger toward his chest. "You are exactly the type of person I plan on avoiding here. I want to get into Columbia. I want to be a journalist. And I'm not going to let some Don Juan Casanova get in my way."

"'Casanova?' Did you grow up in the nineteen thirties?"

"You're a casanova," I said definitively.

"A casanova who saved your honor today."

"By dragging me to a secluded bathroom! On my first day!" I closed my eyes and shook my head, and when I opened them I gave him what I hoped was a determined look. "Raf, it was nice to meet you. Thank you for the duct tape. I will repay you by buying you a new roll. Not by kissing you."

As I walked toward the door, he glanced up at the ceiling. "This is what I get for helping the less fortunate."

"Who says I'm less fortunate?" I asked, indignant.

He just shrugged. It was probably written all over me. Not to mention the fact that I'd just admitted I get more wear out of socks by using duct tape.

I sighed, determined not to say anything else, and pushed through the swinging door, where Fritz was standing guard.

"You'd better go in before your boy slips out the window," I said. I turned to search for signs leading to the front office and nearly ran into a woman in a brown pantsuit.

"What are you doing here?" she said, her eyes narrowed.

I was suddenly at a loss for words. "I . . . I fell, and then there was a tear . . . and I'm new here."

"What's your name?"

"Piper Baird."

"New or not, I assume you can read?"

"Yes," I said, not sure if the question was rhetorical.

"Then I can also assume you simply chose to disregard the numerous signs forbidding entrance to this hallway."

"I . . ." I fell silent, not sure how to explain that I didn't see the signs because I was glued to the backside of the tall boy in front of me.

"Welcome to Chiswick, Miss Baird. Enjoy detention."

4

"What?" I'd never had detention before. Never ever. I started to hyperventilate. There went the bullet point on my college résumé that said I'd never been sent to detention. I loved that bullet point.

The restroom door behind me squeaked open, and the woman in front of me tugged at the bottom of her jacket.

"Mr. Amador," she said.

Mr. Amador? I looked over my shoulder expecting to see a professor, but it was just Raf.

He gave Mean Pantsuit Lady a killer smile. "Ms. Wheaton, I'm sorry. It's my fault Pip is in this hallway. She had a wardrobe incident that would have been embarrassing had anyone else seen her. She doesn't deserve detention."

I nearly snorted at his audacity, speaking to an authority fig-ure like he had any power to change her mind.

But Ms. Wheaton nodded. "Very well. Get to class, both of you." She walked away at a clipped pace, her sensible heels click-ing on the floor. She didn't get very far before I called out to her, "What? We both broke the rules. We should both have deten-tion. *Both* of us."

She turned on her heel slowly and narrowed her eyes. "I was prepared to let you both go. But if you want detention so badly, Miss Baird, you've got it. After school. The Potomac Room." She produced a yellow notepad from her pocket, wrote my name on the top page, tore it off, and handed it to me. Then she stalked away.

My eyebrows crinkled. "What just happened?" I asked.

"I believe you were about to owe me two favors, but then you basically asked the Beast for detention."

"The Beast?"

"That's what we call Ms. Wheaton. She's the assistant prin-cipal," Raf said.

"I'm more interested in why she didn't give you detention with me in the first place," I said emphatically.

"So you *want* detention with me?" He raised an eyebrow.

"No!" I lowered my voice back down to calm levels. "I'm just saying we both should've received the same punishment for breaking the rules."

He looked at me as if I weren't too bright. "She wouldn't

punish me. She knows who my dad is."

"Who's your dad?"

"The Spanish ambassador to the United States."

"Oh," I said. That explained the security detail. "That's impressive, but doesn't everyone here have a powerful parent?"

He leaned toward me and said in a low voice, "My father is also scary."

"*My* dad can be scary too. He can be totally scary. Especially when his union is threatened with new overtime guidelines." I shook my head at how stupid and nonscary that sentence was.

He smiled. "My father gets people fired."

I sighed. "We still should've had the same punishment."

The corner of his mouth quirked up in a way that probably came from hours of practice, perfecting the smolder. "You're cute."

"What?"

He ignored me. "Welcome to Chiswick, Pip. Where some of us don't get punished." He gave me a confident grin, as if he didn't grasp the gravity of my outrage.

"I have to go," I said.

I wadded the detention slip in my fist and followed the signs to the front office. I really hoped someone would have a needle and thread. This was my favorite pair of jeans.

This was my *only* pair of jeans.

* * *

As I walked away from Raf, I finally noticed the school itself. I couldn't get over the marble in this place. Clarendon High was all industrial tile and cinder-block walls. But Chiswick Academy? Marble floors, marble banisters, marble walls. Portraits of prestigious men in tuxedos and women in pantsuits, with gold plates on the frames noting their achievements. I didn't know whether the paintings were of donors or graduates or the board of directors, but they all looked down on me and my peeling cowboy boots and duct-taped jeans.

I checked in at the office and the secretary printed up my schedule and my locker assignment, and although she didn't have a needle and thread, she did give me a safety pin. As I left, an electronic gong sounded, which meant five minutes until class. I hurried to the bathroom, replaced the duct tape with the safety pin, and then tracked down my locker.

The one to the left of mine was open. A girl with long black hair was standing in front of it, rifling through what looked to be a series of drawers and shelves that seemed custom-made. I glanced around at other open lockers. Many of them had similar custom carpentry inside. Others had jeweled mirrors. Minifans blowing. Electronic displays of nature scenes and weather forecasts. Paintings. Real ones, not prints.

I turned the dial on my locker. What would I find inside mine? A butler, perhaps? The crown jewels? A personal masseuse?

I pulled the door open, and found . . . nothing. Just an empty shelf and metal walls.

The girl on my right had a simple calendar and a framed picture of herself and two people I assumed to be her parents hanging on her door. Nothing spectacular. "What's with the other lockers?" I said.

She grimaced. "Locker bling. Parents get a day before school to 'decorate'"—she used air quotes—"their kid's locker. It's a tradition, although it's gotten out of hand. And usually it's not parents. It's servants."

"Why isn't your locker 'decorated' like theirs?" I said, using air quotes again.

"Scholarship," she said. "I have no servants. My actual parents decorated mine. I'm guessing you're scholarship too?"

I nodded.

"It's not like my parents don't have better things to do than 'bling' as a verb," she said.

I laughed.

"My name's Una," she said.

"Piper," I said.

"What's your first class?"

I checked my schedule. "Chemistry?"

"Me too. I'll show you the way."

I sat next to Una in class. She leaned over several times during the lecture to whisper page numbers. Raf Amador was sitting at the front of the room. His hand shot up each time the professor asked a question. Rich and hot, and now smart. Some things were so not fair.

Una caught me staring at him.

"That's Rafael Amador," she said.

"I met him this morning," I whispered.

"His locker is stocked with Pellegrino every day. Orange, lemon, and plain."

"Of course it is," I said.

Raf's security detail, Fritz, was standing silently against the wall, looking dark and forbidding and ready to tackle students if necessary.

English was next. We'd be reading a classic book each month, which seemed daunting, given the time I'd spend on the paper and at my yogurt job.

Gym was the only part of Chiswick that seemed comparable to my old school. Same wooden floor, same expectations for coordination. Coach Lambourne dragged out a net of basketballs and told us to divide up into teams of three. Everyone seemed to immediately clump together. I glanced around nervously and then made my way toward a tall, lanky girl in hand-me-down shoes. I figured she was scholarship too. I'd recognize hand-me-downs anywhere.

"I'm Piper," I said.

"Julia," she said. "Basketball scholarship."

"I'm *scholarship* scholarship."

She nodded as if she could already tell.

"What position do you play?" she asked.

"I don't," I said.

She frowned. "Can you set a screen?"

"Is that a basketball term?"

She laughed. "Stick with me." A blond girl joined us and we passed the ball around us until Coach Lambourne called us to attention and began the three-on-three matchups. It was a disaster, but at least I could say I'd scored for the opposite team. Twice.

I spent lunch hour in orientation, where I learned how to use the lunchroom credit cards and where not to park my crappy Corolla.

By economics, I'd started to realize something. The only people who had acknowledged my existence, or my newness, had been other scholarship students. The rest had ignored me. I hated to judge a school by its cover, but there seemed to be a pattern developing here that had nothing to do with IQ.

By the time journalism rolled around at the end of the day, my bag was heavy with books and notes, and my brain was heavy with class divide, but nothing could erase my anticipation.

The entrance to the journalism class was right by a painting of a woman named Hilda Reginald, founder of Reginald Assembly Hall, platinum donor. She glanced sideways as I walked in, as if to say, *Are you sure you belong here?*

"No," I answered her, stopping in front of the portrait. "No, I'm not sure I do."

"Did you just talk to a painting?" someone whispered in my ear.

Standing behind me was Rafael Amador. Making fun of me. Again.

"Yes," I said defiantly. "But at least it didn't answer back." As if that proved my sanity.

"Whatever you say, Pip," he said with a smirk as he walked away.

I rolled my eyes and entered the state-of-the-art newsroom of the *Chiswick Academy Journal* and *Chiswick Academy News* and instantly forgot my annoyance with Rafael Amador because this was heaven. My heaven. This was what three years of applying for the scholarship was all about. This room, with the monitors and computers and cameras and expensive equipment even the local TV stations would envy. This was my ticket to the middle class.

I tried to calm my butterflies. *Just do your thing*, I thought. Things were different here, but journalism should be the same. Journalism was universal.

When I walked in, the students were gathered at the conference table in the center of the room. A guy with long shaggy dark hair and headphones around his neck sat at the head of the table, while an older man with gray hair—Professor Ferguson, I assumed—sat among the students.

The professor cleared his throat. "Piper Baird?"

I nodded.

"Welcome to Chiswick. Have a seat. Everyone, this is Piper Baird. Piper, why don't you tell us a bit about your experience."

He was the first teacher who had acknowledged my newness.

I sat in an empty chair and pulled out a notebook. "Well, I was editor in chief at my school paper for two years. We produced a weekly gazette."

That got a couple of patronizing smiles from the room. My cheeks turned red.

"What was your best story?" the professor asked.

I tapped my pencil nervously on the table and tried not to freeze up in the face of all the scrutiny. I made sure I didn't blink excessively. "Um, I uncovered a dognapping ring when my elderly neighbor reported her Yorkie-poo missing."

"A dog story was your biggest break?" the guy at the head of the table said.

"It was a big ring," I said. The table waited expectantly. "Lots of money being exchanged. Even dogs deserve justice."

This got a few snickers. "Because dogs are people too?" someone murmured.

"Okay, thank you, Piper," the professor said. "Here at Chiswick, we produce four twenty-minute newscasts per week, and we update the website daily, in addition to printing a weekly newspaper." Then he turned to the guy at the head of the table. "Jesse, take us through the rundown."

Jesse clicked a button on his laptop and a large monitor at the front of the room turned on.

"Our top story is the freak ice storm, and whether our groundskeepers were ready for it."

I felt like raising my hand with a definitive *No, they were not!*

"Next we have the information for the SAT prep courses." Jesse continued on, and after about eighteen stories, he nodded his head toward me. "New girl, the school is shutting off the water system tomorrow for an hour. I'd like a ten-second voice-over on it and two paragraphs with the information for the paper."

Hmph. The world's most boring story. I guess it was to be expected on my first day, but I still wanted to try for something better.

"Um, at my old school we found our own stories," I said.

"Welcome to Chiswick, where we don't," he said. "And remember, Professor Ferguson says there are no boring stories. Only boring reporters."

What I wanted to say was *I believe this story proves you wrong.* What I actually said was "Got it. Thank you."

If I just did my job for the next couple of weeks, I'd get something meatier. Eventually. I found an empty desk and started to look over the information. There was no way this piece would set me apart, unless, by some unfortunate accident, a student died from dehydration.

I studied Jesse. He was wearing a vintage T-shirt that looked more hand-me-down than fashionably old. He was probably scholarship like me, which meant he probably needed the Bennington, like me. Maybe Professor Ferguson already thought of him as the front-runner for the scholarship. I tilted my computer screen away from the rest of the class and typed Jesse Monson's name. He'd had a story published in the *Washington Bugle*. The *Bugle* was no *Washington Post*, but it was a sizable regional paper, and it was more than I'd ever done.

If he was the favorite, at least now I had a target.

I made a call to Chiswick's head office and got the date and time of the water shutoff from a woman on the administrative staff, and then I called the plumbing company and interviewed one of their employees about the process involved.

It still wasn't a satisfying story, so I used one of the computers to research tips on how to survive when your water is turned off. Maybe it was time to add some drama to all the boring angles. I researched the worst tragedies that had occurred during shutoffs. A woman in Alabama had died soon after the water department had closed her pipes due to nonpayment, but the death couldn't totally be blamed on lack of water. Then I found a story from the *Detroit Free Press* about how their water department was criticized for shutting off the supply to thousands of people below the poverty line.

A good reporter will often find a story that happened somewhere else and try to make it matter locally, so I started the article off with this headline:

IS CHISWICK ACADEMY PREPARED FOR EVERY POSSIBLE OUTCOME FROM SHUTTING DOWN THE SCHOOL'S WATER? THE CITY OF DETROIT WASN'T.

I wrote two pages on the story, ending with a warning and the Alabama woman's death. I handed it in to Jesse at the end of the first hour.

A few minutes later, he came to my desk.

"This is some interesting stuff," he said, plopping the papers down in front of me. "I've never been so scared of a water shutoff."

"Right?" I said with a smile.

"Yes. The problem is, I asked for two paragraphs."

"Two paragraphs would've been boring," I said.

"Two paragraphs would've been just the right length to alert students to the shutoff. But with this"—he pointed to the story— "the readers have to make it through a Detroit scandal and a dead woman before they find out the school's water will be out."

I glanced down. "But our water shutoff is going to happen after school's out. When no one's here."

"That's the point. We want to make sure that if someone *is* here, they'll know to plan ahead. And that's it. End of story."

A few of the other students glanced in our direction.

"But this is a good story." I put my finger on the headline. "This is the kind of stuff I'm used to writing. I'm not very good at fluff."

Jesse sat down in a chair next to me. "Here we write everything. No matter how small or unimportant we think it is. Plus you're new. You've got to earn it."

I sighed. "I'm already a senior. I don't have time."

Jesse ran his hand through his hair. "If you want to be on staff, you don't have a choice. Got it?"

I nodded.

"Then give me two paragraphs."

The electric bell rang, signaling the end of school.

"I can't right now," I said.

He raised his eyebrows. "This is important. Our reporters usually stay late. I hope that won't be a problem."

"Normally, it won't. But today, I have . . . a thing."

"A thing?"

I winced. "A detention kind of thing." I scratched the back of my head.

"Detention? You've been here one day."

"Oh, I wasn't here even a minute when I got it. But don't worry, it's not a habit. It's my first and last time." I felt my cheeks go hot. This was not the first impression I was hoping to make.

"Then after detention."

I bit my lip. "I have a shift at the Yogurt Shop."

He just shook his head and walked away. I put my forehead in my hand and squeezed my eyes shut. Maybe this was a bad dream. Maybe I would wake up soon. Maybe cats and dogs would start living together. I shook my head.

I gathered up my things and made my way toward the Potomac Room, or at least I thought I was making my way there, but another annoying thing about this school was that the rooms didn't have room numbers. They had names. The Jefferson Room.

The Lincoln Room. The Avery Cafeteria. And just to make outsiders feel like outsiders, the names weren't even in alphabetical
order. If anything, they seemed to be ordered by prominence,
and you had to have at least a working knowledge of American
history to guess which room was where. The Washington Room
was the assembly hall, so I assumed the Potomac Room would
be one of the smaller ones, since it was a river and not a hero of
American history, but my first few tries turned out to be dead
ends. By the time I finally found it, the teacher checking the
detention roster was about to shut the door.

"Piper Baird!" I said. "Sorry, I got lost."

"You're ten minutes late. I shouldn't admit you."

My shoulders sagged. "Please. I have to get this over with
today."

He groaned and stood aside. There were about eight students
there. I didn't know any of them, except a skinny girl with black
hair and pale skin who I recognized from the journalism staff.

I sat next to her.

"Hi," I said.

"Hey," she said without a smile.

"You're in journalism, right?"

"Video editor. And I do the graphics."

"Whatcha in for?" I said.

She shrugged. "They found my ID locker."

"ID locker?"

"I get people fake IDs. Run the business out of an empty

locker. I change its location periodically, but they usually find it. And then I get a week's detention."

"You know how to make fake IDs?"

"My dad's in the CIA. He taught me everything he knows."

"Wow," I said. I didn't know anyone at Clarendon who had a fake ID.

She took in a deep breath. "It's a living. Most of my clients are the rich kids here." She finally lifted her head up from her desk and looked at me. "You in the market? Three hundred." Then she looked closer at my outfit. "Or I could give you a discount."

"I barely have three hundred cents, let alone three hundred dollars." Actually I had a few thousand dollars in savings, but I wouldn't waste any of it on a fake ID that could lead to real criminal charges. "Why aren't your clients in detention?"

She raised her eyebrows. "'Cause they're rich." I was about to ask if she was on scholarship too, but she seemed to anticipate me. "I have a wealthy aunt. Gives me tuition money and nothing else. Not the same as a rich parent. I'm in a weird no-man's-land in this school."

That was the second time today I'd heard that the difference between detention and freedom at Chiswick Academy was a powerful parent.

"I'm Piper Baird," I said.

"Yeah, I heard. Mack Ripley."

I stared at her for a moment. "That's, like, the best name ever."

She sighed. "Lemme guess. You're an *Aliens* fan."

"Yes! Favorite movie. Hands down."

"I hear that a lot. Mostly from older people." She shrugged and went back to carving her initials into the desk.

I spent the rest of detention making a list of possible story ideas that could win me the Bennington. If I had any hope of beating out people like Jesse, I would have to come up with brilliant stories, preferably not the kind that dealt with dates and times of water shutdowns.

I started to write down ideas that could put me over the edge—maybe human trafficking at the school? OxyContin-selling ring? Could Chiswick be a front for raising superspies?—but that was the thing about stories. It was hard to find them without some sort of inspiration, and inspiration was in short supply in the Potomac Room.

"What are you doing?" Mack said.

"Trying to come up with stories. I want to win that Bennington Scholarship."

She kept her eyes on her desk. "Good luck with that." She didn't sound very optimistic.

"You don't think there's a chance?"

She shrugged. "I've never seen someone who wasn't here all four years win it. But there's a first time for everything, right?"

We were quiet for a moment. A month ago, I would've thought getting into Chiswick was impossible. Now wasn't the time to start believing the odds.

I leaned toward her. "So what's it like to be a have-not among all these haves?"

She looked up from her carving. "This school has train tracks running right through the middle, and either you're on the right side or the wrong side."

"How do you know which side you're on?"

She shrugged. "As if the blinged-out lockers aren't enough of a sign, every week, the people on the right side of the tracks get a text with a secret password and location for an exclusive party. They treat their parties like knowledge of the specific where-abouts is a matter of national security. You'll know you've made it if you get one of the texts."

"Have you ever gotten a text?"

"Nope." She sighed. "We go to the same classes. Have the same homework. Walk the same halls. And yet we live on differ-ent planets."

I thought back to my encounter with Raf, and how he'd made such a big deal out of helping the "less fortunate." He probably regretted momentarily crossing the train tracks.

That night at work, I tried to calmly tell Charlotte about my day, but I couldn't help ranting.

"There's marble everywhere, and the lockers look like apartments and cute boys drag strangers into bathrooms and tape cheerleaders to walls and want to make out with you for booze . . ."

Charlotte tilted her head. "I'm not following."

"And then they give you detention."

"You got detention?" Charlotte froze with a spoonful of choc-olate chips over a medium vanilla cup.

"Yeah."

"Was it research for a story?"

"No! It was actual detention."

She stayed frozen.

The customer waiting for the yogurt cleared his throat. She finally dumped the chocolate chips on the yogurt and finished the order.

"So, any cute guys to report on?" Charlotte said.

"No. At least none in my price range."

"Since when do guys have price ranges?" she asked as she rang up the customer.

"Since Chiswick."

She gave the customer change, and he pocketed it instead of tipping. At least that meant we didn't have to sing.

5

The next day, I experienced my first lunch in the Chiswick cafeteria. And I say "experienced" because that's what it was. An experience.

The cafeteria was a swanky affair. Aged gouda and brie with sliced baguettes, crusted tilapia, roasted edamame and shiitake mushrooms, marinated and grilled asparagus topped with shaved Parmesan . . . My scholarship included the meal plan. Otherwise, I never would've been able to afford to eat like this.

The tables and chairs were actually made of wood. Not plastered with faux-wood laminate like at my old school.

I put some cheese and bread and tilapia on my plate and looked for a place to sit. Rafael Amador was at a large table full of the shiniest people at the school. Had he already told them about my embarrassing first day? Probably. The girl sitting next to him looked as though she had just walked off the runway. The model kind, not the jet kind. I hadn't seen her yesterday. I would have remembered.

The entire group, with their manicures and sleek buns and designer handbags and bodyguards, screamed, *Go away.*

Una was sitting with Julia and a few other people who I assumed were also scholarship students. They had the kind of look that would've blended in at Clarendon but stuck out at this place, which was filled with designer labels. Not a knock-off in sight. I started toward them, but then I spotted Mack sitting at a small table with a guy I didn't know. She gave me a kind of nod that I took for an invitation.

I walked over and put my tray down next to her and tilted my head toward Raf's table. "This school . . ."

"I know, right?" she said.

"Who's the girl next to Raf?"

"Giselle Bouchard."

I nodded. "So she's not only gorgeous, she's also French."

"Yep. If it makes you feel better, she sucks at math."

I nodded. "That does make me feel a little better."

She raised a celery stick in the air. "Piper, think of this school as a stepping-stone. You have to suffer through it, but it will get you where you want to go. By the way, this is Faroush." She pointed the celery to the guy next to her. "Faroush, Piper."

"Nice to meet you," I said.

He simply nodded.

"Faroush isn't so much about the talking as he is about the staring off into space in an angsty way."

Faroush smiled and softly punched her in the arm.

"And he's my boyfriend," Mack said.

"Ah," I said.

We ate for a few minutes in silence.

"So, where is Chiswick going to get you next year?" I asked.

"MIT," she said. "I'm kind of a genius."

I nodded as if I knew what that was like. "And what about you, Faroush?"

"I go where she goes."

"That's commitment for you," I said. "So, Faroush is an interesting name."

"It's my last name."

"What's your first name?"

"John." He squinched his nose as if the name disgusted him.

We ate the rest of our lunches in silence. In literal silence. These people loved their silence.

Despite my hope for being promoted to scandal or tragedy, my first two weeks at Chiswick were full of fluff pieces like "Most Productive Study Techniques" and "Best Power Foods for the High School Student Brain," and incredibly short on anything meaty.

The more I worked with Jesse and the rest of the staff, the more it confirmed my earlier suspicions that Jesse was, indeed, the front-runner for the Bennington Scholarship. He oversaw every editorial meeting, he had the final say as to content and assignments, and the way he convinced Professor Ferguson to run one of the weekly editions in color made me think he could sell beef Popsicles to a colony of vegans.

I'd hoped he'd see I was "earning my stripes," but on my third Monday at Chiswick, he handed me yet another dry informational pamphlet, this one about security systems.

"The school is updating their security. One paragraph and a twenty-second voice-over, please."

I tried not to roll my eyes as I opened the pamphlet. Another nothing piece.

After the meeting broke up, I went to the administration area to interview the principal about the new security systems. He welcomed me into his office.

"Miss Baird," he said, holding his hand out. "Nice to meet you in person. How are you liking Chiswick?"

"It's good," I said, omitting the fact that I'd received detention from the Beast on my first day. "I wanted to ask you a couple of questions about the new security system."

"Of course," he said. He leaned back in his chair and the leather squeaked.

I sat down and pulled out my notebook. "First off, why are you changing the old system?"

"It's always smart to keep everything updated."

I nodded and scribbled notes. "And what does the security system entail? What equipment?"

"Well, the intercoms. The telephones. The camera feeds, et cetera."

"And when was the last time you updated the system?"

"Um . . . uh . . ."

I looked up from my notepad.

"Last year." He frowned.

We were both quiet for a moment.

"Last year?" I repeated, the scent of a story prickling at the back of my brain. "I'm all for keeping current, but is it typical to do it so often?"

He sighed and was suddenly very intrigued by the books on his bookcase. "We have a lot of generous donors. We can afford to be extra vigilant."

"Vigilant? Is there a reason to be extra vigilant at Chiswick?"

"An administration should always be vigilant."

I took a breath and tried to slow things down. "Right. So one last question."

"Okay."

"Do you change the system every single year? In the name of vigilance?"

He sniffed. "I don't know what you're implying, Miss Baird—"

"I'm not implying anything," I said.

"The purpose of your story is to educate students about the new system."

"Respectfully, sir, I disagree. The purpose of any story is the story." That had sounded better in my head, but I hoped he got the gist.

"What's that supposed to mean?"

"It means that I follow where the story takes me."

He pressed his hands onto the top of the desk. "Look, Miss Baird. There is no story here. It's a simple system update. That's it."

He stood and ushered me out the door, practically slamming it shut behind me.

"Oh, there's a story," I said under my breath.

I glanced toward the receptionists in the office. One was on the phone. I walked up to the other. "Hi, Ms. Preece?" I read the name off her nameplate. "I'm Piper Baird. New girl. I just interviewed the principal about the new security system at the school. He said I could talk to you next. Would that be all right?"

She looked mildly unsure but didn't object.

I pulled out my notebook. "The principal told me the reasoning behind the change. What do you think? Will a new system solve the problems?" A good reporter acts like she knows more than she does.

Ms. Preece nodded as I spoke. "I don't know. Personally I feel a lot safer with the change, but I guess it's always possible someone could hack the new system."

Hack? I tried to keep my face calm as I took notes. There it was. The answer to my real question.

"I thought they caught the person," I said, taking a chance.

She shook her head. "No. In fact, I'm surprised the principal told you about it, although I will say I'm glad. The students deserve to know."

Right then, the Beast came out of an office next to the principal's, and I scooped up my bag and mumbled something to the secretary that resembled *Thank you for the help with my schedule.* Then I ran back to the newsroom and made a few phone calls to the new security company and then the local police departments and eventually confirmed that there was a case of stalking at Chiswick Academy, which had prompted the installation of the new system.

Finally, after weeks of slogging through fluff stories, I had a scoop.

6

I turned to the nearest computer and began typing.

SECURITY BREACH IN CHISWICK'S COMMUNICATIONS SYSTEM CALLS INTO QUESTION SAFETY OF STUDENTS

Chiswick Academy is updating its security system following an incident involving a hacker breaking through the firewalls and gaining access to the school's private video feed.

I looked over the lede, verifying each piece of information.

Once I was satisfied, I wrote some more.

> The hacker has not been apprehended. According to
> sources close to the incident, the breach might have been
> an inside job. Possible motives include stalking, but the
> school administration is hesitant to talk about it.
>
> The principal maintains that he will continue to be
> vigilant about the safety of his students, and that there is
> more than enough in the budget to invest in a more secure
> system. Already employees in the head office feel safer.
>
> The police investigation into the matter is ongoing, and
> officers say they are following all leads.

Voilà.

It wasn't the most complete story, but if Watergate had taught us anything, it was that reporting even the minimum of facts could get otherwise cautious people talking.

With about twenty minutes of the school day left, the journalism room began to fill back up with reporters ready to write and edit their stories. I waved Jesse over.

"Hey, Piper. How did your story go?"

I turned the monitor toward him. "Read this."

He spent a few minutes staring at the monitor and then sat back in his chair. "Whoa."

"Right?"

"You got this stuff confirmed?"

I nodded. "From the receptionist, the company installing the new system, and the police PIO."

"Any clues as to the target of the alleged stalking?"

I shook my head. "If it's a student, their identity is protected because we're all minors. And I don't think I'll get anything out of the principal until we run this and he starts to feel the heat from concerned parents."

He looked impressed. "Wow. You've only been here a few weeks and already you're taking on the administration."

I smiled. "Just following the facts."

He blew out a breath. "All right. Give me something for the front page. Above the fold."

"Yes, sir."

Above the fold. *Above the fold.* It's what every reporter wants to hear. The lead story. The one that will kick off a newscast. The one that will sell the papers. My heart went all fluttery.

Who knew where this story would take me? Maybe it would stop right here. Or maybe, with a little luck, one clue would lead to another, one discovery would lead to another, one corrupt official would lead to another, and I'd be looking back on this story as the one that changed it all.

The following day, I woke up eager to check out the school's news website, and when I logged on, there it was. In black and white.

My headline and my story. My name in print beside it.

I ran to the kitchen to show my parents.

"Nice work, honey," my mom said, looking over her shoulder as she washed dishes. I was pretty sure she hadn't read it, but it was okay. She rarely had any time to sit down and read anything, what with taking care of us and her part-time job at a bakery.

"Good job," my dad said as he grabbed his sack lunch out of the fridge and blew us all kisses good-bye.

I sat down to a bowl of oatmeal and watched as my phone downloaded forty-two new messages. Even accounting for spam and promotional stuff, forty-two was a lot for me. My story was making waves. My heart got all jittery.

I scanned the subject lines. Some people wanted to know more about the stalking. Other messages were from students in the journalism program congratulating me on the scoop. One was from Raf, who said I should change my name from Pip Baird to Woodward-and-Bernstein Baird. I wanted to shoot him a reply to remind him my name wasn't Pip, but then I saw an email from Principal Wallace. The subject line read: "Meeting before school."

Miss Baird,
Please meet me in my office before the beginning of homeroom.
Principal Wallace

Uh-oh, that did not sound good. I tried to calm my sudden nerves by reminding myself that the price of a free press would always be censure, scrutiny, and disapproval. Back at my old high school, Mr. Peters had said that any good story was bound to ruffle feathers.

Still, when I got to the front office, my heart sped up with trepidation.

Maybe it wouldn't be bad. Maybe he was going to congratulate me on outfoxing him.

Okay, that was a long shot.

"Miss Baird," Principal Wallace said, opening his office door, a stern look on his face. He held the door for me. I sat down in silence.

"I assume you know why you're here."

"You aren't pleased with my story."

"To say the least." He pulled up the story on his computer screen. "You've placed me, and the school, in a very difficult position."

"Is the story accurate?" I asked.

"That's beside the point."

"For a journalist, that's the only point."

He pressed his lips together and squeezed his eyes shut briefly. "Miss Baird, you are not at the *Washington Post*. You are at Chiswick Academy, under my jurisdiction."

"A free press doesn't fall under anyone's jurisdiction." Okay, sometimes my mouth could run away with me.

"You printed that story without my permission."

"Does the school paper need your permission for their stories?"

"No, but it's a courtesy."

"Courteous behavior is not required with a free press." Mr. Peters had taught me that.

"But it is if you want to get information, yes?"

I sighed. He had a point. I wouldn't have any stories without grooming contacts.

I hadn't planned on coming in here and being so contrary, but this wasn't the pro–First Amendment atmosphere I was used to at my old school. I tried to tone it down. "I'm sorry if the truth was inconvenient for you."

"Inconvenient? I've had dozens of phone calls from parents asking if their daughter or son was the target of the stalker. Demanding to see details of the latest security upgrade. Threatening to withdraw students if the perpetrator isn't caught, and we aren't even sure there *was* a perpetrator in the first place!" His face was rather red by this point.

"I understand, sir. I was just trying to earn my place on the staff. I really need that Bennington Scholarship."

"I'm afraid the stunt you pulled yesterday has set you back for that."

I got a pit in my stomach. "Why?"

He leaned over his desk and intertwined his fingers. "Because I'm on the Bennington committee. Next time do your research." He sighed. "You're excused."

He started writing on a notepad on his desk and I let myself out. I was surprised I was able to walk so well, considering the tiny new dagger in my heart.

At lunch, I saw Jesse sitting at another table with a couple of other students from the journalism department. I went over and put my tray down by him.

"Hey, Pipe," he said.

"Hi. You could've told me Principal Wallace was on the Bennington committee. Is that why you were so quick to put my story at the top?"

He put down his sandwich. "Look, you did a good job on the story. It deserved the spot it got. Putting you on the outs with the principal was just a bonus."

"Why?"

"The Bennington is still a competition." He took a big bite of his sandwich as if to say there was no point competing with him. Or maybe I was reading too much into a bite.

"Okay. Good to know. So let me just say this: it is *on*, Jesse . . . whatever your last name is." What was it again? "Monson."

"Right," he said. "That might have had more of an impact if you'd remembered my last—"

"I know," I said. Infuriating nonphotographic memory.

I spotted Mack sitting at her usual table, so I headed over toward her.

"Looking forward to working with you," Jesse said from behind me.

I set my tray down next to Mack and Faroush a little harder than I'd meant to.

"What's up?" Mack said.

"Just frustrated." I scrunched up my face. "The principal wasn't happy with my story, which is fine except he's on the Bennington committee."

"Ah, man," Faroush said. Those two words were about the most he'd ever said to me.

I was about to continue lamenting, but before I could get any words out, loud guitar music echoed through the cafeteria.

We turned toward the sound. A man in a dark tuxedo stood just outside the cafeteria doors, holding a guitar. He strummed a few more dramatic chords, then slowly stepped inside as he continued playing a song with a Spanish beat. A striking woman in a red dress followed him in. Her hair was tied back in a low, tight bun, with a huge red flower attached.

She started dancing to the guitar music.

"What's going on?" I whispered to Mack.

"Rafael Amador's birthday, I would guess," she said. "Last year, his parents hired a Spanish chef to take over the kitchen here. And let me say, you haven't lived until you've tried Puchero Andaluz de Verduras." She said it so dryly, I couldn't tell if she was being sarcastic. "Looks like this year, we all get to celebrate Raf's birth by watching the flamenco."

"His parents do this every year?" I asked.

She shook her head. "More like they pay a servant to do this."

The woman stomped her feet and clapped and twirled, and pretty soon the entire cafeteria started clapping along, going faster and faster as the dance neared its dramatic finish.

At the end, the woman took a rose from behind her ear, bowed, and handed it to Raf. Everyone clapped, and then Raf bowed as if he were the one who'd just finished the dancing.

"Seriously?" I said to Mack. "I'm sitting here worried that I may have blown my chance for a scholarship, and thus my future, and that guy over there is chomping on a rose stem as if he's never had to worry about anything a day in his life."

Mack nodded. "Same school. Different planets."

I turned toward the table where the other scholarship students were to see if they found it off-putting too, but Una was clapping and Julia was standing on tiptoes to get a better view.

Jesse waved to me from a few tables away. I went over and he said, "Grab a quick interview with Raf and the dancer. It would make a good story for page six. Take Will with you to get some pictures."

A guy with black hair stood up and produced a camera from his bag.

And there I was. Relegated to fluff again, covering the birthday parties of the rich and infamous.

7

I worked my way through the crowd of well-wishers around Raf. It was like his birthday was an international affair.

"Excuse me," I said. "Pardon me. Raf?"

I guess I said it a little loud, because the group went quiet as Raf turned from Giselle to face me. Then everyone else's gaze followed his. And my pulse started racing.

"Yes, Pip?"

"It's not—never mind." I focused on the amount of blinking I was doing. "Can I ask you a few questions for the paper?" Suddenly this felt so demeaning. As if I were the paparazzo to his celebrity. And why was everyone so quiet?

"Like what?"

Then just as I'd feared, my mind went blank. "Um . . . birthdays," I stammered. "Am I right?"

Raf frowned. "Right about what?"

Geez, pull it together, Pipe. "They're yearly." *Damn.*

Raf squinted his eyes. "Yes. In that case, you're right."

I shook my head and pictured everyone around me naked and when my imagination got to Raf, I blushed. So then I pictured myself naked, and that didn't work either.

I felt a hand on mine. It was Raf's. He led me away from the crowd to a corner of the cafeteria. "Is this better?"

I nodded.

"Do you want to ask some questions now?"

I nodded again, my heartbeat finally slowing down. "Okay, was that dance something from your country?"

"Yes. It's the flamenco. From the Andalusian region in southern Spain. *Ahi donde mi familia es de.*"

"Huh?"

He smiled and shook his head. "I'm sorry. It's the music and the dance. Makes me speak *en español.*"

"Happens to me all the time," I said, making a few notes on my notepad. "I go see *The Nutcracker*, suddenly I'm talking in Russian."

Raf chuckled.

"So what was the Spanish stuff you just said?"

"I said my family is from the Andalusian region of Spain."

"Ah." I made a note. "One last question. Don't you think

having a flamenco performance in the lunchroom was a little over-the-top?"

Oops. Filter fail.

Raf raised an eyebrow. "Well, I tried to restage the running of the bulls, but it got too complicated."

"There's always next year," I said.

"Except we'll be in college."

"Right. Well, I think we're good. Thank you for your time. Will? Can you get a picture of Raf with the dancer?" My cheeks were warm. I felt like Oliver Twist, asking for *more, please, sir?*

Raf waved the dancer over. She sidled up next to him, draped her arm around his neck, and struck a dramatic pose. I left because, seriously—same school, different planets.

When I walked into journalism class, Professor Ferguson said, "Nice scoop on the security update, Piper."

"Thank you," I said, for a moment forgetting the humiliation of covering Rafael Amador's birthday.

Then the professor called the class to attention, and Jesse pulled up the rundown on the monitor. "We're starting off with the system breach. Josh, give me a two-minute package and some B-roll for a voice-over—"

"Wait, what?" I interrupted.

"What's the problem?" Jesse asked.

"It's my story. I got the scoop."

"Yes, but it's Josh's beat. He has the contacts."

I glanced at the professor, but he didn't say anything. "But—"

"Let's finish the rundown," Jesse said.

He continued, and I ended up with a story about new security protocols for the national parks. I walked over to Jesse's desk. "I know we're both going for the Bennington—"

"Everyone here is going for the Bennington," he said.

"Okay, but that's no reason to give me the dreck."

He sighed. "The principal requested that you be taken off the story. I'm sorry."

I sank into a chair. "Is this paper going to kowtow to every demand from higher up?"

"When it's from the principal, yes. We don't have much of a choice."

Mack caught my eye from across the room and shrugged. I suspected that was her way of showing sympathy.

I sat down at my desk and wrote up a quick summary of the lunchroom flamenco incident. Then I researched the new protocols at the national parks. Maybe there would be a story to crack wide open.

There wasn't.

I went over to Professor Ferguson's desk and plopped down in the chair opposite him.

"Yes, Miss Baird?"

"I need help."

He put down the book he'd been reading, opened the bottom drawer of his desk, and produced a folder. He spread the contents on his desk. I recognized the papers inside.

"Those are my stories," I said.

He nodded. "I never got the chance to tell you how impressive your portfolio was. But I'm assuming you're here to talk about your latest work."

"Please don't judge me by that. I'm not used to covering small stuff."

He waved a hand. "Your work is solid. So what do you need?"

I took in a deep breath. "I need some insight. This school, and the potential for a scholarship to a journalism program, is very important to me. And I feel like I'm not grasping what it is you're looking for."

He closed the folder and put his finger on it. "You have a good feel for writing like a journalist, Piper. I would even go so far as to say it's textbook."

I smiled, feeling proud of myself for the first time since I'd gotten here.

"But every student in this class could've written the same articles."

I frowned. Back home, Mr. Peters had made me editor in chief after I'd been on staff for three months. I was the youngest editor in chief the school had ever had. And now Professor Ferguson was basically saying I was ordinary.

"As you approach your writing assignments, I want you to keep something in mind. Three questions."

"What are those?" I said.

"Why am *I* the right person to write about this? What's the story that I can get that no one else can? Why am I not only a good person for the job, but the *only* person? That's what's going to set you apart here at Chiswick."

I nodded. "I understand, Professor Ferguson. It's just hard to ask myself why *I* am the only person who can write about the new rules for flushing the toilets in the third-floor bathrooms. I mean, maybe I could've done what you say if I'd been allowed to stay on the security system update story."

"But that's exactly my point," he said. "Josh was able to take over seamlessly. I want you to find a story that would be impossible for Jesse to give away. So that if the principal comes to him, he has to say, 'I'm sorry. There's no one else who can write that story but Piper.'"

I nodded. "I guess I understand. But that's not how the national networks do it."

"I'm teaching students to be better than what's out there now."

I forced a smile. "Okay."

"Okay. Keep up the good work."

I left the newsroom to get the afternoon edition of the *Washington Post* at the front office. As I walked back to class, I looked at the stories from the first few pages. All of them could've been written by numerous reporters. How was someone like me—a scholarship student who had only just started at Chiswick—supposed to find a story only *I* could write here?

For a moment, I had the fleeting thought that maybe I should just go back to Clarendon High, where I could stick out. Where I had a real shot at being the best.

That's where my head was at when I ran into Raf in the hallway.

I guess I was wearing my frustration on my face, because when he saw me, he said, "Hey, Pip. What's the matter?"

I sighed. "You wouldn't understand."

"Why?"

"Because you duct-tape cheerleaders to walls and dance the flamenco in lunchrooms, and you've never had to worry about paying for a thing." I shook my head. "You do not know what real life is."

"Sure I do," he said with a smile.

"No. You sit on the top of your marble staircase, with your maids and your chauffeurs and your dad who gets you out of every bind you've been in, and your diplomatic immunity, and you look at the commoners like me, and my used car, and my money worries . . . you look at us with an unaffected curiosity."

He rocked back on his heels a bit. "Wow, Pip. Don't stop there. Tell me more."

I knew I should stop, but I couldn't. I was too frustrated.

And I was high up on my soapbox. "If you keep going like this, you won't be able to face any struggles in life, and . . . without struggle, you won't know the feeling of . . . overcoming struggle." This was all sounding better in my head. I wasn't yelling, but I sounded a bit manic, even to my ears. "And overcoming struggle is a really good feeling. Believe me. Also, if you limit your circle of friends to only those with trust funds, you'll miss out on life. Because real life happens with the peasants." Did I just use the word "peasants"?

"I know peasants," he said with a smug grin.

I frowned. "You don't even know where they sit in the lunchroom."

He went quiet.

"I'm sorry," I said. "I had a bad day . . . week . . . month, and I took it out on you."

"No one's ever spoken to me like that," he said. His lips curved upward.

"Because you're surrounded by yes-men who are too scared to tell you no."

He stared at me for a few moments, silent again.

"Okay, well, I have to go. I have a job." It wasn't my paying job at the Yogurt Shop. It was in the newsroom, but I didn't tell him that.

He grabbed my arm. "Tell me more. I can take it."

"Get someone else to tell you."

"But it will mean more coming from a peasant."

I shook my head. "No. You don't want to hear more." I shook my arm free and walked away, irked.

Irked. Rafael Amador irked me. No peasant wanted to hear they were a peasant. Even if I had used the term first. It was bad form.

I went back to the newsroom, where Mack was working on the layout of the paper. I peeked over her shoulder and saw the picture of Raf and the dancer on page one. One!

Normally, I loved being above the fold, but a spoiled boy's birthday bash did *not* warrant above-the-fold treatment.

Suddenly, Raf and his richness and his entitlement and his no-need-for-scholarship money and his quick comebacks didn't feel like a random problem. It felt like a personal attack. Like he embodied the complete injustice of my situation.

I turned to my computer and impulsively tried out a headline.

THE PRIVILEGED ELITE: AN UNDERCOVER EXPOSÉ OF THE WORLD'S RICHEST TEENAGERS

The injustice needed to be documented. The table of scholarship students needed to realize the inequity, not applaud it. I wasn't going to get better stories from Jesse anytime soon. My next assigned story would probably be an investigation into the most effective locker organization techniques, if you have the money. The headline would be: "Don't Just Wing It . . . Bling It!" Or something equally stupid. Professor Ferguson told me to write something only I could write. Who better to expose the rich and privileged than someone on the flip side of the coin? A *peasant*. No one else in this newsroom could do it like me. The only other scholarship student on the journalism staff was Jesse, from what I could tell.

Maybe the principal would never allow such a story, but undercover exposés were hot-ticket items for most magazines. There's a reason the Hiltons and the Kardashians make millions off exposing their lives. If the school didn't want it, I'd take it wide. And if I did it right, I'd get the Bennington. They'd have to give it to me. Even if they didn't want to.

8

At home that night, I was stewing in my room. I couldn't get the story idea out of my head, but I didn't know how to approach it. Getting an invite to one of their parties seemed as likely as stealing nuclear codes from the CIA.

Besides, for now, it was just research.

My dad seemed to sense that I was fretting, because he knocked on my bedroom door with a cup of hot chocolate in his hand.

"What's on your mind, Pipe?" he said, setting the mug on my desk and taking a seat on the edge of my bed.

"How do you know something's on my mind?"

He reached over and grabbed a pencil from my desk. It was

riddled with bite marks.

"Okay, maybe there are a few things on my mind," I admitted.

"Like what?"

I took in a deep breath. "Like how I'm going to pay for college. And why I'm not totally the editor in chief already. And president of the *New York Times*. And why a show like *The Bachelor* is still on television."

My dad nodded. "That's some heavy stuff." He took a sip of my hot chocolate. "First off, there's nothing either of us can do about *The Bachelor*, so let's leave that one alone. Second, your school record is impeccable. I have faith you'll get a scholarship."

"But every student who gets into Columbia will have an impeccable record. I need more than that to get a full scholarship there. I need the Bennington."

"You know, there are other colleges besides Columbia," my dad said. "You could get a full ride to eighty percent of them."

"Eighty percent?" I said skeptically.

"Yes. I conducted a study." He grinned.

"Maybe. But Columbia's my dream."

He nodded. "I know." He pointed to one of my bedroom walls. "The Columbia poster hanging above your bed was my first clue."

Right then, Michael burst into my room, tears filling his eyes. When he saw me, they started to flow down his cheeks. He rarely expressed this much emotion, and so I dropped everything else.

I stood up and held my arms out. "What's the matter, bud?"

He gave me a little head butt to my stomach—his way of making contact—and I put one hand on his chest and the other on his back and pressed. Sometimes the pressure helped to calm his storm.

"Mr. Flannigan said I sweared, but I didn't," Michael said.

My dad gave me a look like *You got this?*

I nodded and he stepped out.

"Shh. It's okay. What word did you say?"

Michael said the F-word. "That's not a swear, right?" he asked, desperate.

I sighed. The rules of social behavior were very important to Michael. From an early age, his therapy had focused on social skills and "fitting in," so the fact that he'd done something that was not generally acceptable was distressing for him. "It *is* a swear word. But it's okay. We'll work on it."

"Will you teach me the swears so I know not to say them?"

Michael liked charts and ranking systems, so we got out a pen and paper and I wrote down every curse word I could think of and helped Michael with their pronunciations and then we took turns using them in sentences.

Afterward, we ranked each one from most worst to least bad, and by the time we were finished, his storm had subsided.

"If I swear, will I go to jail?" he said. Jail was the scariest punishment Michael could think of.

"No, bud."

"If I say the swears in my videos, will they get flagged?"

Michael loved to make videos of himself, narrating while playing his favorite video game, Clan Wars.

"They might."

"Okay, then I won't swear." He took a deep breath. "Until I'm eighteen."

Michael grabbed his hanger and began spinning it and wandering around my room and eventually meandered out without saying anything else.

I went down to the kitchen to grab day-three leftovers (meat loaf), brought it back to my room, and turned on my computer. Time to do some research. First I looked up past Bennington winners to see whether my story idea would fit in with the stories that had won previously. But the stories in the general media that kept coming up were less about alumni achievements and more about the rich kids of Washington's elite and their late-night clubbing and partying habits.

Rafael Amador popped up in more than a few of these. In one, he was pictured with a joint in one hand and a drink in the other. In another, he was onstage, playing a duet with John Legend. That one bugged me more, because I had a thing for his music. Another story showed him on a motorcycle with some glamorous girl on the back. She looked familiar, and I realized I'd seen her face on magazine covers.

How was this boy not in jail?

Probably the same reason why he'd gotten out of detention that first day.

Powerful dad.

Charm.

Money.

Diplomatic immunity.

Like Michael, I was into lists too.

As I went on, my research started to look a little less like research and a little more like stalking, partly due to curiosity and partly due to the face that kept popping up. Rafael's face. Even caught off guard, he was beautiful. Just looking at a picture, I found it hard to remember how annoying he was. There were a lot of stories about him, lots of pictures, but there was one article with no pictures. It didn't even seem to be about Raf specifically. It was about a recent surge in teenage binge drinking. It mentioned a boy who had nearly died of alcohol poisoning at a party at an embassy. The Spanish embassy. Rafael was quoted in the article as a friend of the victim.

"He is American. Americans don't know how to drink."

That seemed so callous. Maybe diplomatic immunity meant he was also immune from manners. My story, if I pursued it, would be a mirror for him to take a good hard look at himself.

I started to notice that most of the articles on the internet were from last year, but hardly any were more recent than that. I kept searching until I came across a gossip blog with a story about Rafael's father. The entry claimed the ambassador had ties to the Spanish mafia—I didn't even know there was one—and through these ties, he got the editor in chief of *Star Lives* fired.

Raf did say his father was scary. But I didn't realize he was mafia scary.

I exited out of the article and did a general search of diplomatic immunity. Basically, it was a perk among countries that had been around since ancient times, and diplomats had been abusing the system for just as long. Defense attorneys had invoked immunity numerous times to get diplomats off for the crimes they'd committed.

I closed out the window and got back to looking for the Bennington-winning stories, and that's when I came across a story from the winner five years ago. Liam Rathbone wrote an article about how he had pretended to be a paparazzo and embedded himself with a group of photographers who hounded the rich and famous. But he turned the story around and made the tactics of the paparazzi the story.

Readers love a good story about someone who dares to embed themselves. One of my favorite books I read as a young girl was the story of a reporter named Nellie Bly. She exposed the horrors of Blackwell's Island Insane Asylum by pretending to be insane herself. She was admitted, and once inside she documented the inhumane conditions. After she was released, she published her story.

She was one of my heroes. She made me want to act insane and embed myself everywhere I went. That's who I could channel in my story. I would be the Nellie Bly of the DI kids. The next night, at the Yogurt Shop, all I could think about was my story, and because of that I messed up four orders in one hour. Charlotte wasn't working tonight, which was too bad, because I could've used another person to bounce ideas off. At the end of my shift, the tip jar was empty, but my head was filled with the exposé. And if it got me the Bennington, I wouldn't need the tip jar.

Except now I had no gas money.

The next morning at breakfast, my mom was checking her emails when she gasped.

"Four hundred sixty-two dollars?" She squinted at the screen. "For gems?"

Michael's face went ashen. "I'm sorry. I'm sorry."

"What are gems, Michael?" my mom said, trying and failing to keep her voice calm.

"They're for his game," I said.

I thought she was going to blow up, but then her lip quivered and she burst into tears. Michael started pacing and spinning his hanger faster. He was upset.

My dad put his hand on my mom's shoulder. "It'll be okay. We'll explain the situation to the credit card company. I'm sure they'll expunge the charges."

Why would she burst into tears instead of scolding Michael?

I didn't think now was the time to ask questions, especially if one of the questions was going to be *Can I borrow some money for gas?*

Mom got up quietly from the table and went to her room.

"She's feeling a lot of pressure," my dad said.

"At the bakery?" I asked.

He didn't answer.

9

The rest of the day, I readied myself for my plan to embed with the diplomatic immunity kids. A reporter's best weapon is the art of conversation. Without sitting down for a formal "interview," any reporter worth her salt knows how to get the most out of a casual conversation, as long as she follows a few simple guidelines.

Ask open-ended questions. Avoid yes or no. Don't ask, *When you have diplomatic immunity, do you get away with things other students don't?* Instead, ask, *When did you first realize you weren't like the rest of us?*

Start with broad questions to get the interview subject comfortable. Establish trust. Then, as the conversation goes on, narrow the questions.

Don't be afraid of silence. Silence may make some people uncomfortable, but it will also provoke expansion on answers.

Never let the subject get the questions ahead of time.

Do some background work. Get to know your interview subject *before* the interview.

I started with the background work. One of the keys to embedding yourself with an exclusive group is to make sure they think it was their idea to invite you, so I tried to find some common interests.

I memorized the DI kids' class schedules. (It's not stalking if it's in the service of a story, by the way.) Monday morning, I walked down hallways convenient to the schedule of one of the diplomatic immunity kids, Mateo Lopez, but by the time lunch rolled around, I'd failed to bump into him. Maybe his security detail was making him take less obvious routes. Which meant that probably everyone else's detail was doing the same thing.

I decided to try to make friends with Giselle. But every attempt of mine looked like:

Me: *Hey, Giselle! I want to be friends!*

Her: *You sound like a loser! Please leave!*

I found myself watching the DI kids at lunch.

"Quit staring," Mack said.

"What?"

"At Rafael. It's kind of obvious."

Faroush nodded in agreement.

"No, it's not. I'm looking out of the corner of my eye," I insisted. "And I'm looking at all of them. Not just Rafael."

Mack gave me a skeptical look. "Look, you think he's hot. You're not the only one. But try to be a little more subtle." She crunched on a piece of celery. Her lunches were always made up of water and water-based foods like celery and watermelon. I wasn't sure where her actual calories ever came from.

"I don't think he's hot. I'm thinking of a story idea."

"'Hot Boys and the Girls Who Pine for Them'?" she said.

I threw a piece of cheddar popcorn at her. "No. This isn't *Us Weekly*."

I turned to subtly glance at Raf from the corner of my eye, only he was suddenly standing two feet in front of me.

"Gah," I said, surprised. But a good reporter can gather herself after a surprise. "Hey."

"Hey, Pip." He stood there for another moment and glanced at Mack and Faroush.

"Oh," I said. "This is Mack. She's brilliant. This is Faroush. He likes Mack. Guys, this is Raf. He has . . ." What could I say that didn't make me sound like I already knew a lot about him? "Very white teeth."

The three of them awkwardly shook hands, and then Raf said, "Actually we've all gone to school together for three years. We've met."

"Ah," I said. "I guess that makes sense."

"I was thinking about our conversation the other day," he

said. "The one about how I'm out of touch with the peasants?"
He smiled as he said this.

Mack raised an eyebrow.

"It happens with royalty," I said.

Raf grabbed a chair, swung it around, and straddled it. "Tell
me more."

"About what?"

"About my problems."

"I'm not the kind of girl who goes around telling people what
their problems are."

"All evidence to the contrary," Raf said.

"You don't know me," I said.

Mack chimed in. "She is like that." At my glare, she added,
"But in a cool way."

"Give me your best shot," he said.

I tried to remember my rules of interviewing through conversation: Open-ended questions. Silence. No aggression. Trust.

"Okay, for starters, how many people are involved in getting
you out of bed and through your day?"

"What do you mean?"

I shrugged and remained silent. At least I could count on
Mack and Faroush to remain silent too. They were good at that.

"Well, my father's assistant, Lidia, posts my schedule. The
house butler wakes me up. The cook makes me breakfast. Then I
get dressed. The chauffeur takes me to school, where I spend all
day actually fending for myself."

"With your security detail."

"Yes." He looked wary. "Then the chauffeur takes me home. The cook makes dinner, which is served by the waitstaff. Then . . . sleep."

"Cook, chauffeur, assistant, security, waitstaff . . ." I ticked them off on my fingers and I could feel that earlier frustration, the tension between the haves and the have-nots, creeping up inside me. Reporters weren't supposed to succumb to their feelings, and yet here I was, succumbing all over the place. "My only other question is, who wipes your butt?"

Mack took in a breath.

Raf frowned. "You're not the only person who gets to complain about their lot in life," he said. "Maybe I'm sitting at the top of a marble staircase, but I'm staring straight across at someone who is on a very high horse."

With that he stood up and smiled, but the smile was lacking his usual swagger. "See you guys around."

When he was gone, Mack leaned over. "Okay, that was awesome."

"What, my shredding the school's most popular guy?"

"No," she said shaking her head. "His comeback."

She was right. His comeback about the high horse was really good. He'd probably planned it. And I'd just lost my first chance to embed because I'd let my resentment get in the way.

10

At journalism after the rundown (I was assigned a story on the school's "Street Art" unit, and whether it's art or graffiti, which was a step up from the fluff, in my opinion), I sat next to Jesse and leaned in close.

"What comes to your mind when I say 'diplomatic immunity'?" I asked.

"Free pass," he said, not taking his eyes off his monitor. "Why?"

"Just a story idea I was thinking of."

"If you're looking for controversy, Google 'diplomatic immunity and human trafficking.'"

"Really?"

He looked at me and nodded. "Good luck."

I went to my computer and did as he suggested, and story after story popped up about diplomats taking advantage of the help in their houses, and prosecutors unable to do anything about it. The *Washington Times* ran a story about how Hillary Rodham Clinton was taking a stand against what she called "modern slavery."

School ended, and I wasn't embedded. The week ended. I still wasn't embedded.

That Friday it was my rotation for Chiswick's horseback riding program. The school provided several monthlong units for things like horseback riding, watercolor art, CPR and EMT training, and other subjects that fell outside the jurisdiction of a regular high school. The property had a large stable at its west end, where a forest and hills provided plenty of riding trails.

I reported to the stables and looked around at the other students in my rotation.

There was Raf, talking to Giselle. Since my attempts with other people had failed to get me embedded, maybe approaching the most notorious of the DIs was my best shot.

"Hey," I said.

"Hi," he said.

"So, I'm sorry about the other day. You wanted to talk to me, and I was mean. I shouldn't have acted like that. What did you want to talk about?"

He sighed and shook his head slightly.

"Come on," I said. "Don't you ever speak without thinking?"

"I try not to," he said. "It tends to get me in trouble."

I snorted. "Like you've ever been in trouble." He frowned, and I realized *I* was speaking without thinking. "I'm sorry. I'll stop."

Raf gestured to Giselle. "Have you two met?"

"Not officially," I said.

"This is Giselle," he said. "Her father is the French ambassador. She is France, I am Spain, so historically we should be at war, but instead we're friends. Giselle, this is Pipper Baird."

"It's Piper," I said, holding out my hand.

"New scholarship student," he added.

"Is that a necessary part of my introduction?" I asked.

"I could already tell by the shoes," Giselle said. The way she said it wasn't totally mean, though, just matter-of-fact. She took my hand. "Nice to meet you, Pip."

"You too," I said.

"Pip talks to paintings," Raf said, starting to loosen up again.

I gave him a look. "Not painting*s*, plural. Just the one."

Giselle shrugged and turned away.

There were two other students who had the same riding times. One was Mateo Lopez. I waved and he waved back. The other was a girl, a short, chubby redhead whose name I didn't know. But I'd seen her around. She bounced over to me like a big red ball.

"Hi! I'm Katie." The girl had what sounded like an Irish

accent. "You're Pip, yeah?"

I cut a glance over at Raf, who shrugged.

"Nice to meet you, but it's Piper."

She raised her eyebrows. "Really? Everyone is calling you Pip. You *are* the girl with the unfortunate tear in her jeans, yeah? A few weeks ago?"

I glanced down at my jeans. Despite my best sewing work, the tear was still obvious. I squeezed my eyes shut and rubbed my forehead. "Yeah, that's me. I'm also the one who talks to paintings."

"Oh. Okay," she said, as if that totally made sense. "Pip. So great to meet you! Good to have you in our riding group. We're the best group, although it's weird not to have Rachel here anymore. Isn't it weird, Raf? She moved away. But you'll fit in nicely. Do you ride western or English? Most of us ride English, but there are a few outliers. Raf, for one. Anyway, follow me, and you can pick your saddle and your horse. . . ." She continued chatting away at the speed of a gallop as she dragged me to the equipment shed.

I glanced behind me and caught Raf giving me a sympathetic smile. I got the feeling Katie talked a lot.

Once we were all saddled up, we met in a group at the north end of the stables, where there was a trail leading out into the hills behind the school. I was in a western-style saddle. Before today, I hadn't known there was a difference. Riding was riding. But now I could see that the English saddles were missing the horn, and the English riders held one rein in each hand. The most I'd ridden a horse was for a weeklong horse camp when I was eight years old. I'd learned to hold both reins in my left hand and keep my right hand on my thigh, which made me a western rider.

Raf was also in a western style, but he held the reins in his right hand. He must be left-handed.

Since I'd had the least amount of experience of the group, the stable master gave me a small horse named Gidget. She was so tiny I worried I would squash her, and when it came to walking, she couldn't keep pace with the others. Which gave me the option of enduring an uncomfortable trot over the course of an hour, or relaxing with a walk and falling behind. I chose to walk, and tried not to think of it as a metaphor for my life.

Until I saw Raf and Giselle walking farther up ahead on the trail, and I remembered this was my chance.

I kicked Gidget and she added an extra boost in her stride. After a few minutes and an uncomfortable trot/walk, the two of us had caught up with Raf and Giselle.

Raf's horse was a stallion with hooves the size of small Volkswagen Beetles.

"Hi!" I said a little overenthusiastically. I tried to calm my voice down. "Hello. Hey."

Giselle looked uninterested in my existence.

"Hey," Raf said. "How did your story on the dance turn out?" he said.

It had been on the front page. He should've known how it turned out.

"Great. It made me want to learn the flamenco."

"Marta would be happy to teach you." At my confused expression, he said, "She was the dancer."

"I didn't know you knew her."

"Oh, I've known Marta for a long time. She used to teach me." He raised an eyebrow as he said this.

Did this guy ever *not* imply something? "You make it sound like she taught you more than dance."

"Let's just say she taught me many moves." He looked mischievous.

Giselle snorted. I thought back to the way the dancer had posed with Raf for the picture. She did seem very familiar with him.

"That sounds . . . statutory."

Raf burst out laughing. "You're funny. But no, Marta is only two years older than me."

"Really? She seemed older."

"It's the makeup," he said.

"Ah."

The three of us rode for a few minutes in silence—Giselle didn't seem anxious at all to break it—and I stole a glance at Raf's profile. His profile alone could've been a ten-o'clock headline.

"What's your horse's name?" I said.

"Spartacus."

"Of course it is. C'mon, Gidget." I clicked my tongue.

I ducked as we approached a low-hanging branch and, in doing so, nearly lost my balance. Raf shot out a steadying hand. He rode his horse as if he were as easy to master as riding a tricycle. Giselle cut a sideways glare toward me.

"I would ride Spartacus everywhere if I could," Raf said. "I would switch him with my own car, if possible."

"Sure," I said. "You could avoid those high gas prices. Hay is cheaper."

Giselle rolled her eyes. Loudly.

"And with Spartacus," Raf continued, "you would never find yourself in those annoying high-speed chases."

I looked at him. "You sound like you speak from experience."

He pressed his lips together and nodded, making his hair flop perfectly over his eyes. You wouldn't think hair could flop perfectly, but his did.

Remember the story.

"What happened?" I said.

"Just last weekend, as it turns out. We were in Georgetown, perhaps exceeding the speed limit, when we saw the flashing lights behind us."

"And you led them on a chase?"

"Goran Kovic was driving. He cannot afford to get another speeding ticket. He would be deported back to Croatia."

"So what did you do?"

"We found the nearest embassy—the Russian embassy. And we pulled in. The guard at the gate knows me, and he saw the diplomatic plates and opened up. At that point, there's nothing the police can do."

I just stared at him. This was the kind of stuff I needed. It was also the kind of stuff that infuriated me.

He shrugged in this totally European way. "Diplomatic immunity has its perks."

I thought about my three speeding tickets. There were no special plates or embassies to help me avoid three hundred dollars in fines.

"Where are we going tonight?" Giselle asked.

I had to assume she wasn't talking to me.

"No text yet," Raf said.

I remembered the passwords Mack had told me about. There was no way I would be getting a text with the secret party information, but Raf would have a phone and he would most definitely get the password. If I could get his phone . . . I thought about where it was right now. Maybe in his back pocket?

I decided to distract him. "What else do you get away with?"

"Well, there's drinking."

"What drinking?"

He held his right hand out, palm up. He did that a lot before speaking. I wondered if he'd developed the habit while his brain translated Spanish into English.

"Here, you cannot drink until twenty-one, yes?"

I was learning that when Raf said *yes?* like that, he rarely meant it as a question. He meant it like someone would say *you know?* or something like that.

I still answered it like a question. "Yes."

"So the embassies are technically built on the territories of the countries to which they belong. And most countries outside the US allow drinking at the age of eighteen."

"But you aren't eighteen yet," I pointed out. I spotted a phone-size bump in his back pocket.

"Yes, but most countries are more relaxed than the US about underage drinking laws. In Spain, for instance, we grow up having wine at the dinner table. I had my first glass when I was two."

I thought about what my dad would say if I ever brought wine to our dinner table. A few years ago, he'd headed up the "Not a Drop before Twenty-One" neighborhood volunteer campaign. And so far, it had worked for me. I hadn't had one drop.

"Last year, another American, Jackson Everett, came to a party at the French embassy. I remember he had used a mayonnaise jar to smuggle vodka from his parents' liquor cabinet. The jar still had remnants of mayo in it. Within fifteen minutes of arriving at the party, he'd drunk the entire thing. He spent the next two hours retching in the toilet. Perhaps if he had grown up with accessible alcohol . . ."

I shrugged. "I'll have to try that theory out on my dad."

Raf nodded encouragingly. "Yes. Tell your dad to call my dad, and they can discuss."

I drove within five miles per hour of the speed limit. I made the full S-T-O-P at the stop signs because if I got another ticket, I wouldn't be able to afford the insurance on my car. More proof that this was the story I was meant to write.

"Have you ever had to work a day in your life?" I said.

His eyebrows furrowed. "No."

"Of course. Because you have people for that."

"You know, Pip, you get this little dimple in your cheek when you're being condescending."

"Well . . . I . . ." I huffed a breath out. He was right. I was being condescending. I was supposed to be unbiased.

"It's not like I don't want to work. Work actually seems like it could be fun."

I tilted my head skeptically. "I spent the summer before my sophomore year dipping pinecones into red cinnamon-scented wax for rich people to use in their fires. Two months after school started, my skin was still dyed red and my pee smelled like Christmas."

"See? What could be better than holiday-scented urine?"

This made me laugh, despite myself.

"Finally," he said. "A smile."

At that moment the sun was shining on Raf just so, making him unfairly stunning. He gave Spartacus a click-click with his tongue, and suddenly I thought about his tongue. *Whoa. Where did that come from?* I flicked my cheek with the end of my rein, to slap some sense into myself. This was not a cute boy. This was the personification of my life's struggle.

Raf arched an eyebrow.

"It was a bug. On my face," I said.

"Okay. Like I was saying, I would get a job if I could. If my dad would allow it."

"Well, singing for tips isn't all it's cracked up to be," I said skeptically.

"I didn't ask to be born into privilege."

"Your dad won't let you get a job?" I said.

"Part of it is because I'm not a citizen here. But the bigger part is my dad won't let anything get in the way of my education." Raf frowned. I think it was the first time I'd seen him frown. Really frown. It made his whole face darker. "My dad has a plan for me, and a job would get in his way."

"What's his plan for you?"

He shrugged, but not in the European way. More in a brush-off way. "Rule Spain. And then, if there's time, take over the United States as well."

I got the feeling he wanted to stop talking about it, so I changed the subject. I didn't want to push my luck.

"Did Jackson Everett survive the night?"

His face lost a little bit of its darkness. "No one knows. What happens on Embassy Row . . ."

"Stays on Embassy Row?"

He tilted his head. "I was going to say 'could fill a book,' but your way is good too."

Giselle kicked her horse into a higher gear. Even on horseback, she still looked like she belonged on a runway. Her horse, too. They could do a fashion spread for *Horse & Hound*. I wasn't sure whose calf muscles were more defined, hers or the horse's.

"Raf!" She said his name almost like an exotic dog bark. *Rrruff.* "What's with the pace?"

"Just helping our new friend feel at home."

Hearing about his life of privilege had the opposite effect from making me feel at home. Raf had no idea what real exhaustion was. He didn't have to figure out how to pay for gas. He thought having a part-time job was . . . cute.

Giselle flipped her hair as she guided her horse back to join pace with Spartacus. She nonchalantly handed Raf a silver flask. "We're good for Chang's yacht tonight."

Raf took a swig and then handed it to me.

"What is this?" I said, holding the flask up to the light.

"It's Ambassador Bouchard's twenty-five-year-old single-malt scotch."

I sniffed it and made a face.

"Smells good, yes?"

"It sort of smells like . . ." I closed my eyes. "Band-Aids."

Raf looked thoughtful. "Maybe that's because of the cresols from the peat."

I shook my head slowly. "I have no idea what you just said."

"It's chemistry," Giselle said. "Raf is kind of obsessed with it."

I handed the flask back to Raf. "Thanks, but I think I'll pass."

Raf took it, glugged another gulp, and handed it back to Giselle, who threw her head back in a most unladylike manner and swigged some. She was every guy's fantasy. Gorgeous like a model and yet could chug like a frat boy. There was no competing with that type.

Not that I was competing with her.

"So, you guys are going yachting?" I said.

Giselle snorted. She even made that sound eloquent.

"I've never been on a boat," I added, as if it weren't obvious.

It was awkwardly quiet for a moment.

"Good luck with that," Giselle said.

"Thank you?" I said.

Raf seemed like he sympathized with my boatless plight, but in the end, he just shrugged.

Clearly they were going to be stingy with the invites. Raf's phone was sticking up from his back pocket. How hard would it be to grab it and find out the code word for tonight's party? Unfortunately, picking pockets was one journalistic skill I had yet to hone. But maybe if I distracted them, and then reached over . . .

"Pip?" Raf said.

Uh-oh. He'd caught me staring at his butt. "Uh, there was a . . . thing." My cheeks flushed and I turned away.

Apparently, it was time to stop pandering to the new girl,

because Giselle and Raf took their horses to a faster pace that poor Gidget couldn't match. I didn't bother trying to keep up.

High-speed chases. Drinking on school grounds, not to mention on horseback. (Did drinking on horseback count as a DUI?) Parties on yachts. Not inviting the new girl. Seemed to be a typical day in the life of the privileged. How did these guys get away with it all?

Giselle and Raf were going to retire for the evening on some exotic yacht while I had to go home and admit to my parents that I was failing to excel at this school and then ask them if I could borrow some gas money. Where was the justice in this new world?

Same school. Different planets.

Maybe they didn't deserve me poking around their lives, but poking around couldn't do any harm for now.

Saturday, Charlotte and I went to see *His Girl Friday* at the dollar theater. It was an old Cary Grant movie about two reporters who fell in love and were working to get the biggest scoop of the year. Even though it was decades old, it captured the spirit and competition of the journalism world. Plus, Cary Grant. Afterward, I told Charlotte about my idea to do an exposé on the DIs.

"Going undercover?" she asked.

"Yep. I'm posing as a scholarship student and everything."

She laughed. "And you think this will be *the story*?"

"I think it's my best shot."

She raised her water bottle. "Then I say, time to go Nellie Bly on 'em."

I clinked my water bottle with hers. Next week, I would be so convincing, Nellie Bly would be sitting up in her grave and giving me a high five.

The next time I saw Raf, it was Monday morning and we were on the same bus for a field trip to the National World War II Memorial. He didn't sit next to me, and I worried maybe my unrestrained opinions might have turned him away for good.

I looked for an empty seat and spotted one in front of a guy named Franco. I'd seen him with the DIs, and he was also in my economics class. We hadn't been formally introduced, but maybe he could be another source. He was sitting next to a guy named Dembé who was from somewhere in Africa.

I sat down. "Hey, Franco."

He looked up. "Pip," he said.

"It's 'Pipe,'" I said. "So where are you from?"

"Brazil," he said. Then he turned to Dembé and continued whatever conversation they'd been having, completely ignoring me.

Mack got on the bus then, spotted me, and sat next to me. "Hey," she said.

"Where's Faroush?"

"He opted out of the field trip. He has asthma, so he gets to use that excuse whenever he wants. I wish I had asthma. I hate these things."

"Why?"

She nodded toward Professor Berg—the school's most boring teacher. As the doors shut and the driver pulled out the professor stood up and started telling us the history of the World War II Memorial, and I began to wish I had asthma too.

The memorial consists of fifty-six granite pillars, arranged in a circle around a plaza and a fountain, with two arches, one each on the north and south ends. Each pillar is engraved with the name of a US state or territory. When the bus parked, Professor Berg gave us a quiz and fifteen minutes to wander around and find the answers.

I started right in on it.

"Don't waste your time," Mack said. "We never have to turn them in." She glanced over my shoulder as something caught her attention. "That guy is gonna kill himself."

I turned around and saw a bunch of students at the base of one of the pillars looking up at Rafael Amador, who was scaling the granite.

"What is he doing?" I asked Mack as we ran over to join the spectators.

"Besides desecrating a national monument?"

A couple of guards in blue uniforms ran over to the pillar and started yelling for Raf to come down. He didn't look like he was about to comply. I thought about how someone should be documenting this, and then I remembered that Jesse had given me the staff camera to take pictures of the memorial.

I pulled the giant thing out of my bag and started clicking away and didn't realize my powerful flash was on until Raf jerked his head my way, blinking. There was a moment where the entire crowd seemed to hold their breath, and that's when Raf lost his grip. He fell fast and hard to the ground with a sickening thud.

I gasped.

My flash. My flash killed Rafael Amador.

I turned to Mack, speechless.

"He would've fallen anyway," Mack said.

The guards rushed over to him. One of them spoke into a walkie-talkie, and I got a glimpse of Raf's left hand, which was hanging limply at a disturbing angle. I felt a twinge of guilt. But then his finger twitched and I realized he was at least alive.

"That doesn't look right," Mack said.

Raf didn't seem to be bothered by the pain. In fact, he was smiling. Maybe he was in shock.

"Do you think anyone else noticed the flash?" I asked.

"Um, yeah," Mack said.

I followed Mack's gaze over to where Giselle was giving me the stink eye.

"He would've fallen anyway," I said loudly.

"Keep telling yourself that," Giselle said.

The paramedics arrived on the scene. One looked at his wrist while the other checked out his eyes with a flashlight, saying something about a concussion. By the time they carted Raf away, the excitement began to die down, although everyone was talking about it for the rest of the day. They all said how epic the stunt was.

But I couldn't help thinking Rafael Amador had some sort of death wish, and maybe I shouldn't embed myself anywhere near him.

That night my mom made creamed tuna on toast. It was one of her go-to dinners, but I noticed she'd switched out our regular tuna for the store brand. I don't know why I noticed. It was still creamed tuna on toast.

Michael cut his toast into perfect little squares and arranged them in a row so he could eat them from left to right.

"How is the journalism program going?" my dad asked.

"It's okay," I said.

"It better be more than okay," my dad said with a smile. "You're this family's great hope."

I ruffled Michael's hair. "I want to go on record that I think Michael is going to make more money than all of us put together."

My mom smiled.

I stabbed my fork in my toast. "A weird thing happened today, though. This boy—"

"What's his name?" my dad interrupted.

"Rafael Amador."

"Is he cute?"

"Too gorgeous for his own good."

"Does he like you back?"

"No—that's not my point. He's one of the spoiled rich kids, and he was trying to convince me his life is harder than it looks, but I totally didn't agree, and then today, during a field trip, he decides to scale the pillar of a national monument. I took some pictures and it distracted him and he fell and broke his wrist. Why would someone do that?"

My mom frowned. "You broke a boy's wrist?"

"No. He totally would've fallen anyway. The monument is superhigh and he had no climbing gear, and that's not the point. The point is, why would someone who has everything do something like that?"

My parents met my question with blank expressions.

"Why were you taking pictures?" my mom asked.

"It's this story I'm working on. An exposé on all the stuff the rich DI kids get away with."

"DI?"

"Diplomatic immunity. It's a big thing at Chiswick. The DI kids basically run the school. So I figured, like any good reporter,

I would expose the corruption."

"It doesn't sound like the best way to make friends," my dad said.

I looked at him, confused. "I'm not there to make friends."

"I remember high school as the perfect time to make friends."

I shook my head. Same world. Different planets.

Right before bed, I called Charlotte and told her what had happened at the national monument.

"It's perfect," she said.

"What are you talking about?"

"Offer to help him. To write his notes and share yours and stuff. Tell him it will make you feel better about making him fall."

"He would've fallen anyway."

She ignored me. "It will give you an in."

I shook my head. "Do I still want to have an in? Raf seems a little crazy. What with scaling monuments and all."

"Do you think that's what Nellie Bly said when she saw Blackwell's Island? *I can't go in there, because they seem a little crazy*? C'mon, Pipe. What would Nellie say?"

I sighed. "She'd say, *Get your crazy on, girlfriend*."

12

When Raf showed up at school the next day, his left arm in a sling and a brace, he was immediately surrounded by admirers. Giselle was next to him, holding his books.

I wasn't going to be able to get near him now, so I went in the opposite direction, to my locker. Just as I raised my hand to turn the dial, Raf's voice came from behind me.

"Hey, Pip! Remember that one time you flashed me?"

I turned around and faced his grin.

"It's one of my favorite stories," he said. "I was climbing a national monument, set to make history, and this girl with the biggest camera I've ever seen sets her flash to 'stun.' And then I fell and broke my wrist."

"Shouldn't you be in jail right now for, like, desecration of a national monument? Or wait. Don't tell me. Diplomatic immunity."

He Euro-shrugged.

"Can I just ask you something?" I said.

"As long as it's not on the record."

"Why did you do it?"

He frowned. "Same reason Mallory climbed Everest. Because it was there."

I shook my head but then remembered Charlotte's idea. "I'd like to make it up to you."

"Hmm. I'm intrigued."

"Since the argument could be made that my actions triggered events leading up to the breaking of your wrist, I'll help you with your notes and homework and typing and stuff."

He put a finger on his chin thoughtfully. "Pip repays me and I get to try to knock that chip off her shoulder. I'm in."

"I don't have a chip on my shoulder."

"Oh, you have a chip the size of Alaska there. You'll see."

By the end of the week, Raf had switched around his schedule so that our similar classes were taken at the same time, all in the name of sharing notes. I didn't think it was that easy to change classes, but of course, because he's Rafael Amador, he got exactly what he wanted.

Our English teacher, Professor Wing, let us shuffle seats so that Raf and I were sitting close to each other. Raf even went as far as to push our desks together. Una glanced back at us, and I felt the train tracks running right between my desk and Raf's.

I turned my attention to Professor Wing. I was pretty sure he wanted to be an actor, because he loved to do dramatic readings during class. He would stand front and center, and before reading, he would close his eyes and take a deep breath in through his nose. To assume the character.

I dreaded these readings, not because he wasn't any good. (He really was.) But because after he finished, I couldn't help the urge to clap, even though no one clapped. So there was always this really long awkward pause.

Today, he was doing a dramatic reading of the beginning of *Moby-Dick*.

He took in a deep breath and cleared his throat. "'Call me Ishmael. Some years ago—never mind how long precisely—having little or no money in my purse, and nothing particular to interest me on shore . . .'"

It was really loud, too, I guess to reach the audience members seated in the mezzanine.

"'. . . I thought I would sail about a little and see the watery part of the world. It is a way I have of driving off the spleen and regulating the circulation.'"

At the word "spleen," he motioned toward his belly.

Raf leaned over. "That's not where his spleen is. Do you want to tell him, or shall I?"

"Don't you dare interrupt him. If you do, it'll go on forever," I whispered.

Raf sat back. Then leaned over again. "I've never felt the need to drive off my spleen. Have you?"

Professor Wing's gaze flitted in our direction, so I started scribbling notes.

"No," I whispered out of the side of my mouth. "I always thought my spleen was something necessary for survival."

"Actually, you can live very happily without your spleen. It's not one of the vital organs."

This made me turn. "How do you know?"

"I learned it at the kung fu marathon at the Tower. Ninjas are always going for the spleen." He made a slight karate chop motion. "Inflict the most damage. Keep your opponent alive."

There was a hiccup in Professor Wing's reading, and this time he narrowed his eyes at us before continuing on.

Raf sat back upright. Then he leaned over again and opened his mouth, but before he could get any words out, I cut him off. "My notes aren't going to be any good if you keep talking to me. Which means *your* notes aren't going to be very good."

He gave a short nod and turned his attention back to Professor Wing. "'. . . cooled by breezes, which a few hours previous were out of sight of land. Look at the crowds of water-gazers there.'"

At this, he gazed upward and to the left. So the rest of us turned to follow his gaze. He was staring at an old metal fan.

Raf sighed. "And we fall for it every time."

* * *

After class, my phone beeped with a text. It was from Charlotte.

How's the story coming? Is there any THERE there?

I frowned. So far all I had new to report was how Raf smelled when you sat by him for an entire hour.

He smelled really good, by the way.

"Who's it from?" Raf said from behind me. He'd been peeking over my shoulder.

"A friend," I said, clicking the screen dark. Charlotte really should've known better than to text something about the story where the subject of that story might be able to read it.

"What friend?"

"Her name's Charlotte. She goes to my old school. She wants to be a journalist too."

We started down the cement sidewalk that bisected the campus. I was sure I would appreciate the outdoor parts of this school come spring, but right now it was freezing.

"I've been in the news, as you know." He tilted his head, as if waiting for reassurance.

"I've heard," I said.

"Why do you want to pursue such a demeaning profession?"

My mouth dropped open in annoyance. "It's not demeaning. Journalism changed the face of war during Vietnam. It brought down a corrupt president. It keeps politicians in check."

"It thrives on intrusive pictures of celebrities."

"Sure, some magazines do, but there's a difference between

investigative journalism and tabloid fodder."

He nodded, considering my words, and then opened his mouth as if he were about to divulge some big life lesson, but right then Giselle strode by, using her perfect long legs and short skirt to make a statement to the world on just how perfect legs can be. She put her arm around Raf's neck and pressed her cheek against his. "Good-bye, lover. See you at Mass?"

Raf smiled good-naturedly, making no effort to disentangle himself, and for the first time, I realized they weren't just close friends. They were a couple. Was this new? Why hadn't I realized that before?

She'd called him "lover."

"Bright and early," Raf said, answering her question.

Okay, Raf and Giselle were together. So what? That made it easier to stick to my task and not get caught up in emotions, even though the two of them seemed completely wrong for each other. It was better for the story. It would go under the part subtitled "Revolving Door of Hookups."

It was perfect. Just perfect. Yay.

Giselle kissed him on the cheek and walked away, not once acknowledging me. Even better.

I squinted up at Rafael, all the while not thinking about how Giselle had called him "lover." Who used that term, anyway? What was she, some middle-aged housewife? "So, Mass. As in church? You guys go to church?"

He nodded solemnly. "We never miss Saturday-morning

Mass. Father Mannion expects us."

I'd never been very religious. I guess you could say I was raised believing there was a God, but he probably didn't care how I spent my Sundays. But this was an opening. A chance to see Raf outside school.

"You go to Mass, yes?" Raf said.

"Yes. Lots of times. All the time."

He cocked a skeptical eyebrow at me.

"They still hold Mass on Sundays, right? Not Saturdays?"

The corner of his mouth quirked up in this cute way, and I reminded myself he was with Giselle. For some reason, it was throwing me, the fact that they were together, and then it was throwing me that their togetherness was throwing me, and to keep myself from asking Raf about it, I did that thing where I overcompensated with what I lovingly referred to as "word vomit."

"Back in the day, I was totally close to my pastor. Father. Preacher man. But not in an inappropriate way. You know. Not in the way that makes the news nowadays." *Whoa. Get off that track.* "I was one of the first altar girls in our community. And don't get me started about . . ." My mind went blank. What was something Catholic? "Confession. Confessing, telling all my sins . . . paying for them. Making payments on them. Working out payment plans." What was the word I was looking for?? "Retribution!"

"Are you thinking of repentance?"

"Yes! That."

Raf just watched me as if he were thoroughly entertained and hoping the word vomit would continue. When I finally shut up, he said, "You've never been to Mass."

"No. Never. Not once. Not even on Christmas Eve. But I saw one on television." I frowned. "Okay, that's a lie. But I've seen the pope on television. He drives that Ford Focus, right?"

Raf tugged on a clump of my hair. "Come to Mass tomorrow, Pip. I promise it will be unforgettable."

An invitation. An official one. Granted, it was Saturday-morning Mass, and not one of their legendary parties, but it was something. And what better place to procure an invite to one of their legendary parties than during an ancient religious ceremony?

I wondered if this was how Christiane Amanpour felt when she closed in on one of the Taliban.

13

The next morning, at the ass crack of dawn, I stood in front of my mirror assessing the situation. What does one wear to Mass? I'd opted for a black skirt, black tights, black mary-jane pumps, and a black T-shirt with a black cardigan over it. I looked so severe. But church was a serious thing, wasn't it? Eternal salvation was not to be taken lightly.

Michael stopped by my room. "Today's Saturday. Are we going to Costco?"

He and I liked to go to the warehouse stores to get the free food samples on the weekends.

"Not today, bud," I said.

"But it's Saturday."

"I know. I can't go today, though."

He paused for a moment and looked like he wasn't sure what to do next.

"I'll go next week. Why don't you go get your list of swears and go over them with Mom and Dad."

He nodded and walked away. I was glad the change in routine hadn't caused a storm.

On my way out of the house, I passed my mom and dad, who were in the kitchen having their morning cup of coffee.

"Off to a funeral?" my dad said, taking in my appearance.

"Nope. Mass." I grabbed my car key off the hook by the door.

"Sounds great," my mom said. "Except you know we're not Catholic, right?"

I blew them a kiss, and just before I went out the door, I glanced at a stack of small, rectangular papers peeking out of an envelope on a small table. The top of the papers read, "Food Coupon."

Food stamps.

I left before I could process the discovery. Maybe they were for someone else. Some other family. Maybe they were free samples from the government. Maybe food elves had left them in the middle of the night.

By the time I got to Saint Ann's, I was resigned to the fact that no, the food stamps weren't meant for anyone else.

Except us.

Were we really in such dire straits?

Maybe I would ask my mom when I got home.

Maybe I wouldn't.

The cathedral was down the street from Chiswick, but the traffic was unexpected. I was five minutes late. The heavy wooden doors squeaked as I entered, making everyone already seated turn to stare at the person who'd dared show up late to Mass.

Ugh. I waved my hand in an apologetic way and quickly scanned the crowd for Raf and Giselle. When I finally saw the backs of their heads, I sighed. They were dead center in the front row. A girl with red hair was next to Giselle. It was probably Katie.

All at once, the congregation opened hymnals and stood to sing, following the music leader, who had to be at least a hundred and ten. I walked as quietly as I could up the aisle, but my blasted mary janes echoed off the stone walls with each step.

Heads turned as I passed by. Basically the only way I could've attracted more attention would be if I were a bride walking down the aisle.

Once I was seated, Raf leaned over and said, "Quite the entrance there, Pip. Wasn't the marching band available to accompany you?"

"Shut up," I said.

The singing ended and everyone sat down to listen to the sermon.

Father Mannion, bespectacled and wrinkled, droned on and

on about the evils that tempt us as teenagers, and after twenty minutes of his monotone, I started to drift. My last thought before dozing was wondering if research for my story was really worth enduring Mass.

A sharp elbow in my arm woke me.

"You were snoring," Raf said.

"I don't snore," I muttered.

Katie leaned over. "You have the most delicate snore," she said with a grin.

Raf cough-laughed.

"Why did you wake me up?" I said.

"You were about to miss the best part," he said.

"How can anything beat that sermon?"

He didn't answer as a line of altar boys dressed all in white filed in, the last one carrying a chain with a silver ball attached at the end. Smoke escaped through vents inside the ball and swirled above the boy's head. I recognized him. It was Gabriel Martínez, the son of an Argentinian diplomat.

He swung the smoking ball back and forth, and as he passed the front row, our row, he arced the ball perilously close to our faces.

I flinched away. Why hadn't anyone warned me church was dangerous? Were you considered more faithful if you didn't flinch?

I was about to comment on it when a familiar odor reached my nose. I'd smelled it only once before, and that was at a bluegrass festival my mom took me to.

"Breathe it in, Pip," Raf said.

The odor seemed to be emanating from the silver ball.

"Is that . . . is that . . ." I sniffed in what I'm sure was a most unattractive way. "Pot?"

"It is something of the cannabis family, that is certain," Raf said. "Gabriel has a greenhouse in his basement."

Giselle and Franco, who were on the other side of Katie, leaned forward in their seats, inhaling as much as they could. After a while, Giselle let her head fall onto Raf's shoulder. Gabriel walked back and forth in front of us, his face a solemn mask, never betraying the fact that the holy incense burning inside his silver ball was not, in fact, incense.

Father Mannion looked on with a faint smile of approval. Was he high?

"Did I mention that Father Mannion lost his sense of smell due to nasal polyps?" Raf said.

My mouth hung open.

"Close your mouth, Pip. Inhale."

"But I've never smoked pot," I whispered, turning my head to see if anyone of the police variety was coming down the aisle.

"And you still haven't. You've only inhaled."

Pot in the church. Now I could see why no one missed Mass. But how was it that no one had gotten caught, either?

As if I'd asked the question out loud, Raf leaned over and said, "Gabriel's dad has a good relationship with church security. It's part of his distribution network."

Distribution network? Those were charged words. Those were words around which a reporter could frame a story. Those were words rarely spoken on the record. That was the tricky thing about reporting. Unless you say "off the record" before the interview, anything is fair game. Normal people didn't know that.

But I did.

In the stained glass interior of a cathedral, I'd found my first possible headline.

CANNABIS IN MASS . . .

HOW DID ARGENTINIAN DIPLOMAT CONVINCE
POLICE TO TURN THE OTHER WAY?

14

It was a headline, to be sure. But not enough for the kind of exposé I needed. Not only that, it was obvious Raf seemed to trust me enough that "off the record" went without saying. But it didn't.

When Mass was over and we were all outside, a handsome couple was waiting. "Gigi," the woman called out, waving to Giselle. It must've been her mom, but she looked too young. Giselle took Raf's hand.

"See you around, Pip," he said.

"Oh. Are you guys all going home? For . . . the day? And night?"

He shrugged. "Not sure. But we'll catch up Monday, yes?"

"Yes."

"Are you good to drive?"

"Yeah. I don't feel anything."

He smirked. "You might want to take a little walk anyway. See you later."

I tried to mask my disappointment. As I walked away, I wobbled a bit. I grabbed the bag at my shoulder, as if it would steady me.

The pot had affected me more than I'd thought.

Raf and Giselle waved as I left.

I was disappointed on an investigative reporter front, but I sensed I was also disappointed in other ways. Ways I could feel inside my chest, just underneath my ribs. Ways that had to do with Giselle's perfect face. So instead of letting myself explore those feelings (because every good reporter knows there's no room for those kinds of feelings, those ones you feel in your chest under your ribs), I sat down on one of the benches lining the sidewalk and texted Charlotte.

Me: Guess what? Pot in the incense balls at Mass!

Charlotte texted back immediately.

Charlotte: Is that a euphemism?

I rolled my eyes.

Me: No! I went to Mass. There was pot in the little silver ball thingies they swing around!

Charlotte: You went to Mass??

Me: How is that the bigger question?

Just then, I caught Raf walking alone out of the corner of my eye. I looked up. Maybe now was my chance.

Me: brb

"Hey, Raf! 'Sup?" It came out loud and clumsy.

Raf stopped and smiled. "What did you think of Mass?"

His smile was sort of brilliant, and my breath caught a little in my throat. "It was interesting, to say the least."

"Mass isn't normally held on Saturday mornings, but Father Mannion knows none of us would show up on Saturday night. He likes to feel hip and brag about catering to the younger crowd."

"Apparently," I said.

Probably because of the pot, Raf seemed a little floaty. And slightly blurry around the edges. And a little distorted.

"But still beautiful," I said, finishing the conversation I'd been having in my head.

"Huh?" Raf said.

"Oh, um . . . Mass. It was beautiful."

"Okay." He glanced at the ground and his hair did that perfect thing where it fell across his perfect eyes perfectly. I could see why he got in trouble with so many girls. If I were into perfect floppy hair, I would probably be affected by the floppage. But I wasn't. Because I knew this was the pot talking. It was replacing Raf's annoying habits with attractive ones, because pot can do that. This is why pot was dangerous. Pot made you irrational.

"So can I borrow your phone, or what?" I said.

He raised his eyebrows, as if the question was unexpected.

"Weren't you just texting on your own phone?"

He'd been watching. I scrambled. "I was, but then it ran out of all the batteries." Yes, it was a lie, but not a bad lie, because it was in pursuit of a story.

Raf looked wary, but took his phone out of his pocket and handed it to me.

Now what? How was I supposed to find the password with him looking over my shoulder?

"Um, could you give me a little privacy?" I said. Raf didn't move. "I need to text my brother about our upcoming Scrabble game."

He looked to be suppressing a smile but turned away.

His phone was like mine, so it was easy to find the text messages. Once I did, I scrolled down past all the Giselles (okay, there was just the one Giselle, but she'd sent lots of texts, and maybe I clicked on one of them for a second) to a text sent to a group. It said:

SPAIN 15-11

Luchar contra el hombre

15-11. In America, that was 11/15. November 15th. That was next Saturday.

"Ha!" I said.

"What?" Raf said.

"I . . . just beat solitaire. Thank you." I handed him back his phone and left him to go for a long walk. Because I really shouldn't drive in my condition.

* * *

That night I told Charlotte about my detective work, and she came right over with some "educational material," which consisted of a flash drive of clips from Christiane Amanpour making the Taliban talk and Joyce Latroy making dictators cry.

"You see how they use empathy as a tool?" she'd say.

"Look how she lets the silence fill the room," she'd say.

"Nobody acts desperate," she'd say.

"See how she tries to analyze the subject's behavior? That's a good opening. Everyone loves to be analyzed."

When we were done studying, we decided to visit the Post-Anon site.

"Ooh," Charlotte said, pointing to a poem titled *I Lost You*. I clicked on it and read.

> *I am ugly without you to tell me I'm pretty*
> *I am lost without your hand on my back*
> *I am drowning in all of this space you now give me*
> *I would do anything to get you back*

"Love sucks," Charlotte said.

"I couldn't agree more."

Around one in the morning, we fell asleep to the dulcet tones of the twenty-four-hour news channel.

15

The following Monday, I felt a little bad about my deception, but I had more digging to do.

Bob Woodward always said, "You get the truth at night, and lies during the day." And he broke Watergate, so he knew what he was talking about.

That's why I stole the code off Raf's phone. So I could find the truth at night. At a DI party.

When I got to Professor Wing's class, Raf saw me and smiled, and I swear somehow he'd gotten cuter since Saturday. He didn't annoy me as much as he used to, and that realization annoyed me.

I sat down next to him. "Scale any monuments lately?"

"Nope," he said. "But as soon as this heals"—he pointed to his brace—"I have plans for the Washington Monument."

"Because it's there?" I said.

"Naturally," he said.

"You know, there are professionals who can help you curb your appetite for seeking thrills."

"Why would anyone want to do that?"

I shrugged. "Survival? No broken bones?"

"That doesn't sound like living."

I shook my head and decided to try out Charlotte's advice about analysis. "I have a theory about you."

He raised his eyebrows. "I'm flattered you've given me so much thought. What's your theory?"

"I think you do stupid stuff so you can feel."

He scratched his head. "Feel what?"

"I don't know yet."

He nodded. "It's not a very well-formed theory yet, is it?"

Professor Wing closed the door as the bell to begin class rang, and we didn't get a chance to continue.

The next day, in chemistry, Professor Ferron was demonstrating what happens when sodium reacts with water. Raf and I were sitting in the front row of desks (his choice). And I was madly taking notes.

Raf wouldn't need to borrow these notes. He was really good at chemistry, and he kept everything in his head. But he needed my help for the finagling of doohickies during labs. Not that my finger dexterity was something to write home about, but it was marginally better than that of a guy with a brace on his wrist.

Then again, who would ever write home about finger dexterity anyway? That was why it was important to steer clear of clichés, because what would the letter look like?

Dear Mom,
I met this boy who can pick up a single grain of sand between his thumb and forefinger! Dexterity!
Love, Piper

Dear Piper,
Marry that boy!
Love—

"What kind of notes are those?" Raf was reading over my shoulder. I'd started absentmindedly doodling the "letters to home" on my paper.

I swept the paper off my desk and got a fresh one out. "Nothing. Just practicing my shorthand."

The crack of an explosion came from the front of the classroom. Professor Ferron had taken a tiny piece of sodium and dropped it in a petri dish of water. The class clapped unenthusiastically and ironically, and Professor Ferron took a bow. I liked Professor Ferron. He was simultaneously obsessed and unimpressed with science.

A knock came at the door, and the school secretary poked her head in, motioning for Professor Ferron. As he was momentarily preoccupied with whatever news she'd come to deliver, Raf leaned over toward me.

"Tell me, Pip," he said, "do you think I can make it rain?"

"What?"

"Shall I make it rain?"

I rolled my eyes. "I know you think you can do anything, Rafael Amador, but I highly doubt you can control the skies."

"Not the skies." With the flick of his wrist, he took his water bottle and threw the water on the slightly larger lump of sodium on Professor Ferron's desk.

I jumped out of my chair as a flash of light, much brighter and louder than the first, exploded.

Professor Ferron lunged from the doorway and threw a handful of sand onto his desk, and the bright light and crackling explosions stopped.

The entire classroom heaved a sigh of relief.

Then the fire alarm went off—much later than I would've considered safe. Maybe that could be my next exposé: "Why the Alarms Are Delayed at Chiswick Academy." And then the sprinklers on the ceiling turned on. Streams of water pelted the desks.

Giselle held her backpack over her head. I wanted to tell her not to bother, because even with makeup streaming down her face, she still looked great. Other students would start wearing makeup streaming down their faces just to look as gorgeous as Giselle in this downpour.

The students rushed toward the door, and I realized that I wasn't as wet as I should've been. Raf had been holding his folder above my head.

"And you thought I couldn't make it rain," he whispered.

16

Did I mention Raf held his folder above my head?

No. Because why would I? He's just a story.

The school closed early because of the "incident," and evacuated us all, which I was pretty sure was the reason Raf had done what he'd done.

I kept practicing writing the story of the explosion in my mind. It should've started out with a headline like "When the Privileged Get Bored: A Simple Lab Experiment Turns into an Explosion."

But instead, the only headline I was coming up with was "Rafael Amador Holds Folder over Head of Scholarship Student."

Maybe he was just trying to be nice. Or maybe he had seen

the beginnings of my smeared makeup and thought, *No more. Please, no more.*

He probably wouldn't have held his folder above my head if he'd known he was the focus of my exposé.

But for now, the exposé was still just in my head.

Once we were outside, I stood there awkwardly as Raf took a moment longer than necessary to lower the folder.

"What is wrong with you?" I said. "You could've burned the school down."

He didn't answer me. Instead, he took out a pack of gum (some foreign type, because I couldn't read the label), popped a piece into his mouth, and balled up the wrapper. Then he held it between the thumb and forefinger of his left hand, and with his right hand closed his fingers around the paper, making a fist around the wrapper. Then, voilà, he opened his fingers and the wrapper had magically disappeared.

With his other hand, he pretended to take it out of my ear.

I rolled my eyes.

"I saw the wrapper the whole time," I said. "It stayed in your left hand."

"You're just assuming that."

"I'm not. Do it again, and switch hands or don't, and I'll tell you which hand it's in."

He did it again.

"Left," I said.

He did it again.

"Left again."

He did it again.

"Right."

He sighed. And then he did it again.

"Left."

"Hmm. Maybe it's because I have a brace," he said.

I shrugged. "I told you. I'm very observant."

"You are. Has anyone ever told you you should be a reporter?" He smiled.

"So, back to the fire: What is wrong with you?"

He looked upward at the blue sky. "It's too beautiful a day to be trapped indoors, wouldn't you say?"

"Is that what you're going to tell the judge? *It was a beautiful day, so I burned down the school*?"

"What judge?"

I sighed, frustrated and flustered. "Oh, yeah. Diplomatic immunity. No judge. No jury. No consequences. A lifetime surrounded by yes-people and nothing to show—"

He put his finger on my lips. "Can we stop with the prosecution?"

I glanced away. "Sorry. Habit."

"You know, Pip, you have a bright future. There are plenty of stories of those who started with nothing and persevered to great success."

"You think I have nothing?" My mind flashed to the food stamps in my kitchen.

He closed his eyes for a long blink. "Well, sometimes you act like the downtrodden."

Ow.

He walked away.

"I don't act like the downtrodden," I muttered.

Like he would even know what the downtrodden looked like.

I guess that's what the downtrodden would say.

17

I decided to ignore Raf's comments. Maybe I was acting like the downtrodden, but that was only because I *was* a downtrodden.

I shook my head. My dad wouldn't like to hear that.

I decided again to ignore his comments. After all, I'd scored the password to one of their exclusive parties. If I was one of the downtrodden, I would share this moment as the one that changed everything.

The night of the party, I felt the same way Christiane Amanpour must have felt the first time she was allowed to be embedded with US troops in Iraq, except I was now embedded with what could be the biggest scoop inside the Beltway.

I'd been texting Charlotte all day.

Me: Going to the party!

Charlotte: Don't forget to go through the medicine cabinets. 98% of secrets are hidden there. And if you open the closet and find a giant plastic bag full of fingernails, run.

Me: You thought there would be any scenario where I found a bag full of fingernails and didn't run?

I did all the necessary things to prepare for covert investigation: I programmed my phone to record sound with the touch of a button, video with the touch of another one. I brought a notebook and pen in my purse, in case I ran out of battery and there was a power outage or something. I wouldn't be caught unprepared.

As for personal preparations, I psyched myself up. I wanted to play it cool. I would try to be witty and inviting, but not too inviting. I assumed one of the security guards would be taking the password, and as long as I could get by, then I could stay under the radar inside.

I practiced faces in the mirror, working on an expression that hopefully said, *Feel free to tell me all your secrets.*

"What are you doing, Pipe?"

I jumped and turned at the same time. My dad was standing behind me, watching me make faces in the mirror.

"Nothing," I said, short of breath. "Why?"

"You look like you're somewhere between very confused and very hungry."

I sighed. "I was going for trustworthy."

"Ah. Try a little less frown. And not quite so much squint in your eye."

I adjusted my look.

"There. That's a little less constipated looking."

"I thought you said 'confused and hungry'?"

"Yeah, I meant constipated. Why are you practicing a trustworthy face?"

I bobby-pinned a clump of my hair up to keep it from falling into my eyes. Must stay sharp and not obscure my vision!

"I got invited to a party at the Spanish embassy." I didn't tell him I was using the term "invited" loosely. "This, Dad, is where I get the scoop."

He smiled. "I'm glad you have your fire back. I'll leave you to practice your faces."

"Thank you."

I started singing along with the song on my playlist. Michael walked by. "Stop singing," he said. "You're ruining everything."

As he walked away, I smiled. At least I'd never have to wonder what he was really thinking. I worked on my facial expressions again, focusing on the changes my dad had suggested, frowning a little less and widening my eyes. Once I'd settled on a face a nation could trust—I dubbed it the "Walter Cronkite"—I texted Charlotte again.

Me: I'm ready! Recording devices set, facial expressions mastered, notebook in hand.

Charlotte: Great! What are you wearing?

Crap! I glanced up from my screen and looked in the mirror again.

Me: Hello Kitty T-shirt. Jeans. Sneakers . . .

She texted me a "grrrrr" emoji.

Charlotte: You don't want to repel your assets, do you?

Me: Ack! No! What should I wear?

Charlotte: Wear your jeans, those black boots with the silver thingies, and the shirt we bought that one time when your finger got caught in the dressing room door.

Everyone needs a best friend who can say, *Wear that one thing from that one time* and you know exactly what they're talking about.

I rifled through my closet until I found the outfit, changed into it, and took a mirror pic to send to Charlotte.

Perfect. Now get that piece of lettuce between your teeth.

I pulled my lips back from my teeth and, sure enough, there it was. What would I do without her?

I drove my car to the Spanish embassy. I was pretty sure I was the only one who'd driven their own car. The lot was jam-packed with long black sedans and drivers leaning against doors, drinking coffee and smoking.

I pulled up to the gate. A man in a blue security uniform strode out of a guard station and over to my car.

"Yes?"

"Um . . . *Luchar contra el hombre?*"

I'd looked up the phrase at home. It roughly translated to "fight the man." Whatever that meant to someone like Raf.

The guard nodded. "Reason for visit?"

To uncover and expose the underground network known as "diplomatic immunity."

"A party?"

He frowned. Then he asked for my license, and after looking at it, his frown deepened.

No way was I going to be turned away at the gate. What would Christiane Amanpour do?

She'd say something in Arabic that would be just the right thing that would convince the guard to let her through. Because that was her specialty.

What could I do here?

I could speak in Spanish.

"¿Dónde está la baño?"

He looked up from my license, and as he handed it back, he said, "There are twenty-two bathrooms inside. I'm sure you'll find one to your liking. And it's 'el *baño*.' Not 'la.'"

I could feel the heat reach my cheeks. "Right. Thank you. I guess you're not available for Spanish lessons?"

He didn't even acknowledge that I'd spoken again. He just pressed a button, and there was a buzzing noise, and he opened the gate.

I parked my old Toyota behind the sea of black sedans. When I got out, a man in a tuxedo approached me and asked for my keys. I handed them over and he started to walk away.

"Wait, don't you need my name?"

He held the keys up with just his thumb and forefinger and said, "I think I'll remember the girl with the Toyota."

I went to the door and looked up at the ornate knocker. The gold in it could've paid for my college tuition, I was sure. Maybe instead of going for the Bennington, I should just steal the knocker.

Okay, Pipe. Slip inside and blend in. Slip and blend. Slip and blend.

Unexpectedly, the door flew open. Even more unexpectedly, it was Raf. My heart did a little twitterpation, and I considered diving into the bushes, but at this point in our relationship, that would be cliché.

"Pip?" he said, looking confused.

"I . . . uh . . . I . . ." *Crap.* What could I say? "I followed a . . . dog."

"A dog?"

I shook my head. "A car. I thought I knew it?"

"The car?"

"The driver."

He narrowed his eyes.

"And I thought it was my cousin. Who has been missing."

"Your cousin's missing?" he said, true concern on his face.

I shook my head. "No. He was found. I just forgot."

Raf scratched his forehead. "Do-over."

Before I could say, *Huh?* he slammed the door shut. I just stood there. I raised my fist to knock, but before I could, the door swung open again.

"Pip! What a surprise." His face showed everything but surprise. "Come in."

He was wearing black jeans and a button-down white shirt with the sleeves rolled up to the elbows.

He looked really good. He gave me a smile that reached from my eye sockets to my kneecaps. I couldn't imagine a happier reaction to a party crasher.

"Hi," I said. It was about all my heart could manage.

No, not my heart. The heart was about love. What was the part of the body associated with simple physical attraction?

Loins.

Ugh. Why was that the first word I came up with? *Stop thinking about loins!*

"Are you doing that thing again where you're having a conversation in your head, and I am merely an intruder?"

"How did you know I did that?" I said.

"Well, it's either that or you have indigestion."

"It's indigestion."

I put my hand in my pocket and felt for my phone. I wanted to keep it at the ready.

"Follow me," Raf said, starting to look unsure as to why I was there and what he was supposed to do with me.

We started to walk out of the opulent entryway when a man

appeared from one of the several hallways surrounding us. He looked like an older version of Rafael.

"Did I hear that somebody has indigestion?" he asked. Before either of us could answer, he motioned to a pretty woman in a dark suit who was following him. "Lidia, could you get some club soda and that powder Mrs. Amador swears by?"

For someone who was scary and had a history of getting people fired, he seemed pretty nice.

Lidia nodded curtly, made a note on the clipboard she was carrying, and rushed off.

My cheeks flushed. I could feel them burn. There was no way I was going to yell and stop her and try to explain I didn't have indigestion.

Raf didn't stop her either, although I'm sure he knew I didn't have stomach problems.

"Papa. I'd like you to meet Pipper Baird. She's new at our school. Pip, meet His Excellency, Leon Gabriel Amador, the Spanish ambassador to the United States."

Whoa. Quite a title.

Raf's dad held out his hand. "It's a pleasure to meet you, Miss Baird."

"The pleasure's mine. Your . . . Highness."

Raf stifled a laugh, but his father merely smiled bigger.

"'Mr. Amador' will do. Especially for friends of Rafael's. After all, you should've heard the names his mother called me as Rafael was being born."

"Papa!" Raf said, looking embarrassed. I'd never seen him look embarrassed. It was adorable.

"It's true. That's why his middle name is—"

"Papa!"

"Leandró. It means 'lion man.' She was sure she had given birth to something the size of a lion."

Raf looked to the ceiling. "Oh God," he mumbled.

"Do you have a middle name?" his dad asked me.

I smiled a little. "Lily. It means, like, the flower."

"And what do your parents do?" he asked.

"Um, my dad works for the Power and Light Company."

"Ah." Mr. Amador looked confused, maybe because he didn't realize I was a scholarship student. "And your mother?"

"She takes care of me and my younger brother," I said. "And she works nights in a bakery."

Mr. Amador's face lost all traces of his former smile. "Well, I'll let you two get to it."

Raf put his arm on my back and started leading me away. "Okay, Papa."

We walked down a series of hallways and parlors and sitting rooms and drawing rooms. Faint music grew louder the closer we got to what I assumed was the "great room" of the house.

"I don't think your dad likes me very much," I said.

"He's like that with everybody," Raf said. He wasn't very convincing.

We kept going in silence.

"Are you going to kick me out?" I asked.

He smiled. "I'm not the type. Besides, you must have gone to great lengths to get here. Maybe it involved stealing phones and such." He gave me a knowing glance.

I looked away, heat filling my cheeks again.

"If you wanted to be friends so badly," he said, "all you had to do was ask."

I doubted it. Besides, this wasn't about making friends.

The music became clearer, but I didn't recognize the song. It sounded like it was in another language. German maybe? And it had a techno beat. Suddenly I imagined a giant orgy in the great room. I'd read about them in articles about the lives of the foreign privileged elite. Orgies. Drugs. Hallucinations. Sex. Cool Euro club clothing. Maybe something really weird like gnome bongs or Oompa Loompa limbo.

We were getting close to the room. What would I say if someone propositioned me?

No thanks, I have the clap?

Honestly, I didn't even know what the clap was, but it did not sound pleasant.

Before I could come up with a respectable rejection, we turned a corner, revealing the largest room I'd ever seen.

18

It wasn't as big as Carnegie Hall. I guess that was the only place I could really compare it to. Except for the room under the dome at the Capitol Building. But as for houses, I'd never seen anything like it.

It looked to be the length of half a football field.

The walls were covered in tapestries and paintings, and there were a dozen chandeliers overhead, but none of them were lit. The room was rather dark, except for the swirling lights from the equipment of the DJ.

The music itself seemed like an additional presence in the room. It filled the empty spaces and pressed into my ears like it wanted to bypass the eardrums and go straight to my brain.

There had to be about a hundred people inside, most dancing to the music, many drinking from clear plastic cups. I recognized a bunch of them. Mateo Lopez, Franco, Gabriel, Katie, two other girls from the paper, Pat Bagley—son of a Scottish diplomat—and a few others. A lot of faces were unfamiliar.

Raf leaned over and shouted something in my ear, but I couldn't make it out exactly. Did he say, *Grab a drink*?

Giselle emerged from the crowd on the dance floor, carrying an extra clear plastic cup. She handed it to me with a smile and then she seemed to register my face. She gave me a confused look.

Hi? I was sure she shouted, but it looked more like she just mouthed the word.

I took the plastic cup and mouthed, or shouted, *Thank you*, even though I couldn't hear which way I'd said it. I was glad the music was too loud for her to ask any questions.

Giselle rejoined the party in the middle of the floor, and I was suddenly alone, holding a cup, so I took a drink mostly because I was feeling awkward and deserted.

Whatever was in the clear plastic cup, it was stronger than my regular juice, and a tad sparkly.

As my ears adjusted to the decibels, a girl with brown hair came up to me.

"You're in my chemistry class," she said.

I had no idea how I was able to make out a single syllable she'd said. Maybe I was getting used to the music. Maybe I'd killed all the fragile ear hair thingies and now I was partially deaf.

"Yeah, I'm Piper."

"I know," she yelled. "Thank you for getting school out early!
I'm Hillary!"

"I didn't do it!"

"What?"

"The fire. I didn't . . . Never mind!"

She sat there, smiling, waiting for me to say something else.
Why would anyone want to make small talk in all this noise?
It would be like aliens came to blow up your city on Independence Day, and during the explosions, you asked your neighbor
if they'd read any good books lately.

I tried to think of something, anything, we might have in
common.

"Loud music, huh?" I said.

"What?" she shouted.

"*Loud music* . . . Never mind."

"Huh?"

This was really pointless. I put a finger against a crack in my
cup and tapped it and Hillary smiled and nodded in an *oh, I get
it* kind of way, even though I had no idea what I'd meant. All I
knew was, I wasn't going to get a story by trying to talk over the
music.

As I walked away, apparently to the emergency cup repair
station, I sipped my drink and tried to check out everyone around
me without looking too suspicious.

THINGS I WAS LOOKING FOR:

1. Drugs. Drug paraphernalia. Drug deals. Manila envelopes
   being exchanged. Joints being lit.
2. Prostitutes.
3. Cops looking the other way.

As for number one, I couldn't find anything that looked like rolled joints, or under-the-table deals, or a bong. I'd seen enough television shows to know what a bong looked like.

Number two, there were several girls on the dance floor about whom one could make the argument that they were dressed like prostitutes. But they really looked to be about my age, and their clothes were designer and tailored. No safety pins or hand-me-downs there.

As for number three, I knew there wouldn't be literal cops in the room, looking the other way. But what about the security detail? Where were *they* while their subjects were partying hard?

I glanced at the walls. Oh. There they were, their dark suits blending against the unlit walls as they stood back and watched their charges.

What, were they going to just stand there while their teenage charges . . . did . . . their thing?

Actually, the thing most of the people in the room were doing was dancing. And sipping responsibly from their cups.

I took another swig, the music sounding twice as loud as it had been before. Wasn't it supposed to sound softer as the tiny hairs in your ears became permanently damaged? What were those ear hairs called? The ones that registered sound waves. Stereo-cilia?

I felt a hand on my shoulder and turned to see Raf. He leaned toward me and put his lips on my ear. *On my ear.*

"You seem miles away!" he shouted. "Are we not entertaining you?"

I used my pointer fingers to make circle motions in the air.

Raf nodded. *Loud.*

He motioned toward the DJ lights and the music went down one decibel. Then he took my wrist and raised the hand holding my cup and poured some more pink sparkly stuff in it.

"Sangria!" he said. "From Spain. My family makes it."

I heard him better this time. "It's delicious!" I took another sip. "Does it have alcohol?"

He wrinkled his eyebrows. "Yes. It's like sparkly wine."

"Ah. I've never had the alcohol!"

His eyes went wide, and he went to grab the cup from my hand, but I yanked it away, the liquid sloshing a little over the sides.

"It's not because I haven't wanted to! It's because my dad used to participate in the 'Not a Drop before Twenty-One' neighborhood campaign." It was a small campaign, consisting of the houses in our cul-de-sac.

Raf still seemed uneasy—or maybe he just hadn't heard my infallible reasoning over the music—and looked like he was ready to pounce on my cup again, but right then, Giselle came up and put her arm around his neck, kissing him on the cheek. At least, I think it was supposed to be a kiss on the cheek, but she ended up very close to his lips. Where was Raf's security guy when I needed him?

I mean, when *Raf* needed him.

"Dance with me!" she said.

He smiled and nodded, but before he left, he quickly switched my cup with his. His had less of the . . . what was it called? Santaria? Santa Maria?

I didn't like the idea of someone else dictating what I could and couldn't drink, even though I guess technically the law did that. But I was in Spain. It was no longer my law. And when in Spain . . .

I switched my cup with the cup of the guy standing next to me. His had more in it. He gave me an annoyed look, which was weird because all the cups looked alike, and he could just go get more of the drink whenever he wanted it. Who was this guy?

"Who is this guy?" I shouted at him.

He looked side to side and then pointed at himself. "Who am *I*? As in, what's my name?"

I rolled my eyes and nodded. He didn't look foreign, but he sure didn't understand English very well.

"I'm Samuel. Why did you take my drink?"

"Well, Samuel, if that really is your name—"

He raised an eyebrow. "Why wouldn't that be my name?"

"You tell me."

He didn't.

"As I was saying, *Samuel*, it's not technically *your* drink until you ingest it. Before then, I believe it's anyone's drink."

He smiled. "That's very philosophical of you."

"I philosophize often. You don't go to Chiswick."

"Huh?"

Seriously, what was this guy's deal with plain English?

"You. Don't. Go. To. Chiswick. It's a simple question."

This time he seemed to be suppressing a laugh. "Sorry. You just change subjects so quickly. And technically, it's not a question. But you're right, I don't go to Chiswick. I go to Sidwell."

I took another drink and turned to the dance floor, where Giselle and Raf were dancing super close. Raf looked over at me and smiled, and then did this double-take thing as he seemed to register that Samuel and I were talking.

I turned to Samuel. "The president's kids go to Sidwell!"

He nodded and looked at me as if I was stating the obvious. "Yeah. How do you know Rafael?"

"See that brace on his wrist?"

Samuel nodded.

"I did that." I made two fists, put them together, and then twisted them apart. "Snap. Care to dance?"

"Um, I think I'm going to go over there." He motioned to the opposite side of the great room.

"What's over there?"

"People. Other people."

"Don't be silly. Come dance." I grabbed his hand and pulled him to the dance floor.

Samuel shouted something from behind me, but it was muffled. Something about how I should be careful with his wrists?

It was at that moment that I remembered I was supposed to be a reporter. What better way to observe than by blending in on the dance floor?

Raf looked at me and smiled and then looked at Samuel and did that boy-greeting thing where he flicked his head upward once. *Hey, dude. 'Sup?*

Samuel did it back. *Not much, dude.*

I always added commentary in my head when guys were being guys.

The good thing about a distinct techno beat is that it kind of dictates how a person is supposed to move on the dance floor. I'd never felt very comfortable dancing, but tonight it was like the music had penetrated my bones, and my mind was somewhere else as my body just danced.

I raised my arms and swung my hips and Samuel was facing me and he was a lot cuter than I'd originally thought, mostly because I hadn't gotten a good look at his face until now. But he was. Cute. And his shoulders were broad.

"You okay?" Samuel said.

I realized I wasn't moving anymore. I was frozen. And staring at Samuel while I studied him. I shrugged.

"You're just cuter than I'd originally thought." I shouted the words. Loud. At what seemed to be the quietest (relatively) part of the song.

The people around us glanced our way. Raf stared for a long moment. He didn't smile.

I felt I had to explain myself.

So I said to Raf, super loud, "It's only because I didn't get a good look at him before. I didn't mean it rudely. If there were better lighting over in that corner over there where we were, I would've noticed."

Were my words slurring together? When I said "would've," it sounded more like "woodiff." And my *R*s were significant. "Where we were" sounded more like "wrrrr wrrrr wrrrr."

I went back to dancing to the music in my bones, and Samuel was smiling, and I was spinning, and bodies were everywhere, and suddenly Raf was dancing in front of me, where Samuel used to be. I noticed it because Samuel was taller than Raf.

"Samuel's taller than you," I said. For a fleeting moment, I realized the filter between my mouth and my brain was malfunctioning. But then that moment passed. "That's how I know it's you."

"Because I'm short?"

"No. You're six foot feet. Which is not considered short. But Samuel's super tall."

"Ah."

We kept dancing, and he was getting closer to me, and his pants touched my pants.

"Your pants touched my pants." Filter officially gone.

He smiled this wry smile. "Yes, I believe they did."

I went to take another drink, but suddenly Raf lunged forward, bumping into me and making me drop my cup.

"My sanataria!"

"Sorry! Someone bumped me."

I looked behind him and couldn't see anyone.

"And it's sangria. Not . . . whatever you said."

Then we were dancing again, and Samuel changed places with Raf, and then Franco changed places with Samuel, and then I was dancing with a guy I didn't know, and that's when the room really started to spin and then I saw Raf kissing Giselle in the corner of the room. Really kissing. Not the kind you can write off as a kiss on the cheek.

I was hot. Really hot. And the room suddenly felt stuffy.

I turned quickly away from the Raf-kissing-Giselle scenario and immediately saw a guy in a gray hoodie, exchanging something with one of the students near the door. He stood out because everyone else here was dressed better than a hoodie. Next to him was a table with dozens of yellow cups. Maybe it was a drug deal. But I couldn't make it out because it was all fuzzy.

I put a hand on my cheek, and it felt warm and wet. The great room was getting smaller and more crowded, which seemed inconvenient for a great room, so I leaned over to the stranger and said something about how he should take over dancing for me and I stumbled out of the crowd and out the door I thought we'd come in.

Only the hallway I was in now didn't look familiar. I tried a few doors on my left and my right, but none of them opened up to a bathroom.

I thought about what the guard had said. "Twenty-two bathrooms, my eye."

I stopped opening doors and decided to put a little more distance between myself and the great room. I was pretty sure it was the general stuffiness and loud music that were making me act the way I was acting.

I turned left then right then I don't know, and ended up in a room that was blessedly quiet. It seemed to be some sort of second parlor to the first parlor. I didn't know what to call it. My mom would've known—she was obsessed with *Downton Abbey*.

I shut the door and breathed a sigh of relief. I would rest here for a bit and then venture back out into the fray. I turned around to face the room, and gasped.

There was a boy at a table in the center of the room, his nose in a book.

"Sorry, I didn't know anyone was in here," I said. Feeling a need to explain my appearance, I added, "I was tired of the music. So loud."

The boy looked up, revealing a face that looked very similar to Raf's. He instantly smiled. "Hi. I'm Alejandro Amador." Just as quickly, he frowned and looked back down at the book.

"Oh. Hi. I'm Piper. A friend of Raf's."

"I know," he said, his face still down. "I've heard about you."

I fanned my face with my hand. "All good things, I hope."

He finally looked up again. "No. I'd say eighty-five percent of what I've heard was good, if you're using the usual measurement for 'good' referring to positive information about one's appearance, countenance, or behavior."

"Huh?"

He Euro-shrugged, although slightly less emphatically than Raf usually did. "My percentages would be better if there were a universally agreed upon basis of measurement for the term 'good.' Since there isn't, I'll define 'good' as I said. Eighty-five percent."

Alejandro lowered his head back to his book.

I scratched my forehead. "So, of the things you've heard about me, eighty-five percent of them were good."

"As I said."

"So, fifteen percent of the things you've heard were . . . bad?"

He looked up again, and this time there was a flash of irritation in his eyes. "Yes. Percentages are based upon a full portion equal to one hundred. So one hundred minus eighty-five is fifteen. Although given what I now know of your rudimentary math skills, perhaps the number is closer to eighty-four."

"Hey! I have good math skills. I did the subtraction right, didn't I?"

"Yes, but confidence is a factor in math skills, and you displayed no confidence. Minus one from the good side."

I looked left and right to see if there was some sort of hidden camera there. Not finding anything suspicious, I turned back to Alejandro.

"Well, how do you know I'm the same Piper you've heard so much about?"

"Pipper Baird. Clumsy, torn pants, western-style rider, astute, easy smile, tendency to speak her mind, even if it's rude."

"Some people like that about me," I said, defending myself.

"Why are you in here?" he said.

"Exploding eardrums," I said, pointing to my ears.

He gazed at me quizzically. "They don't look exploded."

Before I could answer, Raf's voice came from behind me. "He doesn't get exaggeration."

I jumped. "What?"

"Clichés, sarcasm, metaphors, exaggeration. Alejandro is a very literal person."

Raf went around to the side of the table where Alejandro was seated and scruffed his hair in a loving, brotherly kind of way. Alejandro quickly smoothed the messed parts.

"I also don't read facial expressions, but I have an app to help me out." He pulled out his phone, fiddled with it a bit, glanced at my face with narrowed eyes, looked back at the app, then to my face again. "You are bemused."

Raf then studied my face. "I would've guessed bewildered, but I think you nailed it with bemused."

I glanced from Raf to Alejandro and made a mental note not to speak in metaphors.

Alejandro nodded his head toward me. "Pip came looking for refuge from the overly loud decibels of the music you chose."

Raf held his hands out, palms up. "You don't like my music?"

I turned to Alejandro. "Way to throw me under the bus."

Alejandro tilted his head and Raf raised an eyebrow as if to say, *Did you not hear anything we just said?*

"Why would I throw you under a bus?" Alejandro said. "There are several problems with that suggestion, not the smallest of which is the fact that there are no buses nearby."

"I meant . . . when you ratted on me for not liking the music. I felt like you had thrown me under the bus."

"Have you ever met someone who has been thrown under a bus? Because if you do, please don't tell him this story about how I told the truth about your music preferences, and then end with, 'so I know exactly how you feel.' Because I would think the real bus victim wouldn't agree."

"I . . . uh . . ."

Raf looked like he was enjoying the scene before him immensely. "It's great, isn't it? Practicing the literal meanings of words?" He put his hands on Alejandro's shoulders and gently kneaded them. "Makes you think about what you say."

Right then, I wasn't thinking about the literal meaning of words, though. I was feeling a certain kinship with Raf that I wasn't expecting. More than that, I was *feeling* something. Empathy.

"My brother spins hangers," I blurted out.

Raf gave me a confused look, but Alejandro just nodded, as if he had expected no other words but the ones I'd just uttered to come out of my mouth.

The room fell quiet for a moment. Even the usually loquacious Raf had nothing to say, and who could blame him? What are you supposed to say to the whole spinning-hangers remark?

Besides, the story I was looking for wasn't in this room. I'd gotten sidetracked, and now I had to go do some exploring.

"So . . . um . . . sorry for intruding. I think my ears have recovered enough."

Raf followed me out of the room.

"Tell me more about the spinning hangers."

I bit my lip. "I have no idea why I blurted that out like that. I just think your brother and my brother have some similarities."

"Your brother is on the spectrum?" he asked quietly.

"Yeah. He spins hangers to stay calm."

"Self-stimming."

I nodded, a little surprised.

"How do you like the party?" Raf said.

"It's great. How do you like Giselle's mouth?"

Raf frowned.

"Sorry, I have even less of a filter than normal right now. And that reminds me. Is there a bathroom around here?" I said. *"El baño?"*

Raf nodded. He pointed down the hallway. "Left, then right, then the first door on the right."

"Thank you."

He didn't follow as I walked away. "Come back to the party when you're done."

"If I can find my way."

19

I returned to the great room with a slightly clearer head. Giselle was talking to a guy I didn't know.

Samuel waved from across the dance floor and came over.

"How are you feeling, Pip?"

"Who told you to call me 'Pip'?" I narrowed my eyes.

"Raf. We were talking about you after you walked out. You didn't seem to be in a particularly good place."

I closed my eyes and let out a breath. I'd come here for a story. The last thing I wanted was to become a story myself.

"I'm okay." Somebody handed me a yellow plastic cup and I was about to take a drink when Samuel grabbed it from my hand. "Why is everyone grabbing my cups tonight?"

"It's a yellow one," Samuel said. "Yellow means mellow. That means it has a little something extra in it."

"Like what?"

"Like, usually some type of hallucinogen."

My mouth dropped open.

"Not enough to knock anyone out," he said, as if that would reassure me. "Just enough to make the lights dance."

"Do you drink it?" I said, pulling out my phone and discreetly taking a picture of someone with a yellow cup.

"Never," he said. "I prefer the lights to just sit there."

There was a commotion at the entryway. Raf was trying to lunge at another guy but Franco was holding him back. I ran over to see what was going on and heard Raf say, "Get out of here, asshole."

I didn't recognize the guy he was shouting at. He was shorter than Raf and thicker and at the moment he was smirking. Another guy I didn't know was blocking him in front.

"It's ancient history, Amador." He broke free and lunged toward Raf, and I have no idea what made me do it, but I leaped in front of him. He knocked me down immediately, and I heard my head hit the floor.

Things were fuzzy from that point on, but somehow Raf got free from Franco and he landed a few punches on the guy's face and the guy got a hit in just before the guards broke them apart.

And then I was in Raf's arms. A trickle of blood ran from his nose and he looked a little off balance. Samuel came over and put my arm around his shoulders. "I've got her," he said.

Raf stood there panting.

The guards escorted the other guy out, Giselle went to check on Raf, and everyone resumed the party like it wasn't a big deal.

Samuel helped me out to the hallway, where it was quiet. I sank against the wall, and he followed.

He brushed my hair back and kept telling me to look in his eyes.

"I am," I said, feeling a slight headache.

"What made you do that?"

"I'm a pacifist." The words were slurred. "I hate fighting. What was that about?"

"Who knows?" he said. "But it happens. More with Raf than with other people. Sometimes guys need to let off steam. And Raf has a lot of steam."

I shook my head. "It's crazy. These guys fight each other because . . . what, they're bored in their privileged lives full of maids and keepers and chauffeurs and . . . and . . ." I realized I was hyperventilating, so I leaned my head down so blood could get flowing there again. "Do you remember which way out?" I asked, still hunched over. "I have to get my keys."

"Your keys? You didn't have a driver bring you?"

I shook my head. "I'm on scholarship. I have food stamps. I don't belong here." The truth of my money situation felt heavy on my shoulders.

"You're not driving."

"I can't stay."

The door burst open. "Is she okay?" It was Raf.

"She's fine," Samuel said. "I've got her. Go take care of your guests, Amador."

I couldn't exactly tell how Raf reacted, but the door closed.

Samuel turned back to me. "My driver can take you home."

He put an arm around my shoulders and navigated the hallways and parlors as if he'd been there a bunch of times before. We went out the front door and he led me to one of the dark sedans. His driver was named Longborn, and he didn't seem to mind an extra passenger.

"What do I do about my car?" I said.

"Trust me," Samuel said. "Your car has never been safer."

As we pulled out of the drive, I looked through the window, back at the Spanish embassy, and thought about the headlines I had now, but my brain was still too cloudy to come up with actual words. As it disappeared from view, I could've sworn I saw the front door open and someone with dark brown hair watch our car as we left. Maybe I was imagining it.

I turned to Samuel, who'd been looking at me. The fact that he was watching me made me flush.

"So, have you ever been to an embassy party before?" he asked.

I shook my head and felt the clouds in my brain. "I've never been to anything like that before."

Sangria and dancing and yellow cups and fights and blood.

I put my hand on my head to keep it from spinning.

"I met Raf's dad at a fund-raiser for something," Samuel was saying. "It was crazy—he and his wife had this shouting match halfway through dinner, and this team of security guys swooped in and disappeared his wife."

"'Disappeared,' like a verb?" My words were all a-tumble.

"Exactly like the verb. You'd think it would be this big commotion, but it was more like a soft breeze coming through and quietly carrying her away. I only saw it because they were sitting at our table."

"So what were you doing there? Who's your dad?"

"My dad's the secretary of state."

"Secretary of state of what?"

He smiled. "The union?"

My eyes went wide. "Your dad's Scott Morrison?"

Samuel nodded.

"Wow. He's big."

"Yep."

"*Literally* big too. He's like six four."

The car went over a bump and I held my head again and Samuel seemed to sense it was a good time for quiet.

Before too long, Longborn pulled up in front of my house.

"Thanks for the ride," I said.

"Hey, Pip?"

"Yeah?"

He glanced down. "It was nice to meet you."

Ask for my number. Ask for my number. Why isn't he asking for my number?

I paused for a moment before opening my door. "Nice to meet you too."

20

The next morning was ugly, from my bloodshot eyes to my angry stomach to my brain, which seemed to be bursting through my skull. All I could think about was Raf's bloody face. And the drinks.

Sangria? More like *pain*gria.

I emailed Gramma Weeza to tell her I'd had my first drink, since she'd been dying for me to "live life a little." She had yet to master texting, and probably never would, but she could definitely email.

Then I wandered into the kitchen and grabbed the pot from the coffeemaker, but there was nothing in it.

"There's no coffee because it's no longer morning," my mom

said. "It's one in the afternoon. But the more troubling problem is, where's your car?"

I closed my eyes and grunted. "The Spanish embassy. I got a ride home from a guy with a driver."

I went to the fridge and took out a bottle of seltzer, poured a cup, and drank most of it in one breath.

"Sit down, Pipe."

Uh-oh.

"How was the party?"

"It was okay."

"Have you been drinking?"

I sighed. "Spain's drinking laws are different than ours. Eighteen is the legal drinking age."

"You're seventeen."

"But it's not strictly enforced. And apparently since they have this one province in Spain where the drinking age is still sixteen, it's okay to do it at the embassy."

I squeezed a lemon into the seltzer, took another sip, and instantly felt a little bit fresher.

My mom put her hand over mine. "Here's the thing, Pipe. Underage drinking might fly in Spain—"

"It's technically not underage drinking there."

"Don't play your word games with me. Underage drinking might be okay in Spain, but you still live under my roof."

I nodded.

"You did the smart thing by not driving."

I decided not to tell her about the part where I would have driven home if it weren't for Samuel.

"But I'm not sure it's any smarter to go home with a boy you don't know."

"Technically, I didn't go to *his* home—"

The look in my mom's eyes made me stop.

"He wasn't just any boy. He was the son of the secretary of state. Scott Morrison. And it was his driver driving."

My mom nodded as she took in this new information. As if it were every day her daughter was driven home by the son of the secretary of state. "Listen. I trust you. I've never worried about your choices. I like seeing you making new friends and putting yourself out there. But we're going to have to set some ground rules. Number one, tell me first if there's going to be drinking. Number two, if you drink to the point of puking, that will be the last time you drink. Number three, you do it only on international soil, where it's legal. Am I clear?"

"Warn you. Don't puke. Stay out of the country."

My mom smiled. "More or less. And if I ever see the sunrise before I see you . . ."

"I know, I know." I put my wrists together the way someone would if they expected to be handcuffed.

"Good. I'll put another pot of coffee on. So, did you have fun last night?"

I thought about my night. Met Raf's dad, drank sangria, danced with Samuel and then a bunch of people, met Raf's autistic brother, watched Giselle put her lips all over Raf, saw the yellow cups, got in the middle of a fight, was knocked to the ground—

I drew in a sharp breath. "Ohmygosh."

"What?"

"I . . . my story. Bye!"

As I ran out of the kitchen, I heard my mom give a confused "Bye?"

I went to my room and called Charlotte and told her to come over, and when she did, I told her everything.

"Whoa," she said. "Where do these people come from?"

"I have no idea." I pulled out my laptop and opened up a document and started typing.

THE QUEST FOR DANGER IN THE LIVES
OF PRIVILEGED KIDS

"I'm not sure 'quest' is the right word there," Charlotte said. "It's a little *Lord of the Rings*."

"You're right."

THE LIFE OF THE PRIVILEGED TEEN:
DRUGS, DANGER, AND DIPLOMATIC IMMUNITY

"Oh yeah, that's much better," Charlotte said. "Good alliteration."

I pulled up the footage of the party to show Charlotte the pictures I'd gotten the night before. Students in a daze holding yellow cups. The fight between Raf and that other guy.

"Why would Raf do that to such a great face?" Charlotte said.

I slowly traced his face with my finger. "I don't know."

I started typing again.

"Do you think I can make it rain?" the handsome son of the Spanish ambassador asked me just before he caused a chemical explosion in the school lab.

"Ooh, that's good," Charlotte said.

Exposés were different from regular news articles, in that they were told more like a story—with a little more artistic license—and they required a good hook at the beginning.

"Or what about . . ."

"Don't drink from the yellow cup," the boy said. "It will make the lights dance."

"I like that one too," Charlotte said. "How do people live like this?"

I shrugged. "I don't know. The thing is, it's not always like this. I've seen Raf be pretty normal, too. Especially with his brother."

"He has a brother?" Charlotte said.

I nodded. "Alejandro. He's on the spectrum. Raf is really sweet with him."

Charlotte tilted her head. "You sound like you like him."

I acted all taken aback, although I didn't know if I really was. "Who, Raf? No. Did I also mention he was sucking face with Giselle all night?"

"That doesn't mean you can't like him."

I shook my head. "He's a possible story. Nothing more. Now help me write it."

I typed a few sentences about Raf's need for danger and his scaling the national monument and his broken wrist and his fight.

We were quiet for a moment. I didn't know what Charlotte was thinking, but I was wondering what could be going on inside a boy to make him do the things that Raf did. Was it really a spoiled childhood and the need for attention? Or was it something more?

I had a hard time believing a boy who'd been given everything had some deep, dark wound to numb.

So I tried to focus on the story, not the boy. I'd successfully infiltrated a DI party (with minimal physical harm) and I'd gotten some headlines. That had to be something, right?

"Who's that?" Charlotte said. She was looking out my window.

I leaned over and saw two cars pull up to the curb outside my house. One was my red Toyota, and it was followed closely by a black sedan. The cars pulled up to my curb, and the driver of the red Toyota stepped out.

"It's Rafael," I said, my stomach fluttering. I wasn't sure if it was due to the fact that we were writing about him and now he was here, or the fact that my mom had left her coupon stash scattered all over the living room floor.

I was bothered I didn't know.

"Ohmygod. I'm dying to meet him," Charlotte said.

I shook my head. "You can't. I'm on the verge of being in with them. If the two of us meet him, looking like crazed puppies . . . ?"

"All right. You go," Charlotte said. "He'll be more comfortable with you alone. I'll slip out the back."

"Okay," I said. I shut my laptop and went down the hall to the front door, opening it just as Raf had his finger up to the doorbell.

"Oh. Hey, Pip."

"Hi."

His cheek was a little swollen, but on the whole he didn't look as bad as I remembered. And he was still beautiful by anyone's definition of the word.

"I was just returning your car." Raf took the keys out of his jacket pocket and put them on the table by the door.

"You didn't have to do that," I said. "But thank you."

"It was no problem. Yours was the only car that needed returning."

We stood there for a few long moments, the security guy in the black sedan watching us through sunglasses and a tinted front window.

"Um . . . am I supposed to tip?" I said.

Raf smiled. "No. The car return service is complimentary. Part of the 'invitation' to the party." He gave air quotes.

"Ah." I waved toward the car. "Hey, Fritz." He didn't wave back.

We stood there for a few moments.

Part of me wanted to invite Raf inside and see what other information I could get out of him, and another part of me wanted to bring him in and tend to his injuries. That part of me was unexpected. I didn't want to appear too anxious. "Um . . . am I supposed to invite you in?"

Raf chuckled. "Well, that would be entirely up to you."

"Okay."

We stood there for another few moments.

"So, would you like to come in?"

He smiled. "Sure, Pip. Thanks."

Raf waved to the black sedan and then followed me as I led him to the living/dining room. I used to call it the "great room." I didn't anymore, now that I'd seen what a real great room looked like.

"Do you want some coffee?" I asked.

"That would be lovely. Black."

I filled a cup for him and one for me and we sat down in my

kitchen. I'd always thought our kitchen was adequate, but seeing Raf here, even in his bruised state, made me acutely aware of the peeling wallpaper and dated wooden cabinets. I spotted the food stamps by the microwave. Hopefully he wouldn't notice.

"Did you get home okay?" Raf said. Then he shifted in his seat. "I mean, I can see you got home okay. But did you?"

"Yes."

He nodded. "I got a text from Samuel. Did you know that was the name of the guy you were with? Samuel Morrison?"

"Yes." What was he getting at?

"Samuel wanted your phone number."

I could feel my cheeks flush slightly. "Oh. Um, you can give it to him."

Raf scratched the back of his head. "I don't have your number."

His voice was soft, hardly that of a guy who had punched someone the night before.

"That's quite the shiner you have there," I said.

"Oh, yeah. That. A side effect of raucous parties." He glanced down. "Are you okay?"

I nodded. "I don't know what got into me. Probably the sangria. What's your story?"

"You're the reporter. Aren't you supposed to figure it out?"

He sipped his coffee, safe in some protective shell. Did he know that he *was* the story? I could tell he wasn't about to let me in. Not right now. And to tell the truth, maybe I didn't want to be let in. Raf was reckless. And he seemed intent on getting hurt.

Maybe Giselle was after the same thing, and that was why they were together.

But *I* wasn't intent on getting hurt. Which is why it was a good thing I was the reporter and not some starstruck girl hanging on for scraps of time with him.

"Well, you could give me Samuel's number. And I could just contact him myself," I said.

I watched for his reaction. He stared hard at his coffee cup, clenching it as if he would fall off the face of the earth if his grip slipped.

Before he could say anything, my phone rang. It was Gramma Weeza.

"Is that the infamous grandma who believes in the power of duct tape?"

I was surprised he'd remembered. "Yes. I told her I had my first drink last night. She's most likely calling to find out how it was."

He leaned closer. "Your grandma is the first person you told about that?"

"Well, the first person I talked to about it was my mom, who put me through the wringer making sure I was okay. But Gramma is the first person I actually *wanted* to talk to about it."

He smiled. "I like that about you. Family is very important to me as well." He stared at his cup of coffee, and we were quiet for a moment. What was going on? What was he doing here? I'd crashed his party. Why wasn't he angry?

"Thanks for letting me stay at the party last night," I said. "Do your parents mind the parties?" I thought about his scary dad.

"The parties? No. Gathering friends and loved ones to celebrate life is a Spanish tradition. My father encourages taking many moments in the day to just sit and soak it all in."

"Soak what all in?"

"The beauty of life."

I raised my eyebrows. "Are all Spaniards this optimistic?"

"Recognizing beauty isn't optimism. It's living with your eyes open." He picked at a peeling piece of laminate on the counter, and I cringed a little bit at the cheapness of our house.

"Is part of the beauty of life beating the crap out of one another?"

Raf frowned, but he didn't get a chance to answer because Michael wandered into the kitchen, spinning his hanger. When he saw Raf, he stopped. "Why are you here?"

"I brought your sister's car back," Raf said.

Michael went over to the window to check and make sure Raf was telling the truth.

"Who's your dad?" Michael asked.

"That's how he categorizes people in his head," I explained. "By parentage."

"Ah," Raf said. "My dad is . . . Leon."

"Leon?" Michael repeated.

"Yes."

Michael went up to Raf and put a finger on his chest. "How old are you?"

"Eighteen."

"Eighteen." He seemed impressed. "So you can make someone."

Raf raised his eyebrows and I stifled a laugh. "Milestone birthdays are very important to Michael. Especially the ones that make you legal. When you're sixteen, you get to drive a car. Eighteen, you're an adult. Twenty-one, you can gamble and vote. Eighteen, in his mind, means you're old enough to . . ." I made circular motions with my hands, but Raf just raised his eyebrows in a confused sort of way. "To . . . to . . . make a baby."

Michael interjected then. "When I'm eighteen, I want to make someone. A boy."

"Ah, okay," Raf said. "I think I might wait to make someone. It's kind of a big responsibility. And it can be expensive."

Michael shrugged his shoulders. "I've got gems."

He didn't wait for Raf's reply. He just walked out of the room without saying another word, off again in another world.

"Gems?" Raf said.

"They're from his computer game. You earn enough gems, you can buy an army. He's pretty sure that will one day translate into real wealth."

Raf smiled. "I like the way his mind works."

"Me too."

My heart twitterpatted as it often did when someone seemed

to appreciate Michael. For a moment, I forgot I was even considering a story. I forgot Raf was the notorious son of the Spanish ambassador who duct-taped cheerleaders and spilled all my humiliating secrets. I forgot that digging into his personal life was my ticket to the Bennington and Columbia.

For a moment, I was having coffee in my kitchen with a cute boy who liked my brother. Light snow had started to drift outside the window, layering the fallen leaves with a thin sheet of white.

"There are people who can help him," Raf said. "He's getting therapy, yes?"

I shoved the feeling back down and looked at Raf. "Therapists cost money. We have to work the state system, and it's not very good."

But how would he know that? I shook my head. Raf represented everything that was wrong with the world. He was reckless and entitled. If I acted like he did, I would have nothing. No scholarships. No letters of recommendation. And I wouldn't have any rich parents to bail me out.

A loud rap came from the front door. Fritz didn't wait for anyone to answer, he just swooped in and walked back to the kitchen as if he'd seen the house blueprints. Come to think of it, maybe he *had* seen the blueprints.

"Mr. Amador. You're needed at the house."

I stood up and Raf stood up and we were facing each other and Raf blurted, "Don't get with Samuel," he said.

"What? Why?"

"Just . . . don't."

I was flummoxed. "Why are we having this conversation? And aren't you with Giselle?"

Raf looked startled for a moment and then closed his eyes for a long blink. "Thank you for the coffee, Pip."

"Are you with her?" I pressed.

He nodded.

"Then . . . why do you care who I date?"

Fritz looked rather impatient, but Raf was standing his ground in my kitchen.

"Because we're friends now," he said.

Maybe that's how they treat friends in Spain. I held out my hand. "Okay. Friends."

He let out a breath. "Good friends."

21

Good friends. Good friends. That was unexpected. Was I supposed to be good friends with an asset? The subject of a story? No. Raf was bad news, and I had college plans. Christiane Amanpour would never have let that happen, would she? I tried to picture it.

Christiane as she's shaking the hand of the leader of the Taliban: "Okay. Friends?"

Taliban leader as he takes her hand: "Good friends."

Not that I was comparing Raf to the leader of the Taliban. That would be ridiculous.

Besides, even if we were friends, his father would probably have something to say about it. If I had been reading him correctly, he definitely didn't approve of my family's status, or lack thereof. Or maybe it was simply me he didn't approve of.

I decided to text Charlotte about it.

Me: Do I come off badly in front of parents?

Charlotte: Not that I can think of. You're great with parents. Although there was that one time you offered to teach my mom the proper uses of the words "lay," "lie," and "laid."

Me: Was she offended?

Charlotte: That a 12-yr-old would be teaching her grammar? No. Not offended at all. ;)

Me: It just so happened that I had a great and easy way to remember it, and to be fair, I waited until she had used it incorrectly at least a hundred times. She likes me, though, right?

There was a long pause this time. I was sure it was just because Charlotte was in and out while getting ready for bed.

Charlotte: Of course. But I think she's had to get used to your ways.

I waited for a moment, because in this instant, I wanted to text her more about Raf, but not in a story kind of way. More about how he'd asked me not to get involved with another guy. And how he'd come to my house. And how he liked Michael.

Instead, I just texted her *Okay, thanks. Good night.*

The following school week meant more fluff stories, which I wrote without complaint because I knew something Jesse didn't know—I had a good story coming down the pipeline. One that could win me the Bennington.

I didn't bother telling Jesse anything about it because, knowing him, he would just assign the rest of the story to someone else. I wanted to wait until I had everything I needed. This was what Professor Ferguson was talking about. I was making this story my own. Making it a story only I could write.

Raf and I continued to share notes. He even started to help me with all the things about chemistry that I didn't understand, which were basically all the things about chemistry.

Maybe now he would invite me to their weekend party himself, instead of my having to steal his phone, but by the time Friday came around, he hadn't mentioned anything about their next party. Didn't "good friends" mean getting invited to parties?

During chemistry, I glanced at his phone peeking out from his pocket. Maybe, if I used enough stealth—

"Come to my house tonight," Raf said.

"Huh?" I said, startled.

"Come to my house. I have . . . notes there I need to type."

I tilted my head. "On a Friday night?"

"And I'd love to play a game of Scrabble with you and Alejandro. And Michael, too. You said he plays Scrabble, yes?"

"Yes," I said.

"Yes," he repeated.

"Yes," I confirmed.

"Okay. So can I bring a car to pick you and Michael up this evening?"

"Why aren't you asking Giselle?"

"She doesn't play Scrabble. Eight o'clock okay?"

"Okay," I said.

Scrabble on a Friday night? Instead of a raging party? The invitation sort of baffled me. Maybe all his friends were going out of town.

I was pretty sure a game of Scrabble with our brothers was not the way to get the story I was looking for, but I wasn't about to turn down a chance for research. Besides, even if it didn't lead to anything, I had to admit it sounded fun. I also had to admit I wanted to see Raf again.

Later that afternoon, my dad caught me fixing my hair in the mirror. "What are you up to?"

"Michael and I are going to Raf's house to play Scrabble with him and his brother."

He arched an eyebrow. "Looks like you're making friends."

I turned toward him. "Yeah, I guess." I didn't want to tell him that they were subjects of a story, and I didn't let myself think about why not.

Michael poked his head into the bathroom. "Scrabble!"

I nodded and smiled. "Yeah, bud. Scrabble."

An hour later, a long black limousine pulled up in front of my house and Raf stepped out of the back, looking like he was ready for a movie shoot and not a Scrabble game.

Michael bounded out our front door and hopped right into the backseat, but I hesitated. "C'mon, Pip," Raf said. "It's just Scrabble."

He was right. It was just Scrabble. Nobody was using any-body. It was just Scrabble.

Twenty minutes later, I was sitting in one of the embassy par-lors with Alejandro, Raf, and Michael. Michael was wandering back and forth, taking in the new surroundings.

"It always takes him a little while to adjust," I said.

Raf nodded. "I get it."

We picked our Scrabble letters and the four of us started a game. Once the game was going, Michael sat down and began to focus. Scrabble was one of his safe areas. When it got to be his turn, he played the word "box" on a triple-word spot.

"What? Are you kidding me?" Michael said, imitating one of his favorite YouTube gamers. He went on to answer himself. "Nope. I'm not."

I smiled, but Raf laughed out loud, which made me laugh too.

Raf played the word "mush" and then I added an *S* at the beginning to make "smush" and to reach the double-word button.

"'Smush' is not a word," Raf said, the corner of his mouth quirking up.

"Yes, it is."

"Use it in a sentence."

I sighed. "Fine. 'There wasn't a lot of room. So we had to smush.'"

He looked to Alejandro. "Help me out here."

Alejandro typed into his phone. "Valid. It is a blended word from 'smash' and 'mush.'"

Raf shook his head playfully. "You Americans and your made-up words."

It wasn't until that moment that I thought about how difficult Scrabble would be in a second language.

We played for a couple of hours. Despite Michael's strong beginning, Alejandro was winning, which didn't make Michael too happy. I was just proud of him for staying in the game. It was hard for him to accept losing.

Raf took another turn. "'Hadj.' For fifty-six points."

Michael snorted. "'Hadj' is a word every Scrabble player knows."

Raf smiled. "You're probably right." He ruffled Michael's hair. Most people were scared to touch Michael, maybe because they were unsure how he would react, but Raf seemed to have a read on him. Which made me like him even more. Which made me confused. Which made me focus on the game extra hard.

At the end, we tallied up the points. Alejandro came in first, followed by Michael, then Raf, and then me. I never was very good at Scrabble. Alejandro then invited Michael to look at a new game he had on his iPad. I excused myself to look for a bathroom.

"Left, then right, then first door on the right," Raf said.

"Hey, bud," I said to Michael, "I'll be right back."

Michael didn't respond. He was enthralled with whatever it was Alejandro was showing him.

"He'll be fine," Raf said.

I left and tried to follow Raf's directions, but the mazelike hallways were confusing and I ended up in front of a wooden door that looked like every other wooden door in the place.

I tried the handle and the door opened up into a large ornate bedroom, decorated in the deep red and mustard yellow of the Spanish flag. On the wall above the head of the bed was a painting of a couple, the man I recognized as Raf's father. The woman on his arm was beautiful, with long black hair that fell in loose waves just past her shoulders. It must've been Raf's mom. Brilliant gene pool, the kind people probably paid for.

On the opposite side of the room, a door was partially ajar, and light streamed through the opening. Maybe this was the bathroom Raf had been referring to.

I crossed the room and as I put my hand on the doorknob, I heard a soft moan coming from the other side. It wasn't a sexy moan, I was pretty sure. It sounded more like someone was sick.

I opened the door and there, crumpled on the marble floor beneath the sink, was a woman with dark hair. Her head was resting on the cabinet doors, and her mouth was slightly open. Her eyes were cloudy and unfocused.

Gripped loosely in her hand was a bottle filled with red pills, several of which were scattered on the floor.

My first instinct was to call for help, but in a split second, her glazed eyes focused on me with laser-sharp precision.

"Who are you?" she said.

"I'm . . . I'm . . . a friend of Rafael's?"

She closed her eyes, took a deep breath, and said, "Get. The fuck. Out." Then her head sank to her chest.

22

I gasped and quickly backed out of the bedroom. But before I got all the way out, I sneaked a picture of the woman. Then I backtracked back down the hall and saw another hallway I had missed on my way, and I figured that must be the one Raf had been referring to.

Did I really just snap a picture of Raf's mom in that state?

I found the bathroom, shut myself inside, and took a bunch of deep breaths. Raf's mother was officially the scariest woman I'd ever met. The scariest. With her dark hair and her pale face and the vitriol in her voice . . . she could've been a vampire. And not the hot, warm-and-fuzzy kind. The kind where you want to take your own blood out of your body and hand it over to her, because you know there's no escaping the hell that's about to rain down on you, and you'd rather just make a clean blood exchange than be torn apart.

She did have pills, though. And didn't Charlotte say drugs are something I should be on the lookout for?

As I got my breathing in check, I rummaged through the cabinets of the bathroom, but it was obviously a guest bathroom, because the drawers and shelves were empty.

I opened the door and nearly ran into Raf's fist knocking.

'Hi," he said. "I was worried you'd fallen in or something."

I shook my head. "Nope. Everything is fine." I tried to forget for a moment the encounter with his mom. "We should get going, though. It's past Michael's bedtime."

Raf frowned but nodded.

I went back to the room and said good-bye to Alejandro and grabbed Michael. Raf guided us to the front door, but before we made it out, his father appeared from a hallway.

"Rafael. I didn't know you had company." He glanced at me and then Michael, and frowned.

Thankfully Michael hadn't mastered reading facial cues yet. But I had. Raf's dad looked disappointed. And now Raf himself looked guilty.

"We played Scrabble with Alejandro," he said. "And now they're leaving."

"Drive safely," his dad said.

"Oh. Um . . ." I didn't know what to say.

"I drove them here, Papa. At least, James did."

"Then James can drive them home. I need to speak with you."

Raf nodded. He was uncharacteristically quiet as he walked us to the limo. He opened the door and we got in.

"I wasn't expecting my father to be home from his trip so soon," he said. "Good-bye, Pip." He shut the door behind us, and that was it.

I walked inside my house more confused than I'd been in a long time. Why was Raf's dad so upset? Why wasn't his dad helping his mom? Why didn't he tell either of them we were coming over? Why did he invite me in the first place?

I took Michael to his room and set out his pajamas, then started toward my own room. I passed the kitchen along the way and overheard something that made me forget the questions running through my head.

"Bankruptcy."

It was my dad's voice. He and my mom were at the kitchen table, speaking in low tones. I crept closer to the door and sat down against the wall just outside.

"It's not an easy choice," my dad said. "But it's starting to look like our only option."

My mom sniffled. There was a pause, and I wondered if my dad had put his arms around my mom. It seemed like something he would do.

"I know you didn't sign up for this," he said.

"I signed up for *us*." My mom's voice broke.

I couldn't listen anymore. I rose and crept back to my room. My earlier confusion disappeared. Money problems had a way of making everything else so small. Despite the fact that the responsibility wasn't mine, I still felt a heavy weight on my shoulders. I couldn't imagine spending the rest of my life supporting the weight.

Now that I thought about it, there was no dilemma. It was simple. We had no money. We had food stamps. And now, maybe we had bankruptcy.

I needed the Bennington. Raf was my way to get it.

End of story. Whatever happened, someone with means and money could survive, and Raf had both. He would be fine. Right now, I had to be more concerned about my own survival.

On Monday, I passed Raf in the hallway.

"Hey," I said.

He looked at me but didn't say anything back. In Professor Wing's class, he took a seat far away from me. I didn't know how he would take notes, but then he took his wrist brace off and just started writing.

I guessed it was healed.

At lunch, I sat with Mack and Faroush, as usual.

"What's with lover boy?" Mack said.

"What do you mean?" I said.

"I mean last week, he couldn't take his eyes off you. This week he's very interested in his own fingernails."

I glanced over at Raf. He was indeed looking at his finger-nails, as if he was choosing which one to bite.

I shrugged. "Don't know. Besides, he wasn't staring at me last week. He's with Giselle."

Mack crunched on a celery stick. "Oh, yeah. Weird that I forgot."

The rest of the short week brought more of the same behavior from Raf. Not only did he refuse to talk to me, but he even refused to look at me. I started to panic. He was still my best source for the story. He'd provided my only in with the DI kids so far. I was pretty sure I wouldn't get anywhere with the others, judging by how much they've never talked to me.

Raf was my best shot.

And for some reason, he wasn't speaking to me.

School let out early on Wednesday for the Thanksgiving holiday. I considered throwing Raf a Hail Mary that sounded something like "Since it's the season of gratitude, I would sure be grateful if you'd just start talking to me again and give me a story."

But he left the campus immediately. As if he couldn't wait to put more distance between us.

Or maybe he didn't think of me at all.

That Saturday, I focused on earning tips at the Yogurt Shop, even though it meant singing. It was better than focusing on how I'd stalled in my story. Maybe I could do with a break from it. Maybe

I was too close. Maybe another idea, an even better one, would come to me if I wasn't thinking about the DI exposé.

Maybe I could do an exposé on the real calorie count in frozen yogurt.

IT'S LOW IN FAT, BUT IS IT HEALTHIER?

Or maybe I could do one on the meager tipping situation.

IS IT POSSIBLE TO LIVE FOR A MONTH
ON YOGURT TIPS? HIGH SCHOOL STUDENT
DETERMINED TO FIND OUT

Maybe.

But neither of those had the sensationalistic pull of the DI exposé.

Later that night, I browsed through the latest Post-Anons and found another section of that *I Lost You* poem.

> *I'm not sure how to walk without long legs to pace me*
> *I am sick like I just ate a thousand baguettes*
> *I am shivering without your arms to embrace me*
> *I'm consumed by the rot of a thousand regrets*

I sighed. Who would ever want to be in love? It sounded so painful.

23

Christmas break came and Raf had yet to speak to me. I tried not to worry that I had lost my source.

I spent my break taking on extra shifts at the Yogurt Shop. I lost my voice due to all the singing of "Have a Very Dairy Christmas," but my calves were becoming more defined from all the dancing. (I found that our tips increased with dancing.)

Gramma Weeza brought her plumber to Christmas dinner. Her face glowed the entire night, and when the plumber fixed a leaky faucet in the bathroom, my parents' faces glowed too.

I didn't ask them about the money situation. I figured it wasn't the right time, considering it was the holidays. But I left small bills on the kitchen counter and in the junk drawer so my mom would find them without suspecting me. It was hardly anything.

Jesse still had us covering stories during the break, although my most exciting assignment was a snowplow ride-along. I was beginning to think that I would've had a better chance at a college scholarship if I had stayed at my old school, but I didn't let myself think it for very long. Chiswick was a privilege.

On my last night of working at the Yogurt Shop before the end of break, an older man with two young kids tipped me ten dollars and requested the song, "I Will Survive."

I started singing, and halfway through the chorus the door to the shop opened and a familiar face walked through. It was Samuel. The son of the secretary of state, Samuel.

I faltered a bit in my singing, and then kept going because . . . tips.

When I finished, the grandpa and his two little ones clapped. And then Samuel clapped. I served the grandpa and the kids.

"Hi," Samuel said.

"Hi." I was a little out of breath. I hadn't seen him since the party.

"You work here?"

I smiled. "No, why?"

He laughed. "That's cool. I thought about getting a job like this."

"Why don't you?"

He went quiet for a moment. "I don't know."

I nodded. *Because you have money.*

"How did you find me?"

"I asked around. I didn't get your number at the party, so I had to do some detective work. "

I nodded.

"So . . . can I have your number now?"

I squinted. "For what?"

"As in to text, maybe even call?"

"What for?"

He smiled as if his words weren't getting through. "For to get to know you. Maybe take you out."

"Okay," I said, waiting for a catch. Apparently, there wasn't one.

I gave Samuel my number, and he plugged it into his phone. I didn't know if he would ever text me. Part of me really wanted him to. Part of me also thought he might be another glimpse into the life of the privileged elite, even though he didn't have the elusive diplomatic immunity card.

When I got home from my shift that night, I checked my phone for anything new.

There was nothing.

When I started back at school, not much had changed except the number of brand-new cars in the parking lot (because that's what Santa brings the rich) and the fact that Mack and Faroush had broken up—though they still sat together at lunch.

And I sat with them.

In awkward silence.

"So, who broke up with who?" I finally said.

"I did," Mack said.

Faroush nodded.

"Ah," I said.

More silence. I glanced around and caught Raf looking at me. I waved. He didn't wave back. So some things had remained the same.

Enough was enough. We were, by most definitions of the word, friends. I'd been to his house. We'd played Scrabble with our brothers. He was being rude.

I picked up the remnants of my lunch, threw them away, and marched over to his table.

He seemed aware I was coming but kept his eyes on his food.

"Raf, can I talk to you?"

Giselle looked from me to Raf and then to me again.

Raf finally glanced up.

"It will just take a minute," I said.

He shrugged and then stood up and followed me out of the cafeteria.

"What's up, Piper?" he said.

"It's Pip. And I think you know what's up. Why are you being so rude?"

His shoulders sagged a bit. "You think I'm being rude?"

"Yes. By every definition of the word. And I've researched every definition."

He nodded. "I am. Being rude. Aren't I?"

"Yes. Is this how you treat friends in Spain? I mean, we were friends, weren't we?"

He sighed and leaned back against a row of lockers. "Yes, Pip."

"Then why are you being this way?"

He closed his eyes. "You wouldn't understand."

"Try me."

He was quiet for a moment.

"Let me guess," I said. "You have a dad who would prefer you stick to your own kind."

"My own kind?"

"The rich."

He shoved his hands in his pockets. "My dad is from a different generation. A different century. And he can be scary."

"But he knows you're with Giselle. So what does it matter who your friends are?"

"My dad has control in all areas of my life. He'd say my friends now will determine my connections later."

"And you can't be connected to the likes of me?" I got a little pit in my stomach. "Look, it's fine. You don't have to be friends with me." In fact, it was better for the story if he wasn't. "But if you could at least be courteous—"

"I'm sorry. You deserve more courtesy."

"Thanks."

I walked away, feeling more than a little confused. Obviously, my friendship wasn't important enough for him to fight for. I guess it shouldn't have been surprising, since he had hundreds of friends.

But why did that hurt so much?

The silent treatment continued through the end of January. Which was fine. It was the incentive I needed to keep writing my story.

And yet, I started to feel something I hadn't felt in a long time.

Lonely.

I was lonely at Chiswick. Mack and Faroush helped a bit, but they were so quiet, and I didn't have the same closeness with them that I had with Charlotte.

By the time February rolled around, silence between me and Raf was the norm. But then, one Friday night, everything changed. It was late, and I was in my bed, starting to doze, when a scratching noise came from my window. The wind must have been blowing hard, making the branches outside hit against the glass.

It got louder and louder and suddenly turned into a knock.

I put my hand over my heart. Someone was outside my window. I was on the second floor. Maybe they climbed the tree?

I couldn't see outside, since it was dark and my light was

on. Without acknowledging the person at my window—*I know you're there, but I'm going to pretend I don't*—I slowly rose and crept to the light switch and flipped it off.

The silhouette of a head appeared at the glass. I clamped my hand down over my mouth to keep from screaming. Then I thought, *Why the hell* shouldn't *I scream?* but before that message reached the muscles in my mouth, I heard a muffled voice through the glass.

"Pip! It's me. Raf."

What? *What?* Rafael Amador was outside my window. Did that still warrant a scream?

I decided no, that didn't warrant a scream. But it did warrant a walk of indignation across my room and some strong words.

24

I threw open the window.

"What the hell, Raf? You scared the crap out of me! You could've fallen again!"

He smiled. "What is it with Americans and their reluctance to use the hard words?"

"What hard words?"

"Shit, damn, fuck."

"Fine. You scared the damn out of me."

He smiled.

"My word choice is not the issue right now. This"—I gestured wildly at him—"is the issue. It's the middle of the night."

Raf looked at his watch. "Hardly. Judging by the fact that you probably go to sleep at ten thirty on a regular school night, and right now it is twelve thirty, it's not the middle. More like the first third."

I rolled up a magazine that had been sitting on the bench of my window seat and bopped him on the head.

"Focus. You are here at my bedroom window. At twelve thirty. Why are you here? You're not even supposed to be speaking to me."

Raf looked right and then left. "I need a favor. And because we're not speaking, you're the only one who can help me."

"I find that hard to believe. You have a billion friends, all of whom are much richer than myself. And you haven't spoken a word to me in months. Why would you need my help?"

"My security detail knows exactly who my friends are. And all my friends have diplomatic plates on their cars."

"Isn't that beneficial?"

"For where we're going, no, it is not. What would be most beneficial is a piece-of-shit Toyota."

"It's not shitty. It's old."

"Please," he said.

I sighed, weighing my options.

"You didn't talk to me. For months," I said.

"I know. I'm still asking for your help." He looked slightly desperate.

I squeezed my eyes shut. Yes, Raf was dangerous, but he was

also a story. And the truth comes out at night. Maybe this was my chance.

"I'll be right out."

My Toyota was parked on the street, which would make it easier to drive away without anyone noticing. I unlocked the doors and Raf slipped into the front seat with the stealth of a Navy SEAL.

"Is your license current?" he asked.

I rolled my eyes. "Yes, it's current. Why wouldn't it be?"

"It's just that most Chiswick students don't have one."

"Right. Why would you need licenses? Licenses are for ordinary folk, and you, by gosh, are anything but—"

"For God's sake, Pip, just drive!"

I pulled out into the road and headed toward DC.

"Where are we going?"

"Jake's on M."

The only thing I knew about Jake's on M was that it was a bar. "And what are we doing at Jake's on M?"

Raf stared out of the passenger-side window. "I don't know how long we have until my security guy finds me. Will you just take me there, please?"

"Why didn't you call a cab?"

"Because with cabs, or car services, or even buses and the metro, there are paper trails."

I automatically glanced into the rearview mirror. "Paper trails? I have to admit, I've never given paper trails a second thought."

We were approaching M Street, and Raf looked as though he hadn't heard a word I'd said.

"Turn right on M."

I put my turn signal on and followed his direction.

"You see where that neon Wild Turkey sign is?"

I nodded. You couldn't miss it. The *I* in the sign was burned out, and so it looked like it said "Wld Turkey."

"Drop me off at the front. Then drive around back and wait for me there."

I nodded. Rationally, I knew why I was following this boy and his crazy directions. It was for the story. But there was something else going on for me, and considering that he was with Giselle, it made me want to run in the other direction.

But Christiane Amanpour would never run in the other direction from the Taliban just because of a girlfriend. I wasn't about to let thoughts of Giselle get in the way tonight.

"Wasn't Giselle available?" *Oops.* Okay, from here on out, I wouldn't let thoughts of Giselle get in the way.

"Giselle's would be the first place they looked. But they all know I don't have contact with you anymore."

I made some sort of hmph noise that was supposed to sound like an agreement but instead sounded vaguely judgy, even to my own ears.

I pulled up in front of the "Wld Turkey" sign.

"I'll try to be quick," Raf said.

"I'll try not to chicken out."

He smiled. "Thank you."

He got out and slipped in through the front door, bypassing the line of people waiting to get in, as if he were a VIP. But then again, he was Rafael Amador, son of the Spanish ambassador, hot troublemaker and paparazzi bait.

Once he was out of the car, I pulled around back and waited.

The back door stayed shut for what seemed like a long time. I had visions of Raf running out, dodging police bullets as he went. *If guns go off, I'm out of here.* I was pretty sure the AP handbook didn't cover scenarios like this, but if it did, it would probably say "run."

I waited. And waited. And I kept thinking the doorknob was turning. I squinted to see clearly, but the door never opened.

I closed my eyes and sighed. What was I doing? Waiting in some dark alley for someone to come through a metal door with a turkey on it? All because a cute boy asked me to?

Why did I keep returning to the hotness factor? Yes, he was cute. That fact was undeniable and nonnegotiable.

"Cute" probably didn't even begin to cover it. Handsome. Gorgeous. With brilliant eyes. And don't get me started on the eyelashes. Is that how they grow eyelashes in Spain? Like, if his nose touched mine, and he tilted his head just so, his eyelashes would probably tickle my cheek.

What the what.

I took a hand and slapped my cheek.

"Snap out of it, Piper!" I pinched the inch of skin between

the corner of my lip and my cheekbone, because: What. Was. Wrong. With. Me?

I turned back to the door. Maybe Raf had started another fight here, and it had gotten out of hand, and maybe he would fly out of the door followed by hordes of angry guys . . .

And then maybe we would take off and drive west and run away together.

I pinched my cheek again, so hard that it brought a little tear to my eye, and that was when I saw the door open. Raf was helping someone walk. I took out my phone and snapped a quick picture.

It took me a few seconds to realize that Raf was hoisting the limp body of his brother.

"Is that . . . is that Alejandro?"

Raf nodded abruptly. "Can you open the door?"

I didn't realize the doors were locked. I pushed the "unlock" button, and Raf and Alejandro fell into the backseat in one motion.

I put the car in drive.

"Where do you want me to go?" I said.

To my surprise, Raf didn't stay inside. Instead, he got back out of the car and shut the door.

"Can you take him to your house for a little while?"

I nodded. "Of course."

"I have to take care of one more thing."

He turned to walk away.

"Wait. I don't feel comfortable leaving you here on your own."

He didn't turn around immediately, but there seemed to be a release of tension in his shoulders and his back.

"I'll be okay. Alejandro is safe. That's all I care about." He looked over his shoulder at me. "Promise me you'll take care of him."

I didn't know what exactly he was asking of me. Was I covering something up? Lying for him? Was I a pawn in some sort of game he was playing?

At that moment, it didn't matter. I wasn't about to leave Alejandro in a heap on the street.

"You have my word."

Raf turned to go back inside the "Wld Turkey" place, and that's when I noticed a woman dressed in barely there glittery material holding the steel door open for him. As he walked in, she put her arm around him. She was hot. She was probably college age. She'd probably never set foot in a college.

"Shit," I said.

25

A half hour later, I was sitting on my darkened porch with Alejandro. He kept running his hand through his hair as he sipped his third cup of coffee.

"I promised Rafael."

That was all he'd been saying since he'd gotten there. *I promised Rafael. I promised Rafael.*

I couldn't get him to expand on that sentiment. I couldn't even get him to say any other words.

I promised Rafael.

So I just put my hand softly on his shoulder. "I know you did. It's okay."

He shook his head. "I promised Rafael."

"I know. I understand. Everything will be okay."

Alejandro leaned closer, staring into my eyes. "How do you know?"

Finally, he'd said something other than *I promised Rafael.* But I had no idea what Alejandro was talking about.

I rubbed his shoulder. "Because I've seen the plan. The master plan. And everything is all going according to plan. Even what you did tonight. You didn't do anything wrong."

Alejandro squeezed his eyes shut, then reached a hand toward my hand and squeezed my fingers. In the world of the spectrum disorder, the need for physical contact was rare, and it made me feel protective of him.

"Do you promise?" he said.

"I promise. Everything you did today, it will be okay."

Alejandro took in a deep breath, deeper than I thought anyone had the lung capacity for, and let out a sigh, which turned into a melting of his entire body.

By the time Raf got to my house, Alejandro was fast asleep, his head resting against my shoulder. I hadn't moved an inch for fear of waking him. Raf was on foot.

"Hey," Raf said.

"Hi," I whispered. I took the blanket that had been wrapped around me and wadded it up and slowly lowered Alejandro's head onto the cushion.

"I gave him coffee, but it didn't make a dent."

"Yeah, coffee has the opposite effect on Alejandro for some reason."

"Seriously? I'm so sorry! I didn't know that was an option." I watched Alejandro's chest rise and fall. "If I'd had that much, I would be a shaking mess right now."

Raf sat on the stair below the one I was sitting on. My knee rested against his upper arm.

"It's probably better he's asleep."

"Do you want some coffee?" I said, reaching for the silver thermos and Alejandro's mug.

Raf didn't answer, so I poured him a cup anyway and handed it to him.

"Thanks, Pip." He took a sip and set it down. "Where is your family?"

"Asleep. Dead to the world. My parents' room is in the back. Michael's is that window over there." I pointed toward the second window to the right. "He's medicated at night. He won't be awake until seven. Well, seven-oh-six, to be exact."

"He's medicated at night?"

I nodded. "When he was six years old, he decided he was tired of being bored at night. So he would go to the kitchen and raid the refrigerator. Then he would spend the next morning puking. We couldn't figure out what was making him sick. The doctors ran all these gastrointestinal tests, allergy tests, celiac . . . It took us a while to realize that the food in our kitchen was disappearing. We didn't notice until one night I'd stayed up so late finishing a school project and I'd fallen asleep on the couch next to the kitchen. Three o'clock in the morning, in walks Michael. He opens the fridge and begins eating. I said, 'What are you doing, bud?' He's all, 'I'm eating. Because I'm bored. And I read that people eat when they're bored.'"

I smiled, remembering his logic. "He was bored, and all his life he's had to learn what people do in certain situations . . . reactions that come naturally to typical people who aren't on the spectrum. So he read somewhere that people eat when they're bored—probably in some fitness magazine—and he had trouble sleeping, and was bored, so he decided to be like everyone else when everyone else was bored."

I let out a breath and closed my eyes. I think that was the most I'd ever talked about Michael in one sitting.

"Alejandro is the same way," Raf said softly. "People claim to value uniqueness, and yet we spend so much time and energy on facial expression apps and occupational therapy to try to get the ones like Alejandro and Michael to act the same as everyone else."

The wind kicked up a light snow on the brick pathway leading up to the house, and the crystals made me shiver. In lending Alejandro my blanket for a pillow, I'd given up my source of warmth.

Without looking at me, Raf took off his jacket and put it around my shoulders.

I inhaled. It smelled like him. Or maybe the aftershave he used, or cologne, or hell, it could've been deodorant. Or soap. Whatever it was, whoever made that scent should get a raise.

"Are you and my jacket having a little moment?"

My eyes shot open. I didn't realize I'd even shut them. Raf had a crooked smile on his face.

"Yes, yes, we are. And I'd appreciate a bit of privacy."

Raf smiled, and his eyes literally twinkled. Okay, I know it was just from the porch light reflecting off his corneas, but damned if I wasn't sitting on a porch in the middle of the night with the world's cutest boy and his eyes were twinkling.

Get a grip, Piper. What are you going to write a news story about? Twinkling eyes?

BREAKING NEWS: CLICHÉ ABOUT TWINKLING EYES PROVEN TO BE BASED IN FACT. TEAM COVERAGE AT ELEVEN.

Back to being a reporter.

"So what was going on tonight?" I stopped myself from asking follow-ups like *Was it drugs? Illicit shenanigans? Sex trafficking?*

"First off, thank you for helping me. I'm afraid most of my acquaintances have security details that are more imposing than yours."

"My security detail consists of a phone and the option of

dialing nine-one-one." If the phone bill was up-to-date.

"Right. Well, my mom sort of had a crisis. It lasted for a few days. You saw her in her state, didn't you?"

I felt the urge to lie and say I didn't, but he obviously knew I had. He had that ability to intuit the truth.

"Yes. I saw her."

"Probably with a handful of pills."

I hesitated.

"It's okay, Pip. It is what it is."

I nodded. Whether he interpreted my nod as an affirmation that it is what it is, or as an affirmation that I saw her with a handful of pills, I didn't know. But he continued.

"So my dad has this mistress. You met her at the party. The personal secretary, Lidia."

I remembered Lidia. Impeccably dressed and mannered. Beautiful. Young.

"My mom has a hard time with it. To cope, she takes pills. At least, that's her excuse, although she was taking the pills long before there was any mistress."

Mistresses and drugs. This was getting into deeply personal territory.

"Wait." I put my hand up in front of his face. "Stop. You don't need to tell me anything else."

Charlotte would've killed me. The last thing any reporter worth her weight would say was "stop talking." I didn't even understand why I was stopping him.

"I want to tell you," he said. His eyes were wide and desperate. "Because you were there for me, and you deserve to know what you were participating in."

I stayed quiet, not sure which part of me would win out next, the part that knew Raf was vulnerable, and now would be the time to pounce? Or the part of me that knew pouncing would be wrong?

Right. Wrong. Who decides which is which? The story was still just a piece of paper in my back pocket. Besides, Charlotte would say there is no right or wrong when it comes to discovering the truth.

"You can tell me whatever you feel comfortable telling me," I said. I could live with that. I wasn't forcing anything.

"I think I can trust you."

I winced, and for the slightest moment, I felt I should interrupt, but I didn't.

"My father is very protective of Alejandro. I don't know if it's a first-son thing or what, but he takes Alejandro's struggles almost personally. Alex is two years older than me, but with his issues . . . Anyway, when my mom is very upset, she tries to get him in trouble. You see, he has diplomatic immunity, but he already has one strike against him for driving while intoxicated. If he gets one more, he'll be shipped back home."

"Wait, I thought diplomatic immunity was a get-out-of-jail-free card."

"Yes, but it's just one card. It's like three strikes and you're out, except you only get two strikes. Smaller stuff we can get away with, but not a DUI."

That seemed unfair. I couldn't believe I was defending one of the DI elites, but I was. "Why would your mom think that shipping Alejandro back home would get back at your dad?"

"My father would never let Alejandro go alone. He would give up his ambassadorship before he would allow that to happen."

He leaned slightly to the right, which made his arm press against my knee a little stronger. Right then, as the wind picked up and the snowflakes swirled against the brick sidewalk and the breeze blew a tuft of Raf's hair backward, all I could feel in the world was Raf's arm against my leg.

"That's why I needed someone with a car without diplomatic plates. I have some sway with my security team, but if Alejandro got caught at a bar, or worse, got behind the wheel, I couldn't do anything."

I nodded even though I knew nothing about the security and what they could or couldn't do.

Raf sighed and leaned his head on my knee, and I couldn't help but be jealous of my knee for being so close to his head, and then I remembered that the knee was actually a part of me, so I shouldn't be jealous.

But I was. Because my knee was sort of kissing Raf's head right now.

"Can I tell you something?" he said.

"Yes."

"My mom got the idea about getting Alejandro in trouble from me. Because last year I wanted to get back at my dad over Lidia. So I got Alejandro a fake ID. From Mack Ripley. I've seen you with her. You're friends."

"Yeah."

"Her dad is a spy. If you give her three hundred dollars, she'll give you a fake ID that is so good, it works every time. So I had one made for Alejandro, and I took him bar hopping one night, even though I knew with his situation, drinking would lead to trouble. I don't know why I did it. I wasn't thinking clearly. It was just after I'd found out about Lidia."

He stopped talking for a minute, and I had the urge to run my fingers through his hair and stroke his head, but I didn't. Because Christiane Amanpour would never run her fingers through the Taliban's hair.

"My dad lied about Lidia. To everyone. For three years. I wanted to get back at him, so I took Alejandro out, but I didn't know there was someone following us on our bar hop. There was this girl, a public school girl, Tasha Stevens, who I'd taken out a few times. I was just playing, but she got a little obsessive. Her feelings ran deeper than mine, and I didn't realize it. Her dad was a photographer and part-time paparazzo. He got paid by nabbing scandalous photos of politicians. Anyway, he was following us on this bar hop, and he got all these pictures. Alejandro and me chugging beers. Alejandro puking outside the Bourbon House on M." Raf sighed. "My dad had to pay a lot of money to keep those pictures out of the paper, and even more to keep this guy away from us. The worst part was, he didn't get mad. He asked me to do one simple thing: don't hurt Alejandro again." Raf sniffed. I couldn't see his face, so I didn't know what it looked like, but I could hear the pain in his voice. "I never wanted to run away more than I did at that moment. Do you ever want to run away?"

I thought about it. "Sometimes, maybe. I guess it would be nice to pack up and leave this life and start over somewhere fresh, in a different city, maybe in a different country, and I'd change my name to Phyllis . . . Muffler."

Raf chuckled and then raised his head off my knee and looked at me. "That name suits you."

"Does it?" I said.

The way he looked right now, staring at me, making my heart beat a little faster . . . he was in danger of ruining my headline.

He had a girlfriend to get home to. Or the woman from the bar. For all I knew, he had a nightly routine of going from house to house, telling vulnerable girls that they would look good as a "Phyllis."

I stood up fast and wobbled a bit. "You have a girlfriend."

I turned to go inside, but Raf grabbed my hand.

"Things aren't always what they seem," he said. "Please stay, Piper."

"You didn't talk to me for months. Your dad hates me. And you have a girlfriend."

Just then his phone started buzzing. Raf looked at the screen.

"I have to get this." He put the phone up to his ear and turned away. "*Sí*," he said. He looked at me. "No, Papa. He's with me. We're alone." He paused again.

Alone. He couldn't admit he was with me.

I pulled my hand away and shook my head.

He held up a finger.

"*Sí*, Papa. We'll be home soon." He hung up.

"Alone? You're 'alone'? Seriously?"

"It's none of his business," Raf said. He didn't look at me.

Raf had made it clear everything in his life was his dad's business. I pressed my lips together. "C'mon. I'll drive you home."

26

Charlotte: Where have you been?

The text woke me up at the crack of . . . noon. Noon. I couldn't remember the last time I'd slept in so late. Except for the day after the party.

Charlotte: What's the news? It's been forever.

It started coming back to me in bits and pieces.

The scratching at my window.

A dark silhouette.

The rescue of Alejandro.

The porch.

My knee kissing Raf's head.

Raf denying my existence.

How did I not realize I was in trouble at the knee-kissing-the-head point of the evening? I was pretty sure that when Christiane Amanpour secured the first interview with King Abdullah II of Jordan, she wasn't concerned with her knee "kissing" his head.

I started to breathe fast. I felt so lost right now, especially in the light of day. I'd liked being with Raf last night. And I hated that I'd liked it. He'd confided in me. And then he'd lied to his dad about being with me.

I was talking myself in circles. I wanted to pull the covers up and over my head and spend the day in bed.

Charlotte: Did you lose your phone?

Charlotte: Am I texting myself?

Charlotte: Helloooooooooooo

Charlotte: Echo . . . echo . . . echo . . .

I rolled my eyes. Charlotte wasn't known for her patience. She would get suspicious if I put her off any longer.

Me: I'm here!

. . .

Charlotte: Well?

. . .

I hesitated. Should I tell her? I didn't usually talk to her about boys because up until now, there hadn't been any. But last night shouldn't have been about a boy. It should've been about a story, and the truth was, I'd gotten a lot of story last night. I'd also given a lot of my story in return.

And then he'd lied about being with me.

Raf was not a friend. He was a story. I decided the best way to make Raf a story again, and not a boy, was to talk the story part out with Charlotte. I pulled out my computer so it would be easy to text using my keyboard.

Me: Raf came to my window last night.

Charlotte: WHAT???

Me: Needed my help. I drove him to this club where he deposited his intoxicated autistic brother into my car and asked me to take him home and wait.

Charlotte: I can't believe it.

Me: It's true. Then we sat on my porch and talked and I told him things I'd never told anyone before.

But I didn't send that last text. I just stared at it on my computer screen for a while. *Raf was ashamed of me.* Letter by letter, I deleted it so it only read:

Me: It's true. Then we sat on my porch.

. . .

Charlotte: Is the porch somehow important to the story?

. . .

Me: Well, it's where I got some dirt.

Charlotte: Wait! Don't tell me any more. Write it as an article and I'll read it as someone who isn't familiar with the people and the story and edit it for you.

Me: That sounds great!!

Two exclamation points—I was overcompensating. In truth, I wasn't sure how great this all really sounded.

But I started the article anyway. It was good for practice, right? And it was just going to Charlotte. And eventually I would tell her the truth, but not today. Or tomorrow. And probably not this week. Besides, Raf had denied my existence because I was poor. Did he really deserve a free pass?

Then again, did he deserve an exposé?

Just because I wrote it didn't mean I had to do anything with it. Maybe writing it would remind me that he was trouble.

DIPLOMATIC IMMUNITY: ABUSE, BRIBERY, PILLS . . .
AND THIS IS JUST AT THE HIGH SCHOOL

"Don't drink from the yellow cup," the cute boy said to me. It wasn't something I'd heard at any other party I'd been to, but that was because I was growing up in a normal lower-middle-class family where drugs weren't served on a silver platter.

"Don't drink from the yellow cup unless you want the lights to dance."

Later in the night, fists would fly as a rich boy looked for a kind of danger that his privileged upbringing full of handlers and maids and servants and bailouts couldn't give.

This was the life of diplomatic immunity.

It all started when I met a boy.

I wrote about it all. His mom clutching the pills. His dad's ongoing affair. The way both Raf and his mom used his autistic brother to get back at his father. Yes, I was focusing on one family, but that's what makes exposés intriguing: being able to follow one family in an in-depth way.

> They're the same struggles that many families endure, but when kids of privilege lash out, they have the means and the immunity to cause much more destruction, and when there are no consequences, they search for ways to be noticed. To be heard. Ways that escalate to the point of physical pain.

Mack Ripley's secret side job of making fake IDs for the students. (Granted she wasn't one of the elite, but she contributed to them).

> Want to go to a bar for a night of underage drinking? Simply leave three hundred dollars in locker 405 in the morning, and by the afternoon, you'll have a bona fide fake ID, courtesy of the daughter of a spy in the CIA.

The obsessive ex. Bribery of the paparazzi. Getting editors fired.

> Unwanted pictures disappear under the weight of bribes, and papers are brought to their knees with the help of the Spanish mafia.

I laid the article out as if it were the front page of the *Washington Post*, complete with the pictures I'd taken of Raf's mom and the pills, a couple of guys toasting with their yellow cups, Raf helping his drunk brother to the car, and a great shot of blood spurting from Raf's face. I started to realize that what I had might do better in a magazine. Not a trashy one, like *Star Lives*, but maybe *Time* or *Newsweek*. Both were legit publications but also catered to an audience who wanted plenty of pictures and a personal story.

When I finished, I printed it out. I had to admit it looked stellar.

This was a story that could win me the Bennington. This was the story that only I could write.

Maybe I should change Raf's name. Make him anonymous. Make it so that I didn't ruin any part of his life.

But Christiane Amanpour would never kowtow to those in power. If I made him anonymous, I would be yet one more person in his life who protected him from the truth. And wasn't that why he valued me? Because I wasn't afraid to tell him the hard truths?

I emailed the article to Charlotte, and exactly thirteen minutes later, my phone rang.

I picked up. "Hello?"

"Shut up you cannot be serious this is awesome." She said it all in one run-on sentence. "This is good. Like *Time* magazine good. Or *People*. Or the *New York Times*. I mean, I think you still have your work cut out for you. Like, for some reason, you describe everyone very well, except Rafael."

I winced. "Really?"

"Really."

Now that I thought about it, I had been careful not to go into much detail describing Raf, because I was scared my unresolved feelings would find their way onto the page.

"Don't worry, Pip. I can help you. Let me ask you a few questions." I could almost hear her getting out her pen and paper. "So, what's he like?"

"Um . . . you know. He's a boy."

Charlotte went quiet for a second. "Oh. A boy. Thank you for that nice little tidbit. Is your second factoid going to be the revelation that he has boy parts?"

"Well, I can't confirm that personally. But I'm sure there are plenty of girls at Chiswick Academy and the surrounding public schools, and possibly a few bars, who can attest to the existence of said boy parts."

I couldn't help but sound a little disappointed. I heard it in my own voice, but I wasn't sure if anyone else, even Charlotte, would've been able to hear it.

"You sound disappointed," she said.

I rolled my eyes, happy she couldn't hear that as well.

"Of course I'm not disappointed."

"Okay, so what else about him?"

I sighed in an exasperated way. "I don't know. His family

makes sangria. His house is crazy nice."

"That's about his family and his house. What about him?"

I was quiet for a long moment.

Charlotte spoke first. "I'm just trying to be a good editor. I know you don't like what he stands for, but you still need to be able to talk about him. Remember when you said Professor Ferguson told you to write the story only you can write? You're able to write this story because of your close relationship with Rafael. So show that."

Charlotte seemed fine with exposing the secret life of the DI kids. Why wasn't I there yet? Could I do it? Would I do it?

I needed to buy some time to think about it.

"Okay. Looks like I need to do some more digging."

"That's what I like to hear."

That night, when I was lying in bed, my phone buzzed with a text. I was fully expecting it to be Charlotte, but it was Samuel.

Samuel: Hey, Piper! Sorry it took me so long to get in touch. I was in the Alps. I'd like to take you to a little hole-in-the-wall Italian place called Luigi's in Adams Morgan. If you like pasta, you will spend the rest of your days thanking me. 7:00 Friday night?

I clicked the screen dark and went to sleep.

27

Could I do it?

Would I do it?

Two little questions that began to weave their way into every mundane thing I did.

Washing the dishes. *Can I do it? Will I do it?*

Writing a story on the loss of cursive skills in schools. *Can I do it?*

Editing a piece on a local fishmonger and the art of gutting, boning, filleting, and displaying fresh seafood. *Will I do it?*

Singing for tips. *Can I do it?* (Actually, singing for tips made me think I could definitely do it.)

I went over to Gramma Weeza's for coffee and sugar and

more sugar. *Will I do it?*

She noticed the extra sugar. "What's on your mind, Pipe?" Gramma said.

"School stuff," I said.

"Want to talk about it?"

I wasn't ready to put it all into words. "No."

"Hmm. Did I ever tell you about the time I met Patrick Swayze?"

"Yes," I said, rubbing my forehead. "But tell me again."

"It was before he was really, really famous, when he was just semifamous. I went to a dance convention his mom was putting on, and on the last day, in walks Patrick Swayze. Everyone went a little crazy. And at one point, he came up to me and said, 'Would you like an autograph?' And I said, 'No, but I'll give you mine.' And then that night, at the final dance, he was my partner for five songs."

I stirred my coffee and took a sip. "So how is that supposed to help me?"

"Oh, it's not, sweetie. I just like that story, and you said you didn't want to talk about your problems."

I sighed. "It's a good story."

A few days passed, and I avoided Raf. I still wanted more time. If I was going to turn in the article, I needed a little distance from him so I could get some perspective. Maybe I was hesitating because I was too close to it. One of the writers for the *Huffington Post* always said that she leaves a story alone for a while before running with it, so she can see it with fresh eyes. Maybe I needed to leave Raf alone for a bit so I could do the same with him. Maybe some space would help me remember that he was a hot, rich, privileged boy who got away with everything, while I was a struggling wannabe journalist who shopped at thrift stores and had to fight and claw her way to college.

Maybe avoiding Raf would be easier if I had a good excuse. Maybe a good excuse would be to accept a date from Samuel. After all, Samuel was tall and cute and . . . who knew what else? Maybe I should find out.

Me: I'd love to go to Luigi's.

Samuel: Excellent. I was wondering how long you'd leave me hanging.

As I was reading his answer, I bumped into Raf.

"Pip."

"Raf."

"You've been avoiding me."

"You've been disavowing my very existence."

He raised an eyebrow. "What?"

"Look, your dad doesn't approve of you hanging out with me. You have a girlfriend. You have . . ." . . . *everything.* "I'm fine. You're fine. Alejandro's fine. Let's just . . . leave it at that."

He frowned and looked as though he was about to say something else but my phone buzzed with another text. I automatically glanced at the screen. It was Samuel.

Samuel: See you at 7 on Friday.

"Who was that?" Raf said, although something about the look on his face made me think he'd seen exactly who it was.

"See you around, Raf."

I turned and walked away.

When I got to the journalism room that afternoon, Jesse was standing over the monitor showing the layout for today's release. He motioned me over. "You've been phoning in your stories the last couple of days."

I gave it some thought and realized he was probably right. I had been ignoring the journalism staff. "I'm sorry, I've been preoccupied with this bigger story I'm working on."

"Oh, yeah?" He leaned back in his chair. "Tell me about it."

I hesitated. I didn't want to give him facts and details, but I did need some feedback. "I'm not sure how much I should tell you, because I don't know if there's anything there yet, but in a general sense, it's an inside story about the students with diplomatic immunity."

He tilted his head skeptically. "The DIs."

"I'm not the only one who calls them that?"

He ignored me. "You want to do an inside story on the DIs?"

"Yes."

"Do you value a future in journalism at all?"

"Yes. That's why I'm doing it."

He sighed. "Have you noticed that none of them are in the journalism department?"

I glanced around. "No. But yes, I guess."

"And have you further noticed how nobody's done stories on them?"

"I guess."

"Do you think you're the first person to come up with an inside story idea?"

I frowned. "I . . . guess I did. But now I think I'm not."

He went back to his monitor and began typing and clicking his mouse, but he kept talking. "They distrust American media. Journalists, magazines, paparazzi . . . even the school paper. I doubt you'll get anything, and you shouldn't waste your senior year trying. Lots have tried. And they're nowhere now."

I sat down across from Jesse, and Raf's words echoed in my head. *I think I can trust you.*

But then other words echoed in my head. *Duct-taped cheerleaders, escaped detention, kisser of Giselle, yellow cups, fights, acting like he didn't know me . . .* and on and on.

The thing was, even if this article did see the light of day, Raf would probably never have to face any consequences.

"Maybe you're right. But so far, I have a story involving drugs, fake IDs, binge drinking, adultery, pill popping . . ."

As I was speaking, Jesse slowly looked up from the monitor and stared at me. "You have . . . evidence?"

"Pictures. Recordings. Eyewitness accounts. It's nothing ready to print yet, but it's a start."

He closed his eyes and sighed. "You could go somewhere

with this. Or you could disappear."

"I know. But it's a chance I'm willing to take."

He nodded. "Okay. But don't tell Ferguson about it yet. It will be easier to spring it on him so he can have the defense that he didn't know about it in time to do anything. If he needs it."

"Why do I feel like we're dealing with the mafia?"

He smiled. "Because we *are* dealing with the mafia. But if I were in your position, and I had the chance to try what you're trying, I'd go for it."

I paused. "Is this another way for you to knock me down a notch? Like with the internal comm story?"

He shook his head. "I like healthy competition. When I win the Bennington, I want to know I'm the best."

I smiled. "Okay."

"But I'd also consider doing your story anonymously."

Clearly, Jesse was scared of the DIs too.

My talk with Jesse helped give me the perspective I needed. After this year, I would never have to deal with Raf and the DIs again, but the Bennington was my future. I just couldn't let myself drown in the story again. I had to come at it from different angles, safer ones, with slightly less sexy eyes and less persuasive biceps.

I had to find other sources besides the DIs. I texted Mack to meet me after school at the flagpole.

Mack: Did you really just ask me to meet you at the flagpole at three? Are you going to beat me up?

Me: Oops. No. No fighting. It was only for convenience.

Mack: Good. Because in a fight, you'd lose.

Me: I have no doubt.

After school, I headed to the flagpole, where Mack was waiting.

"What's up, Piper?" she said, her hands shoved deep into her pockets.

"How much longer are you going to be running your fake ID racket?"

She shrugged. "The first two months of the school year are the busiest for me. By spring I usually have most of my business taken care of."

"And next year, you'll be at MIT, right?"

"Yeah, if everything goes as planned." She narrowed her eyes. "What's going on?"

"I need a fake ID, and I don't have any money to cover it. And you probably won't be able to keep going with your business afterward. But would you make me one?"

She snort-laughed. "Why would I do that?"

"Because you are on my planet, and you have the chance to even things out a bit with all those pesky rich kids and their privileges."

She looked around as if there were someone watching. "Although I object to anyone our age using the word 'pesky' . . . tell me more."

28

I spent the rest of the week avoiding Raf, which was difficult because we had so many classes together, but my path was getting clearer by the second. My future was on the line. I didn't want to look back ten years from now and regret passing up an opportunity—after all, ten years from now, Raf would be long gone, living in some marble house with his own servants, and what would I have? A mountain of debt that would crush me, and crush any drive I had.

So I avoided him. I didn't share my notes. I ignored his little comments in chemistry. I sat with Mack and Faroush at lunch and didn't once look over.

"He's looking again," Mack would say.

I would shrug.

"Way to stay strong," she said.

When Friday came around, I had put enough space between Raf and me that I finally got some perspective. I realized I had been letting his looks and charm and interest in me affect me. A reporter was supposed to remain unaffected. And I'd been affected.

That stopped here and now.

Besides, I didn't need him.

He passed me in the hallway.

"I don't need you," I muttered to myself. Or so I thought.

"Noted," he answered.

Of course on top of everything else, Raf *would* excel at superhuman hearing.

It didn't matter, though. Tonight, I had a date. Samuel was picking me up at seven. Samuel was cute too. And Samuel would beat Raf every day of the week in a height contest.

That evening, as I was getting ready, my dad knocked on my door.

"Come in!" I said.

He opened the door. "Hey, Pip."

"Oh, no. You too?"

"Michael told me that's what they call you. Who's the special guy tonight?"

I glanced his way as I finished braiding my hair. "I'll make you a hundred chocolate milk shakes if you never call any date of mine my 'special guy' again. But, since you asked, it's Samuel Morrison."

"Morrison?"

"His dad's the secretary of state."

He blinked a few times. "Well, just make sure he's not after you for the wrong reasons."

I rolled my eyes. "What are those?"

"Money," he said, without a trace of a smile. "Fame."

I smiled. "I'll make sure."

Right then, my mom came to the door. "There's a limo for you?"

"A limo?" I got butterflies in my stomach. I'd never been in a limo before.

"Have fun," my mom said. "And don't drink anything from the minibar because they overcharge for those things."

"I'm pretty sure it's his family's limo. Not a rental."

She nodded. "Okay. Right."

"It's the son of the secretary of state, honey," my dad said.

"Hmm," my mom said.

Samuel was waiting in the limo, and I had to admit he looked great. Perfectly tousled hair, dark jeans, brown leather shoes, a purposefully rumpled button-down shirt and a brown jacket.

"Maybe I should change?" I said, although I had no idea what I would change into.

"You look beautiful," he said.

I smiled. "Thank you."

We drove to this tiny Italian restaurant in the middle of this funky neighborhood, with a colorful array of restaurants, clubs, apartment buildings. Adams Morgan is a multicultural landmark in DC. It was named after two elementary schools that used to be segregated. Adams was the all-white school; Morgan was the all-black school. And when segregation ended, the school boundaries blended, and the neighborhood became known as Adams Morgan.

I hardly ever came here, because it was overpriced.

The waiter came and took our order, and after twenty minutes of conversation, I'd learned that Samuel was a straight-A student, he was going to come into his trust fund when he turned eighteen, he regularly saw the president's kids at his school, and his horse's name was Kibble. He wanted to be a surgeon.

"Why?" I asked.

"You're the first person who's ever asked me why I want to be a surgeon."

"Really?"

He nodded. "I guess most people wouldn't bother asking."

"Well, I do."

He drank some of his soda while he thought about it. "I guess I like to take things apart and put them back together."

I scrunched my nose. "Please don't ever describe it like that to your patients."

He laughed. I glanced at the dessert menu and noticed the

prices, which were in the astronomical range, and that made me think of expenses. Which made me think of my lack thereof. Which made me think of how Samuel might be another source for my story.

"So, I met you at a Chiswick party," I said, in a poor attempt at a segue. "Do our schools intermingle often?"

His glass froze on the way to his mouth. "Uh, yes. But I think we'd intermingle a lot less if everyone called it 'intermingling.'"

I smiled.

"I've known Giselle and Raf and the rest of them for a while. Those two are like brother and sister."

He bit off a chunk of hard roll.

"Except they're together," I said.

"Well, some of the best love stories start that way," he said. "Raf would do anything for Giselle."

"What do you mean?"

"I mean, she can do no wrong with him, no matter her history."

I opened my mouth to ask him more, but he put a hand up. "Look, I don't know the details. And really it's none of my business. I only know that last part through my ex-girlfriend, Tasha. She was always jealous of Raf's relationship with Giselle."

"Oh." As I registered the name, my breath caught in my throat. Tasha. Raf had said a public school girl got "obssessive" over him, and that her dad had been the paparazzo who had tried to publish the incriminating photos of Raf.

"Is this Tasha Stevens?"

Samuel raised his eyebrows. "Yeah. She was with Raf for a bit, and he sort of broke her heart. I was the shoulder she cried on. We had fun for a while. And then I realized that on the hot/crazy scale, she was about an eight-slash-ten. You know what I mean?"

"As a ten-slash-ten, I think I understand."

"Ha!" he said. "How are you possibly a ten on the crazy scale?"

I shrugged. "On the first day of school, Raf caught me talking to a painting."

"I've seen those paintings," Samuel said. "They're creepy. I wouldn't be concerned about you talking to one, but did it talk back?"

I smiled. "No."

"See? Not a ten crazy."

"How would you rate yourself?" I said.

He looked down and dipped the last of a roll in some vinegar and oil. "Oh, I don't know. Nine-point-eight-slash-four."

"Nine hot and four crazy?"

"I don't know, yeah." He smiled mischievously.

"I think that zone is so rare, they call it the unicorn zone."

He leaned forward. "Well, Piper Baird, maybe you've met a unicorn. Wait. I think I got the numbers wrong . . ." He pretended to do some math in his head. "Okay, it's a four-hot-nine-point-eight-crazy. Sorry. Math was never my subject." He smiled and held my gaze for a long moment. He definitely wasn't hard to look at. And he was funny. And self-deprecating. And he hadn't tried to do anything like swing from the chandeliers or punch a waiter.

I blushed.

"And now, prepare yourself, Piper Baird, for the most amazing mini-zeppoles you will ever eat."

We kept talking in easy conversation, and where being with Raf was the sizzle of a drop of oil on a skillet, Samuel was a slow burn. Raf wore his confidence on his sleeve, but Samuel kept it in his pocket.

I definitely wanted to see him again. And not for a story.

When I had about three bites left of the not-so-mini-zeppoles, Samuel's phone buzzed.

He looked at the screen and frowned. "It's nine-one-one."

"What?" I said, worried.

"Don't worry, that doesn't mean a terrorist attack or anything, but it might be more of a personal threat to my family, which means I have to go." Security guys filed into the restaurant, faces grim, and I started to panic. "They're supposed to take me straight home. Um . . ."

"It's okay," I said, putting my hand on his arm to reassure him. "I can take the metro home."

He shook his head and pulled out his wallet. "No. Here. Have some cash for a cab. Oh my God, this is so embarrassing. This never happens."

"I'll be fine," I said. "Don't worry."

"I'd really like to do this again," Samuel said. "Say you will."

"I'd love to," I said.

And with that, the security detail whisked him away via the kitchen and probably a back door.

And then I was sitting there alone. Several other diners stared at me. I reached for the bread, but it was all gone. The waiter had taken away the mini-zeppoles.

I hoped Samuel had paid the check on his way out. I know I shouldn't have expected it, given the circumstances, but I really couldn't afford to cover it.

Maybe I could just walk out.

Before I could muster the courage, out of nowhere, Raf appeared in the chair across from me.

29

"What are you . . . Who . . . Where . . . ?" I stammered.

He smiled. "Two more, and you'll have gone through all of the five *W*s." He held his hand out.

"I'm . . . on a date."

"Not anymore, yes?"

"Yeah, but how did you know?"

He smiled, practically bouncing in his chair. "I have ways, Pip. I've told you." His eyes were dark brown and his lips were perfect and his body was yum. But I had to keep my perspective. I had to.

I stood up. "Well, I don't know what you expected, but I'm going to catch a cab and go home."

He frowned. "C'mon, Pip. I know we've had rough times, but we can still be friends, right?"

I looked away. "I don't know."

"What don't you know?"

"How a friendship with you would work. We live on different planets. Your idea of a great night is scaling a monument and getting your face punched in. Mine is watching CNN and correcting the passive voice."

"But you're my link."

"To what?"

"To the truth about myself."

He stared at me with those eyes, the same ones that sparkled so on my front porch, and then I was thinking about moonlight and coffee and knees kissing heads, and I didn't know what to say.

"What did you do with Samuel?"

"Nothing," Raf said.

"I don't believe you." I folded my arms.

"I understand. At least let me give you a ride home," he said, holding out his hand.

Taking his hand wouldn't mean anything. Taking his hand simply showed that maybe we could be friends for a while before my story broke.

"Okay," I said. I took his hand, and we were out of there.

Out of the restaurant and right onto Eighteenth Street, where a motorcycle with two helmets was waiting. Raf grabbed one, handed me the other, then swung a leg over the seat and gave me a leather jacket.

"Ummm," I said, putting on the jacket and shuffling the helmet from one hand to the other. "So, I have this thing where two wheels aren't enough—"

"They're plenty."

"And did you know that seventy-five percent of motor fatalities involve motorcycles with—"

"We'll be fine." He took my hand and pulled me toward the bike.

"And, finally, and most important, I'm wearing a skirt."

"Hike it up. I won't tell anyone."

I buckled the helmet, hiked up my skirt, and we were off. He reached back and pulled my hands around his waist.

He's a story, I told myself. *I'm just hugging a story.*

He wove through the streets of DC and then to Georgetown and started toward the Key Bridge.

"Not the bridge," I shouted in his ear. "It's really narrow."

"My bike is narrow too," he shouted back.

Before I could freak out, the bike was zooming across the bridge and all I could do was hang on.

"No more bridges," I shouted. I hated thinking about a few feet in either direction meaning life or death.

"No more bridges," he confirmed.

"And this isn't the way to my house."

"We're going the long way."

As he wove through the streets of the Virginia side of the Potomac, I abandoned any ideas of conversation. It was too loud and too windy and . . . sort of too beautiful. My fingers were all caught up in the business of Raf's abs. It was hard enough to fight the urge to stroke and caress the six-pack right there, let alone make conversation.

The roads we were on went from business to residential to forestlike.

"Where are we going?" I said.

"You'll see."

He steered the bike toward a heavily wooded road, and I thought back to that day I'd let him drag me into an abandoned bathroom. Now I was letting him drive me into a secluded wooded area. Was I being stupid? Naive?

We reached a gate with a National Park Service insignia on it reading "Great Falls Park." I assumed we'd have to turn around, since it seemed closed and locked, but a guard appeared out of nowhere, and Raf didn't even have to slow down before the guard lifted the gate.

Once we were through, I realized the headlights that had been behind us the entire time followed us through the gate. Must've been his security detail. They kept on us for a few more minutes, but then suddenly Raf darted the bike toward a path I would never have seen in the dark. A loud series of honks came from the car behind us, but that only seemed to make Raf go faster.

"I think they want us to turn around," I said.

"They want me to do a lot of things," he said. "It's only another minute or so."

He guided the bike farther and farther up the trail, and then without warning, the trees disappeared and the dirt below us disappeared and we were on a giant piece of granite overlooking a series of beautiful waterfalls.

Beautiful and breathtaking.

"Please say we're not going to try to jump it," I said. "Or do anything like scale the water."

"Don't be silly, Pip. You can't scale water."

Raf cut the engine, and that's when I could hear the soft roar of the falls below. The height and the scene took my breath away. The park service had put up barriers for a reason. One wrong step could get a person killed.

We got off the bike and I fought the urge to run back toward the forest, but then Raf took my hand and said, "We've got this."

He kept my hand in his as he opened a compartment on the back of his bike and took out a blanket, a bottle, and two plastic cups. He led us to not-quite-the-edge of the overhang and laid the blanket down.

I sat down on the side of the blanket farthest from the edge, and he sat down between me and the water.

He poured us two glasses of pink liquid from the bottle— sangria, I guessed—and we took a couple of sips in silence as my heart calmed down.

"So tell me the truth," I said. "Did you get rid of Samuel?"

"Truth?"

I nodded.

"Yes."

"How did you know where we'd be?"

"Chauffeurs talk."

"Why did you do it?"

He chuckled. "You didn't listen to my warning to stay away from him."

"Well, I can see why you would be worried. He's polite, kind, and survives the evening in one piece. I should definitely stay away from the likes of him." I looked down at the blanket and picked a couple of lint balls off it. "Truthfully. Why did you interrupt tonight?"

Raf didn't say anything for a moment.

"Is it because Samuel used to be with Tasha, and you think he had something to do with the paparazzo following you that one night?"

"Wow. You have a good memory." He gave me a wry smile.

"And good deductive powers," I added.

He looked out over the water and took a sip of his drink. "It's nothing I can prove. But I always suspected."

"He doesn't seem like the type. What does he have against you?"

"It's what he *had* against me. And what he had was a girlfriend who was hung up on someone else."

"'Someone else,'" I repeated. "That's very diplomatic of you."

He gave me a wry smile. "I put the 'diplomatic' in 'diplomatic immunity.'"

We were quiet again for a few minutes, which made the roar of the falls louder and my heartbeat speed up.

"Can I ask you something else?" I said.

"You always ask me something else," Raf said.

"Why aren't you with Giselle tonight? Why are the two of us having a nighttime picnic at the waterfalls?"

He smiled, and my heart fluttered in a way that had nothing to do with the falls. "Because there's something I want to show you." He grabbed my hand, pulled me to my feet, and said, "Follow me."

We walked for several yards parallel to the river and then down a pathway that took us below the overhang and closer to the edge.

"Wait," I said, breathless.

"I've got you," he said.

The pathway got steeper and muddier and a few times I slipped, but Raf held me up. The falls kept coming in and out of view, and just when I thought we couldn't go any farther without actually going into the water, we came to a sign that said "No Cave Access." And Raf did what he always did when he came to a restricted area. He blew right past it.

He pulled a flashlight out of his pocket as we hiked over wet rocks and then we were in a cave, the entrance to which was cov-ered by a sheet of falling water.

"Are you okay?" Raf said over the roar of the water.

I checked my heart rate and it was elevated, but I wasn't dead or anything, because somehow holding Raf's hand made me feel like everything would be okay.

"I'm good," I said.

"Good," he said, but he still held my hand tightly. "Then I would like to present to you a sight you have never seen . . . the *back side of water*." He gestured to the waterfall. "They say you haven't really experienced the world until you've seen the back side of water."

"They do?"

"They do."

"Who does?"

"The all-knowing 'they.'"

We stood there for a few long moments, listening to the roar of the water.

"Are we breaking rules?" I said.

"About twenty," he replied, glancing at me sideways with a smile.

"Are we breaking laws?"

"About three," he said. "But look. It's the . . . Back. Side. Of Water."

The air was cold and wet, but I was warm from the inside

out, maybe from the sangria or maybe from Raf's smile.

"Can I ask you something?" I said.

"Only if you promise to never ask for permission again, and just ask the question."

I smiled. "Deal. Why are you here with me, and not Giselle? The real answer."

He frowned and opened his mouth to say something, but then seemed to change course and say something else. "Giselle hates nature. She hates dirt, rocks, water, trees, and generally being outdoors."

I sighed, a little frustrated. So he was only here with me because his girlfriend didn't like the outdoors? Now who wasn't giving the straight answers?

I took a deep breath. It was okay. If Raf were interested in me, it would only make printing the story harder.

Somehow, he got me home before my midnight curfew. He left his motorcycle where it was and we got a ride home in his black sedan with the Spanish flags. I was cold and warm and excited and frustrated and a little crazy and tired, very tired, even though I was pretty sure I'd never need sleep again.

Before I went to bed, I emailed Gramma Weeza and told her about my night. I couldn't email Charlotte, because she would've been scared I was letting my emotions get in my way. But I had to let Gramma Weeza know I'd done something more exciting than organizing my closet.

* * *

The next morning, I woke up to two texts. One was from Samuel.

Samuel: I'm so sorry again. Turned out to be a false alarm. Let me make it up to you.

The other text was from Raf.

Raf: You haven't really seen the world until you've seen the best view of the Mall you'll ever find. Monday at 7 p.m., yes?

I switched my phone off and put my arm over my eyes.

My choice should've been easy. One was steady. The other looked for new ways to fall. One was disciplined. The other let fists fly. One was safe. The other had a track record of danger. One wouldn't disrupt my plan for the Bennington. The other was my key to the Bennington. One was available. The other had a girlfriend. I guess that should've been the first and biggest difference.

One touched my hand and I felt a tingle. The other smiled and I felt shock waves to my knees.

Before I could talk myself out of it, before I remembered Benningtons and scholarships and debt and college, I grabbed my phone and texted yes to Raf. Maybe it was for the story. Maybe it wasn't.

Then I put my arm back over my eyes and watched as my chance at the Bennington Scholarship teetered on the edge of a cliff.

30

Sunday was a blur. Michael was particularly needy and followed me around peppering me with questions. They were his go-to questions I'd answered a million times before. They were his touchstone when he was anxious.

"Are you going to like it when I go to college and make my own company?"

"Are you excited to play the video games I'm going to make?"

"Will you love me more when I design a weapon with no recoil?"

The answers to these questions were simple. Yes, yes, and I could never love you more.

If only other answers came as easily. Like, why was Raf

suddenly okay with seeing me? Was I still a secret he kept from his dad? Could I trust his change of heart?

That last question wasn't fair. Why did it matter if I could trust him when I knew he shouldn't trust me?

On Monday morning, I ran into Raf. He caught my eye and his face broke out in a smile that spanned the width of the hall-way.

Giselle was next to him. She didn't smile.

But as Raf came toward me, she followed.

"Hey," Raf said.

"Hey," I said.

"Hey," Giselle said.

And there we were, in what was sure to make the *Guinness Book of World Records* for the World's Most Awkward Silence.

Giselle broke the silence. "Have lunch with me today, Pip."

"Oh," I said. "Okay."

And that was it. The bell was ringing. Raf and I walked quickly to class.

All through chemistry, I couldn't stop thinking about why Giselle would want to have lunch with me. I glanced sideways at Raf, who was frowning and staring at the wrist that used to have the brace.

Maybe Giselle had noticed that Raf and I had been spending time together, and she wanted to warn me off, in which case she didn't need to bother because I was going to back off anyway, because Bennington and girlfriend and—

"I like being alone," I blurted out to Raf.

"What?" he whispered back.

"So I'm fine on my own. So there's that."

He turned to look at me and gave me a confused smile. "Okay. Thanks for clearing that up, Phyllis."

Professor Ferron was lecturing on balancing equations. At one point, I was squinting at the board, at a particularly confusing part, and I was trying to read Professor Ferron's handwriting, and Raf leaned over to me and said, "*N H* three."

"Huh?" I said.

"The part you're trying so hard to read. It's *N H* three."

"How did you know I wasn't getting that part?" I whispered.

"I was watching your eyes," he said.

"That's creepy," I said with a smirk.

My phone vibrated right then. I guess I'd forgotten to turn it off. I darted my hand inside my bag and clicked the "off" button, and then, as long as the phone was in my hand, I thought I might as well see who it was.

It was Samuel.

Samuel: Just saying sorry again. And asking you out. Again.

As I put the phone away, I could see Raf had been looking at it over my shoulder.

"Who was that?" he said.

"No one," I said. But judging from the look on his face, he'd seen exactly who it was. He had no right to give me that look. "What did you tell your girlfriend about Friday night?"

"She's . . ." He cut himself off and pressed his lips together.

"She's what? Super hot?"

Neither of us said anything else.

When lunchtime rolled around, I thought maybe Giselle had forgotten her invitation, but nope. There she was, waiting just outside the cafeteria doors.

We filled our trays (mine with lasagna and fries, hers with raw vegetables) and found a table in the corner. Mack and Faroush started walking my way, but when they saw I was with Giselle, they turned and went somewhere else.

I put my tray down and said, "So, why do you want to have lunch with me?"

Giselle popped a baby carrot into her mouth and said, "You and Raf seem to be getting friendly. So I thought I should get to know you."

"Okay," I said. "Thank you. But we're really not that close."

"He likes you," she said.

I wanted to ask her to clarify. He likes me? Or he *likes me* likes me? But it should've been obvious since Giselle was his girl-friend and she didn't seem threatened.

We sat there in silence for a few long minutes.

I took a french fry and drew some circles in the ketchup. "Is this you being friendly?"

She shrugged. "Depends on who you ask. I've sat next to Joe Branson over there for four years now." She jerked her head toward a homely boy two tables over. "Every class with an alphabetical seating chart puts us next to each other. That's a lot of classes over four years."

"And?"

"And I've managed to never say a word to him. So yes, this is me being nice. Because Raf is my best friend."

Best friend. Why didn't she call it like it was and say he was her boyfriend?

I glanced over at Joe again, and he picked his nose. Literally picked his nose. I hadn't seen someone do that in school since second grade. Gwen Stanford. I had made a conscious effort not to touch her fingers ever since.

I looked down at my plate of french fries and focused on trying to find the perfect fry so I didn't have to keep looking at Giselle's perfect face.

"So, how long have you guys known each other?"

"Since freshman year," she said crunching on a carrot. "It's a good story. I had this boyfriend who was a junior."

"That's not such a big age difference."

"In college," she finished.

"Ah. Go on."

"So, one night, we were all hanging out at the Spanish embassy, and my boyfriend got a little drunk and thought he could smack me. He accused me of flirting with someone else, so he hit me. So Raf, who was not as big then as he is now, but was still cut, he grabs this ancient Chinese urn and smashes it over the guy's head."

My jaw dropped. Not quite to the floor, but almost.

"And then the ambassador comes in, and he's all, 'That urn was priceless!' And the security guy whispers something in his ear. And then the ambassador stops yelling and says, 'Perhaps we should all adjourn to the drawing room.' Then he tells his assistant to get me a cool cloth, and before we leave the room, Raf tells his guard to 'get rid of that' and points to my dumbass boyfriend." She laughed at the memory, as if Raf had simply helped her carry her books one day. "Then he says, 'I can hurt him more if you want.'"

"What did you say?" I asked.

"Well, what if you had the chance to teach an older guy that smacking younger girls is not okay?"

"Hmmm," I said, twirling a fry in the air. "I wouldn't ask for permanent damage, but I'd definitely maim a little."

She clicked her tongue. "I guess that's where you and I are *pas compatible*. You're nicer."

And that kind of left me speechless for a minute. So I changed the subject. "Why do you think Raf does the things he does?"

Giselle took a sip of her sparkling water. "You mean the fighting?"

"And scaling national monuments and breaking wrists and such."

"I don't know. I think that's why he likes being around me. I don't ask why."

We ate the rest of our food in silence, and I thanked the

universe when the bell rang.

Raf found me afterward. "How did it go with Giselle?"

"Fine. We're . . ." I paused, trying to figure out how to fin-ish that sentence. We weren't exactly friends. So I said, "We're friendly. Now. A little. She told me about how you guys became friends."

"Oh, yeah. The plane. That story is epic."

"Wait, what plane?"

"Wait, what story did she tell you?" Raf looked confused.

"About a college boyfriend?"

"Ah. Yeah. That one is epic too."

"What's the story about the plane?"

The late bell rang.

"I'll have to tell you later. But it involves Giselle taking her dad's plane, because she was halfway through her piloting course, but she froze when it came time to land. So I stepped in."

"You knew how to land it?"

"No. But I saw it in a movie once."

I rubbed my forehead.

"Don't hurt yourself, Pip."

I nodded.

"So what's the verdict on tonight?"

"I'm working at the Yogurt Shop until nine."

"Okay, we'll pick you up there."

"Where are we going?"

"The embassy."

"Won't your dad be there?"

"Nope. He's out of town. Nine o'clock?"

I must have looked wary, because he pressed on.

"C'mon, Pip. I promise I'll tell you all my secrets."

I couldn't resist that.

Maybe I should've felt a little guilty about meeting Raf to get his secrets, but the fact that I was still being hidden from his dad helped make up for it. At ten minutes to nine, I sang my last song for tips—"Story of My Life," where we added "yogurt" after the line "and time is frozen"—and during the middle of it, Raf walked through the door, looking like he'd gotten lost on the way to a *GQ* photo shoot.

He smiled as I hit my big finish. Charlotte wasn't working tonight, thank goodness.

Then he reached into his pocket and produced a twenty-dollar bill. "Where's the tip jar?"

My other coworker, Seth, looked hungrily at the bill, but I said, "Uh, we're closed. Seth, this is Raf. Raf, Seth."

The two of them did that *'sup* nod with their heads as I untied the back of my apron. Then I followed Raf outside and straight into a limo.

"You didn't tell me you sang," he said.

"I don't."

"What do you mean? You have a beautiful voice." His lips trembled.

"The people with the good voices don't get nearly the tips I do," I said.

"So they are pity tips?"

"Hey, it works."

The limo pulled into the drive of the Spanish embassy, and when we got out, Raf tried to take my hand, but I shoved it into my jacket pocket. I could justify holding his hand when there was streaming water nearby, but now it felt wrong, because of his girlfriend.

Raf frowned.

I looked up at the ornate building. "This is a nice view, but I've seen it before."

"This is not the view I was talking about."

We went inside and Raf whisked me up a set of stairs, then another set of stairs and then a smaller set of stairs. I only had time to think about how I was slightly out of shape for a moment before we went through a metal door that opened to the roof of the embassy.

And the best view of Washington, DC, I'd ever seen. From the rooftop, there was a clear view of the cross-shaped Mall, with the Capitol building on one end, all the way to the Washington Monument in the middle, and the Lincoln Memorial on the other end. Finishing the cross were the White House on the north and the Jefferson Memorial on the south.

Raf led me to a couple of lounge chairs, not the cheap plastic kind you find at a hotel swimming pool but the more expensive ones that felt like they were made of velvet but could weather any . . . weather.

He pushed two of them together, and it didn't seem like any words were needed with a view like this. We flopped down into the chairs and gazed at the lit-up Mall. Soft French jazz floated through the air from hidden speakers somewhere. *"La Vie en Rose,"* I thought. Somebody in a black uniform came through the door and walked over to us with a bottle and two glasses. He poured the pink sparkly stuff and set it down on a table next to us and left without saying anything else.

"What do you think, Pip?" Raf said.

"I think I've never seen anything like this."

He pointed toward the west. "If you squint hard, you can see Iwo Jima."

I squinted into the distance and could barely make out the statue of the six marines who raised the American flag during the Second World War.

"Somebody once told me that if you look closely, there's an extra leg in that statue," I said, taking a sip of sangria.

Raf chuckled. "Maybe when we get a better look, we'll count."

He placed his hand, palm up, in the space between us. And I just stared at it.

"How is Michael?" Raf said.

"He's good."

"I really like him." He smiled. "My favorite part was when we were in your kitchen and he was telling me how he can't wait to 'make someone.'"

I nodded, feeling a little warm from the inside out. One of the uniforms had brought us a blanket, protecting us from the chill in the air.

"Yeah, I love the way his brain works," I said. We were quiet for a moment and I looked at his hand again and didn't take it. "Can I ask you something?"

"You can ask me anything. Free pass."

"Hmm. What to do with a free pass. Gotten any black eyes lately?" I said.

"Nope," Raf said.

"Scaled any monuments?"

"Nope."

"Broken any laws?"

"Not today."

"Why did you punch that guy at the party?"

This made him pause. "He was a jerk to Alejandro. Years ago, when Al was at Chiswick. He was partly right when he said it was ancient history, but that didn't mean I wanted him in my house."

I nodded. "So you punched him."

"He had it coming. For years." He shifted so he was facing me. "Does this stuff scare you?"

I thought for a moment of the blood on his face that night and the image of him falling from the pillar at the monument. "A little."

"When I was a boy, I went to this boarding school, and I would hang out with this one kid Mark, who was bigger and tougher than me. And we got into a fair amount of trouble. This one time, we broke a window at school, and I got caught, and the headmistress took a stick and rapped my knuckles."

"They can still do that?"

"It's a boarding school. They get away with a lot of shit. So my knuckles were swollen and I kept complaining to Mark about how much they hurt. And suddenly he winds up and punches me in my gut."

"What?"

"Yeah. But then, as I'm doubled over and trying to catch my breath, he's all, 'Bet you don't feel your knuckles now.' And he was right."

He poured himself another drink.

"You look for danger so you don't feel the pain that's already there?"

He shrugged. "It's a way to cope," he said.

"It's a stupid way to cope."

He turned to me. "Why?"

"Because sure, pain can be masked by greater pain, but other feelings will be masked as well. Like joy and peace. And love. And I think it would be stupid to mask those."

He smiled. Wide.

"Why are you smiling? I just said you're stupid."

"It's one of my favorite things about you. You're not scared to say what you really think. Remember that time in the hallway when you didn't hold back about how much you disapproved of my lifestyle?"

My cold cheeks went warm. "Uh, yeah. I said I was sorry."

"That was the first time I thought, it hurt, but for a moment I could focus on that pain and forget about other pain."

"So, you're saying my words to you were like a punch in the gut?"

"Exactly."

"Hmm. How do I have any friends?"

He laughed. "I keep telling people to give you a chance. I say, 'Be friends with Pip. She's like a fist to the gut.'"

I smiled and then we lay there in silence for a while. Somehow, in the time since we'd started talking, the bottle of sangria was empty, and my insides were warm and gooey.

"What are you going to do after you graduate?" I said. "Join the sangria business?"

He took a sip before answering. "My father is on the board of directors at IE Law School in Spain. So after I graduate, I'll go there. Study law. Get into politics."

"Sounds like your dad has it all planned out."

He frowned and nodded. "He does."

"What about chemistry?" I said.

"What about it?"

"You love it."

He sighed and looked up at the sky. "I want to study chemistry, which would be useful in the sangria business, because I have some ideas, but my dad would never go for it."

"Why not?"

"Because it doesn't involve ruling Spain."

"So? It's your life."

"But it's his money."

"Are you afraid of making it on your own?" There went my filter.

Raf frowned. "Tell me something, Pip. Do you save any harsh truths for yourself? Or just for others?"

"I probably share my harsh truths with others so I don't have to look at my own."

"What are some harsh truths of yours, Pipper Baird? Good grades. Columbia bound. Will probably one day save the world through journalism. What are your harsh truths?"

I thought for a moment. "Sometimes when I'm doing homework, I have the air-conditioning on and a space heater at my feet. At the same time."

Raf nodded. "Global warming be damned. What else?"

I thought for a moment more. "Sometimes I'm jealous of Michael, because he doesn't have to pretend to be anyone."

Raf smiled. "These are things that just make you even more likable."

I blushed.

"Tell me the real stuff. The harshest truth."

I don't know if it was the drink or the night or what, but I started talking.

"I lie. I have no hesitation lying to get a story. And I don't feel bad about it." He stayed quiet and watched me as I fidgeted with the edge of the blanket. "And I wonder why I don't feel bad about it. Does that scare you?" I said.

"Do you lie to me?" he said.

Crap. "No," I said, and I could taste the lie in my mouth.

"You don't scare me, Pip," he said.

"My mouth can run away with me."

"I love staring at your mouth. Even when it's calling me stupid."

There was that warm gooey feeling again. He was sucking me in. I shook my head because . . . Giselle's face.

"Wait. What are you doing?" I said.

"What do you mean?"

"I mean, why am I here and not Giselle? You can't tell me it's because she hates rooftops. Or views."

"Nope. She hates heights."

"No, she doesn't!" My outburst was louder than I'd meant it to be. Maybe I cared about why I was here and she wasn't more than I'd thought. I wanted him to have a good reason why I was here and she wasn't, and I wanted it to have to do with Raf's feelings.

He turned toward me in his lounge chair. "The truth is, I like you. You are ambitious and hilarious and quirky, and I can't get over the fact that you talk to paintings, and you have this daredevil streak that you work really hard to keep hidden—"

"I'm not a daredevil. I'd never even had detention until that first day of school."

He leaned closer. "You let me show you the back side of water, and I know you were scared of falling yet you went over the edge. Don't tell me you're not a daredevil."

"Falling is not my biggest fear."

"What *is* your biggest fear?"

I looked away and back to the lights twinkling in the city. I took a deep breath. "A crazed man with a gun to my head ranks pretty high. Being caught in an avalanche. Topping the list, though, is probably mayonnaise that's been left out of the fridge for too long."

"Huh?"

"You have no idea what the little things growing inside it can do to the human body."

He laughed.

"Yeah, you think it's funny now, until you have to live with your colon in a bag attached to your hip."

"Ew."

Mental note: if you're hoping for the possibility of romance, don't bring up bagged colons attached to hips.

"See, this is what I mean," he said. "Who says that? More-over, who looks cute while saying that?"

Never mind about the mental note.

"You think I'm cute?"

And that's when he leaned forward and his lips were close to my lips and my heart was all aflutter and then Giselle's face was in my head again.

I put my hand on his chest. "No."

"What?"

"I know it's not a word you hear very often, but no."

He looked confused. "It seems like I hear it from you all the time."

"Do you think that just because your dad cheats . . ." My voice trailed off as Raf's face fell. I couldn't believe I'd taken something he'd shared like that and thrown it at him.

"I have to go." I sprang from the lounge chair, throwing the blanket to the side, and even though my head was a little bit woozy, I quickly made my way to the rooftop door and then every time I saw a staircase, I went down, farther and farther, until I found the opulent entryway.

By this time, Raf had almost caught up. "Wait, Pip, it's not what you think!"

"I doubt that she would say that," I said over my shoulder.

Just as I reached for the handle of the entrance, the door swung open and in walked Raf's dad.

"Papa," Raf said, obviously surprised, and not in a good way.

"Hello . . . Pipper, was it?" His dad frowned.

Raf stopped trying to prevent me from leaving, and that's when I knew I really had to get out of there.

I blew through the front door and said to the driver waiting by the town car, "Take me home. Now and fast."

31

My parents were waiting for me in the kitchen when I got home. They hadn't waited up for me in a long time. I started to worry.

"Hey, Pipe," my dad said.

My mom kept her gaze on the table.

"What's going on?"

"How was your date?" Dad said.

I looked at him skeptically. "That's not why you both stayed up, is it? To ask me how my date was?"

My dad sighed and rested his head in the palm of his hand. "We need to talk to you about something."

My mom raised her head.

"You probably know how our finances have been tight."

"Yes," I said.

"Well, we're behind on the mortgage. Our salaries haven't been able to keep up with our debt. And it's getting to the point where they're going to have to foreclose. Which means moving."

"Moving where?" I said.

My mom looked at my dad. "Cleveland," he said.

I felt a stab to my heart. "Ohio? What's in Cleveland?"

"A new job," my dad said. "And a lower cost of living."

"When would this happen?"

My parents exchanged looks. "Soon," my dad said.

I took a few deep breaths. "I would have to leave Chiswick," I said. Not a question.

My dad nodded.

"How can we stay?" I said.

"I'm not sure we can," my dad said.

"Chiswick is my future. I can't give it up." I closed my eyes for a moment and then opened them. "How can we stay here until the end of the year?"

My dad looked at my mom again, and suddenly I knew.

"You need to drain my savings."

"We are not going to do that," my mom said.

I tilted my head. "You need to drain the money that was earmarked for my college tuition."

My dad shook his head. "It would buy us some time with the bank, but it's not enough to make a significant dent in our money troubles."

"I know." It wasn't enough to make a dent in my tuition, let alone a dent in my parents' debt. "How long have you known about this?"

They were quiet for a long moment before my dad answered, "A while. We've tried everything."

"What about Gramma Weeza?"

"She lives on social security," my dad said.

"But what if I lived with her?"

My dad shook his head. "I checked into that. For you to keep your scholarship, she'd have to legally adopt you."

I squeezed my eyes shut.

"We're not using your money," my mom said.

"Wait," I said, holding up my hand. "Just wait."

What were my options? Leave now and give up my chance for a prestigious scholarship, but keep the meager college fund, or stay and drain whatever was left in the fund, and put everything into the Bennington.

I thought about Raf and how when it came to his dad, he was ashamed of me. And also how he was with Giselle and how likely it was that, given everything I knew about him, he was probably playing me.

I stood. "Drain it."

"Sweetie," my mom said.

"Drain it. I'll gamble on the chance of winning the Bennington. It's my dream. Drain it."

I walked out, and I think my parents didn't know what else

to say, because how could they refuse my offer? Especially when they knew what the Bennington meant to me.

When I got to my room, my phone displayed two texts.

Charlotte: How's the story? Are you getting closer to Raf?

Jesse: How's the story? Any corroborating evidence?

There was no way I was going to admit to either of them the position I'd gotten myself into with Raf, a person who thinks cheating on his girlfriend is no big deal. Besides, I was actually grateful it had happened, because there couldn't be a better reminder of the type of person Raf was, the things he got away with, and the fact that he was just a story, and I would be just a fling. I couldn't believe I'd almost become a girl he wooed and discarded while he carried on a relationship with his real girlfriend.

And now I had no backup. I had no more money. I needed the Bennington more than ever. My parents' financial situation was the clincher. I had to go after the exposé.

There was no better time to finish the story than now, when the fire of retribution was hot, the sangria was getting the creative juices flowing, and the threat of poverty was a fire beneath my feet.

I pulled out my laptop and began adding everything I'd learned since my first draft. Illegal landing of planes. Cracking precious vases over the heads of boyfriends. Ins with the guards at national parks. Faking a 911 call to the son of the secretary of state. I included all the new stuff, complete with information

I'd gotten from Mack about the fake IDs. (She'd decided she was ready to quit for good.) I used it all. It was beautiful. And this time I didn't hold back on describing Rafael Amador.

I sent it to Charlotte before I went to bed. Maybe Raf had made me look like an idiot, but who would look like the bigger idiot when I was holding the Bennington trophy?

Okay, it was a scholarship, not a trophy, but the picture in my head was so much more poignant with me holding a golden trophy of a girl at a typewriter, and Raf wondering what had hit him.

This was all ethical, though. I was leaving out the part about Raf's brother. I would never divulge those secrets. I had standards.

In the morning, I had an email from Charlotte, and a sinking feeling in my stomach that I wasn't sure was from the sangria or the article.

But it must've been the sangria, because Charlotte's email about the article was glowing, using words like "standout" and "fascinating" and "captivating," and I knew I'd struck just the right balance between compelling and tabloid.

She texted me.

Charlotte: What are you going to do with it?

Me: Not sure how to handle it yet. Jesse (news director) thinks anonymous is the way to go. But I want to wait awhile.

Charlotte: I think it will work better in a magazine. You'll get more space. More photos.

Me: Do you think it would work at People?

Charlotte: Definitely.

Me: Okay. I want to sit on it for a bit.

Charlotte: Pipe, are you scared?

Finally, something I could answer honestly.

Me: Yes.

Charlotte: Of what?

Me: People who have tried before have failed and failed hard.

Charlotte: Is that why you're having a hard time pulling the trigger?

I couldn't quite explain my hesitation, except that maybe now in the light of day something was holding me back. And that something was Raf.

Me: I'm having a hard time pulling the trigger because of what it would do to Rafael.

This time there was a long pause on Charlotte's end. And then:

Charlotte: Herbert Matthews didn't let any feelings for Fidel Castro get in the way of his story.

Me: Can't argue with that.

Charlotte: This is your future, Pipe. Your dream. Pull it together.

Me: I'd never let anything stand between me and my dream.

Charlotte: Don't pull a Dave Benoit.

Dave Benoit was a reporter who'd hidden information he'd gotten about a corrupt senator because he'd fallen in love with her. That wasn't me. It couldn't be me.

Me: Never.

Charlotte: Don't worry. We'll figure it out. I'll help you.

Me: Thank you.

I purposely arrived at school with only seconds to spare before the first bell, but Raf still found me.

"Can we talk?"

"No."

I walked past him and to class. The truth was, I didn't need him anymore. I had everything I needed: pictures, interviews, reasonable conclusions. This was another instance where journalism was different from a court of law, especially if it was a magazine exposé written from the viewpoint of the author. I didn't need to prove something beyond a reasonable doubt. There was no such thing as evidence not being admitted because it was obtained in the wrong way.

The article had broad appeal. I thought about the audience. Students without astronomical trust funds would be interested in seeing how the other half lived. Parents in the middle class could read it and pat themselves on the back for not making more money. People who followed the tabloids would love the insider information. I didn't need him anymore.

But Raf leaned over and said, "I'm not with Giselle," just before class started.

"You broke up with her?" I asked. I couldn't resist.

"We were never together."

I stared at him, and he nodded, but there was no time to ask follow-ups because class began. The rest of the morning, he stuck close by and seemed to be waiting for me to ask a question, any question, but for the first time in my life, I wasn't really ready to ask anything.

If they weren't together, why were they kissing at Raf's party? Was this just another thing Raf was saying so he could smooch me? And what teenager used the word "smooch"?

One who had never been to third base, and had been tagged out at second.

I sat at my usual table at lunch with Mack and Faroush (they were back together, although you'd never guess it from the silence at the table). Suddenly Raf plopped his tray down and joined us. He didn't say anything for a long time. He just waited.

Mack and Faroush looked at each other, and after a few moments, they both grabbed their trays. "We're done here," she said. "Because this is weird."

As they walked away, Mack raised her eyebrows, asking if I was okay. I nodded.

"Okay," I said, looking back at Raf. "What do you mean you're not together?"

"I mean we're only together for show." His voice was low and soft. "I'm doing it as a favor, and I couldn't tell you about it because it was Giselle's story to tell. I kept trying to get her permission, but she wouldn't give it. She doesn't trust you. I didn't know if it was just because she didn't like you or because she was scared. Turns out it was mostly because she didn't like you."

I shrugged. "Not surprising."

"But then, last night, she finally gave me permission. Because you walked out on me."

"Why would that make a difference to her?"

"Because she knows how I feel about you." He blurted it out, then winced and smiled. "It was supposed to go smoother than that. But I told her the truth was the only way to get you back."

I tried to ignore the thrill that went through my heart. "Why don't you start at the beginning?"

Raf nodded. "I'm only telling you this now because Giselle said it was okay. And because I trust you."

I didn't stop him.

"Giselle's had it rough. Her mom died a long time ago, and her stepmom is batshit but has her father wrapped around her little finger. Now Giselle is seeing this older guy, and while it's not unusual for her to see an older guy, this guy is the son of one of her father's biggest rivals. The diplomatic community is a very small world. Word gets around, so to hide the relationship, I told her I would pretend to be her boyfriend." He stared hard at his sandwich and ran his hand through his hair.

"Did it work?" I asked.

"So far, yes."

We were quiet for another few moments. By this point, my heart was beating outside my chest.

"When I agreed to the plan, that was when I didn't have an interest in anyone. But that's not how it is now."

My heart leaped to the ceiling and swung around a chandelier.

"So, Pip, I like you. Can we start over?"

"What about your dad?"

"I'll deal with that when we come to it. I won't deny you again." His eyes looked dark and intense. "So, can we start over?"

I had a choice to make, right then and there. I didn't know how I'd gotten into this position, the one where I had let it all get personal, but here I was, and the truth was, I wasn't a bad person.

But this was the Bennington. This was my ticket.

Maybe I could win the Bennington without the exposé and maybe I couldn't, but one thing I knew for sure: in this moment, staring into two big brown eyes . . . I couldn't . . . *I wouldn't* publish my story now. I couldn't live with hurting him. The end.

I turned my thoughts to living on tips from the Yogurt Shop for a month, and turning that into a story. It could be good. And I wouldn't be destroying anybody.

"Can we?" he said.

"Yeah," I said sort of breathlessly.

Charlotte would be so disappointed in me. I had broken a basic rule of journalim. It was a rookie mistake. That's all I was. A rookie. Charlotte had made me promise not to pull a David Benoit, and here I was, doing just that.

No, I couldn't tell her just yet. I would break the news to her when I found another Bennington-worthy story. And they were out there. I just had to look, and it would be easier to do that if I wasn't preoccupied with the DIs. I couldn't stand to dash her hopes without something bigger to get excited about.

I took Raf's hand in mine, and his face went instantly soft. "Let's start over," I said. And then I did what I always did when starting a new project. "First we need a few rules."

He looked wary. "Okay."

"Number one. I don't care how bad you're feeling about yourself. I know I metaphorically punch you in the gut, but no provoking me to actually punch you in the gut. Maybe we should make a list." I pulled out a pencil and piece of paper, and started to write. "One, no punching each other in the gut."

His lips twitched. "You really think that needs to be written down?"

"Yes. Feel free to add things."

"Okay, number two, no talking to paintings about the other person."

I glanced up.

"Let me clarify," he said. "You can talk to paintings. You just can't complain about the other person to them."

"Okay," I said. I added the rule. "Number three, no scaling monuments."

"Wow. You're demanding."

I snorted and wrote the rule.

"Number four," he said. "You said you have a habit of lying. So no lying."

I paused only for a tiny second before writing it down. I would need to come clean about what I'd been up to and why I'd gotten near him in the first place. But not today.

"Number five," I said, "we go on a date in my world. In my crappy Toyota, which I'm probably going to have to sell."

"Why would you sell it?"

"It's a long story. But I will show you how the peasants party on a dime."

He nodded. "Deal. You can show me tonight, on our date in your world."

"Okay. I'll pick you up at your house after my shift at the Yogurt Shop."

I floated about two feet above the ground for the rest of the day. Everything felt exciting and new and hopeful.

32

That night, I drove to the Spanish embassy. Raf was waiting on the curb, with Fritz in tow.

He opened the passenger door. "Fritz, you get in the back."

And we were off. Me driving, Raf at my side, and Fritz sitting awkwardly in the cramped quarters of my backseat.

"No funny business back there, Fritz," I said.

"Like what, Miss Baird?"

My mouth dropped open. "He speaks!"

Raf smiled. "Can we have some music?"

I gestured to the knobs on the console. "It's called a radio. It plays all sorts of stuff."

"What a novel concept," Raf said, stroking his chin.

It took him a while to figure out the difference between AM and FM.

"Where are we going?" he asked.

"I figured we'd start with dinner," I said.

I drove all the way out to Falls Church and wound my way through the streets until I found what I was looking for.

"It's . . . a car dealership," Raf said.

"I know. Follow my lead."

We walked in, Fritz tailing us, and I led Raf to the service repair department and then to the waiting area, where there was a fridge full of soda and a basket with muffins, candy bars, and granola, and another basket full of fruit.

"Fill your pockets," I said out of the side of my mouth.

Raf did as instructed, and Fritz actually turned his back to us and acted as lookout. We were out of there after two minutes, pockets bulging with dinner.

Raf was laughing. "I feel like I just robbed a bank."

"I discovered this trick while I had my car in the shop. And if you liked that, you're going to love where we go next."

I steered the car back toward Arlington and then turned south along the Potomac. As we got closer to the destination, I made Raf close his eyes and I put earbuds in his ears and turned the music up.

"Is this necessary?" he said.

"Yes," I said loudly so he could hear me.

I saw the lights of Reagan National Airport in the distance, and I waved my hand in front of Raf's face to make sure he couldn't see.

I followed the Potomac to a park in Alexandria and pulled my car into one of the spaces.

"Now can I open my eyes?" he asked.

"No!"

I watched overhead at the planes taking off from the airport, and I planned our car exit just perfectly after one plane had left and before the next one had taken off. I led him across the grass of the park and helped him lie down on his back, and only then did I remove the earbuds and let him open his eyes.

We were staring up at the stars.

"Stars?" he said. "That was the big . . ."

His voice drifted off as the engines of a 747 rumbled from behind us. He started to sit up, but I put my hand on his chest.

"You showed me the back side of water. I'm going to show you the bottom of an airplane."

And right then, the departing plane flew above us, so close that it vibrated through my whole body, starting from my chest and radiating outward to my fingertips and toes.

Raf grabbed my hand or I grabbed his and we felt plane after plane from our insides out.

When I dropped them back at the embassy, Raf said, "Best date of my life."

* * *

The rest of the week, it was like we were getting to know each other all over again, except we already knew so much. He seemed to sense my feelings like a piano tuner would pluck a string and close his eyes and listen for the vibration and know from the sound just what to do.

When I saw him the morning after the planes, I had a hard time looking at him. The scrutiny of the crowded hallways felt heavy and dense, and I literally didn't know how to be near him.

I didn't know how to grab his hand.

While I was having this slight mental breakdown, Raf simply came up beside me, put his hand on my elbow, and said, "We've got this, Pip. No worries."

He seemed hyperaware of the nuances of my actions, to the point where it was almost like it was a superpower. During lunch with his regular group of friends, and the addition of Mack and Faroush, we didn't touch an inordinate amount, and we sure as hell didn't kiss or anything like that, but at one point during one of Giselle's stories about the foreign help at her house, meaning the Americans, I was looking around for a napkin, and without even looking at me, Raf handed me his.

Things like that.

After school on Wednesday, we met out at the stables. Raf's horse was already saddled, and so while the others were saddling up, Raf held his hand down to me. "Come on up, Pip."

"I'm pretty sure that saddle was built for one."

Raf grabbed my hand and hoisted me up. He put his hands on my waist and finagled it so I was on the front half of the saddle, facing him, with my legs both falling to one side of the horse.

He gave me a goofy smile. Then his eyebrows started to wrinkle.

"Not as comfortable as the movies make you believe, right?" I said.

"Nope," he said with a grunt. "Is that a pen in your pocket, or do you just really like this position?"

"Oh! Sorry. It *is* a pen." I wriggled so that I could access the pen, but that only made Raf wince more. "How about I get down now?"

He nodded.

Thursday night, I had off work, so we went to the Alliance Française de Washington for a five-dollar showing of the French movie *Amélie*. The frenetic pace and its themes of anonymous love reminded me of the confessions on Post-Anon. I loved it.

Raf walked me to journalism on Friday, and when he walked away, I saw that Jesse had been watching us. "How's the story coming?" he asked with a frown.

I looked down, feeling the weight of my unprofessionalism. "I think I'm going to find a different one to focus on."

He nodded. "I thought so."

I stalked over to my desk. I could do it all. The more I thought about the living-on-tips story, the more I liked it. I could write a kick-ass article and still get the boy. Charlotte had been sending me text after text, wanting to know the latest, and whether I was ready to send it out, and I'd been blowing her off with generic responses. I had already appeared unprofessional to Jesse, but I wasn't ready to let Charlotte know I was giving up such a big scoop. At our shift at the Yogurt Shop, I told her I still wanted to sit on it.

And then I focused my time on trying to figure out a new story to cover while also riding the high of . . . Raf. That night, there was another party at the Spanish embassy.

I got there early, and when the door opened, there stood Raf. Behind him was his father.

I hesitated and then stepped in.

"Papa, you remember Pip?"

"Yes," he said. He didn't expand.

"Pip and I are together."

My eyes went wide, but not as wide as Raf's father's. It was obviously unexpected news.

He recovered quickly. "Ah." His eyes narrowed. "Enjoy your evening. Rafael, I will speak with you tonight."

"I think we're going to be busy most of the night. Perhaps tomorrow."

I'd walked right into a showdown. Would his dad kick me out? Voice his disapproval to my face? *Disappear* me?

Raf took my hand in his and led me away. His father watched us, the disdain emanating from his face almost palpable.

"What made you do that?" I asked when we were out of earshot.

"That was the beginning of a string of choices my dad will not approve of. Might as well start somewhere. I can't hide forever."

That night, when the great room was packed, Raf and I danced mostly together—except for a few times I danced with Samuel and Raf danced with Giselle. Samuel didn't bother asking why I hadn't answered his text. I guessed it was pretty obvious. I felt a little bad. At the end, after everyone had left, I was still there.

It was just me and Raf in the great room by ourselves, facing each other across the dance floor, breathing the same air, tired and sweaty and tipsy and . . . and . . .

Raf strode toward me and took my face in his hands and turned my head up toward his and kissed me. It wasn't a questioning kind of kiss. It was a demanding kiss.

I wasn't sure how it happened—except to say I don't think it was a ninja move where Raf swept my leg or anything—but soon we were both on the floor, on our sides, kissing and grabbing fistfuls of hair (okay, that was me . . . but his hair was so grabbable).

I pulled back a bit, breathless. "Sorry about the hair," I said.

"It's okay," he said with a smile.

He put his index finger on my lips, traced them back and forth, drew a line to my chin, down the front of my neck, down past my collarbone to the top edge of my tank, and down a little farther.

Then he ran his finger across the top of my tank, back and

forth, and he looked like he was concentrating very hard on making sure his finger didn't go any farther south.

I was probably concentrating just as hard on not grabbing said finger and giving it more than the ten-cent tour.

To make not grabbing his finger easier, I busied my hands with the difficult task of unbuttoning his shirt. And then my fingers were busy doing their own exploring. Down his chest. Down his stomach. Tracing a line around the top of his jeans. I briefly imagined scrubbing clothes clean on his washboard abs, and I was going to mention the idea, but I still had just enough wits about me to keep the thought to myself.

Because it was quiet. Gorgeously quiet. No music. No talking. For hours, or maybe just minutes. Only the sound of our breathing, and the noise lips make when they touch other lips and shoulders and necks. And the soft echo the light from the sun makes when it first appears in the windows.

The sun. *The sun.*

Crap. It hadn't been minutes. It had been *hours.* The sun wasn't up yet, but dawn was definitely approaching.

I pushed him away softly. "I have to go."

"What?"

I pointed to the window. "Do you see that?"

"The window? Yes."

"Not the window. The *light.* Basically, if the bottom of the sun rises above the horizon before I get home, you won't be seeing me for a very very long time."

He frowned. "Understood. Fritz!"

"Fritz?" I scanned the room and saw that the guard had been sitting in the corner *the entire time*.

But I didn't have time to be embarrassed. Because dawn was approaching, and I might as well have been a vampire anticipating total burnage.

With the efficiency of a travel agency he got us out of the house, into the town car, and me to my front door with seconds to spare before daylight.

As I settled into bed, I sent an email to Gramma Weeza. Subject line: "I stayed out all night."

33

I didn't sleep much, because . . . feelings.

The truth was, I could still feel Raf's finger drawing lines over my face. My neck. My collarbone. And other places. My shins. My kneecaps. Connecting all the lines. Making the lines come alive.

I looked at my reflection in the mirror, but all I could see were dancing lines, twisting and twirling and entwining.

Last night (or this morning) as we were racing to get me home, he still found time to say sweet things.

"Fritz, drive faster. And see who you can call to slow down the sun."

With eyes closed, I touched my cheek and remembered the

exact feel of Raf's cheek against mine, the way that if I moved in one direction, the hairs on his skin were rougher than if I moved in the other.

I wondered if he shaved with the grain or against it. I wondered if, when he thought back to our cheeks touching, he noticed the white-blond peach fuzz hairs I had on my skin. I wondered if he wished I didn't have them, or if he thought they were just another thing that made me uniquely . . . me.

The way he looked at me, I could tell he wanted to know everything inside my head. He listened to me like my voice was the only sound he would need for the rest of his life. And I talked and talked and spilled my guts because I knew I was safe.

I wanted to savor every tidbit with Rafael. He was like a good book, one I'd been waiting for and anticipating, and once I'd gotten it in my hands, I couldn't bear to read one single page because that would be one fewer page I would get to read.

My dad knocked on my door and poked his head in. "Break-fast, Pipe," he said, and then, looking at my face, he frowned. "What's wrong?"

"I don't want to turn his pages!"

"Whose pages?"

"Never mind. Sorry. I'm fine."

Because Raf was a person. Not a book. He didn't have a beginning and an end. It wasn't like I had a set number of min-utes with him, and every minute spent together was a minute gone that I wouldn't get back.

No. We had infinite minutes. And I was going to savor every one.

At breakfast, the eggs tasted like clouds and the milk tasted like heaven and the crunch of the toast reminded me of the scruff on Rafael's face and the bacon . . . well, the bacon just reminded me of bacon because bacon is good.

Michael's plastic hanger tapped against the wooden tabletop and the newspaper crackled in my dad's hands, and I remembered I wasn't alone.

"Piper? Where are you this morning?" my mom asked.

I was about to ask her what she meant, until I realized I'd been sitting there with a piece of bacon halfway to my mouth, with what must've been a dreamy sort of smile on my face.

"I'm . . . here. Totally paying attention. And eating. And breathing in and out. Totally breathing. Breathing like it's never gonna go out of style."

My phone buzzed.

Charlotte: I took some initiative and got you an early birthday present.

. . .

I sighed. I was going to have to come clean with Charlotte about giving up the story. But not today.

Charlotte: Aren't you gonna ask me what it is?

I couldn't ignore a birthday present. That would be rude.

"Do you mind if I text at the table? It's Charlotte and it's important."

My mom shrugged. "Fine. We're all reading our own stuff anyway."

I texted back.

Me: My birthday's not for six months.

Charlotte: Ask me what it is!

Me: What is it?

Charlotte: Check your email at one o'clock.

Me: Okay!

"Everything okay?" my dad said.

"Yeah. Charlotte with an early birthday present."

"Wow. Six months early. That's some present."

I smiled and clicked my phone off and put it in my pocket. Everyone needed a friend like Charlotte. My mom scooped some more eggs onto my plate, and finally acknowledged the obvious. "You made it home by the skin of your teeth last night. I think you only got fifteen minutes of sleep. How are you even walking right now?"

I bit my lip. "I know. But the point is, I made it home in time. And yes, sometime in the near future, like this afternoon, I will crash."

My dad folded the paper in his hands, kept reading, but I could tell he was paying attention.

He asked, all super casual, "Who were you with last night?"

I cleared my throat. "I was with Rafael Amador. There was a party at the Spanish embassy."

"Oh?" my dad said, in a forced uninterested way that made him seem totally interested. He had not taken to the drinking calmly as my mom had. He'd wanted a strict no-drinking policy instead of her three rules.

"Yeah. I want you guys to meet him."

This time my dad could no longer hide his interest. He put the paper down and leaned forward. "Really?"

I nodded. "I've told him a lot about you."

Now my mom was leaning forward too.

"He's met Michael. He wants to meet you."

My dad stared at me, his mouth slightly open and slightly curved upward. They'd never heard me talk about a boy like this. They'd only ever heard me talk about the news like this.

Several moments passed us by.

Michael was the first to speak. He flicked his hanger toward my dad and said, "Rafael's dad is Leon."

I bit my lip and smiled. "I want you to meet him."

"Then I can't wait to meet him," my dad said.

Raf texted me later that morning, after I'd had a good nap, and asked to come over and and take me for a picnic. There was a strong early-spring snowstorm outside. I texted back, *It's winter out there.*

Raf: Of course it is. I was thinking a picnic in the National Arboretum.

Me: Sounds perfect.

I raced to my bathroom and brushed my hair and tried to think back to the checklist Charlotte used when she was getting ready for a date or an appearance on-camera.

Hair: clean. (And a little shiny because I added that hair oil she gave me for Christmas last year.)

Teeth: brushed. Flossed.

Tongue: scraped. (Okay, that wasn't on Charlotte's checklist, but my mom swore by it.)

Clothes: on. (On? I think that was part of her checklist. If it wasn't, I was making it part of the checklist. Because I most definitely had clothes, and they were on.)

Makeup: five minutes' worth. I remember Charlotte had told me once that makeup should take only five minutes to apply. If it took longer, it was too much.

I had just completed the checklist when my doorbell rang.

Raf.

I raced to the door and barely beat Michael, and then I put my finger on my lips and whispered to him to wait.

"Why?" Michael said.

"Because I don't want to seem overly eager," I whispered so softly it was barely audible.

"Why do you want Rafael to wait?" he said, in a voice that was technically totally normal but under the circumstances, totally loud.

I rolled my eyes and opened the door.

Raf stood there on my porch, with a bouquet of wildflowers and a smile that could broker a peace deal in the Middle East.

"Hi."

"Hi."

"Would you like to come in?"

Jeesh, could I be any more awkward?

"Yes, I would like that very much."

Okay, yes, I *could* be more awkward. Which made me even *more* awkward.

"Um, if you would be so kind as to follow me into the . . . sitting room. Parlor. Drawing room. The place where my parents are."

Because they were there, waiting to meet Raf. When I brought him in, both of them smiled as if he had been the lone human responsible for bringing the sun.

My dad stood up and held out his hand. "Rafael? Robert Baird. Nice to meet you."

"It's nice to meet you too, sir." They shook hands, and it all seemed painfully formal to me, so I broke up their hand clinging with a karate chop.

They both looked at me as if I was weird.

My dad invited Raf to sit down on the couch.

"So, Rafael. You've lived in DC for how long?" my dad said.

Raf put his hand on my knee and everyone in the universe looked at his hand on my knee.

"For four years. We moved from Madrid, although my extended

family is from the southern region. We make wine."

"Sangria!" I blurted out.

Raf raised his eyebrows but didn't lose his composure. "And sangria. It's kind of a family recipe."

"And how do you like DC?" my mom said.

"I like it very much. It gives me a good opportunity to work on my English."

"His English is really good," I interjected. "Except he ends a lot of sentences with 'yes?' It's taken me a bit to get used to, but if you just answer 'yes' when he says it, it makes it easier."

Raf squeezed my knee, and my heart exploded.

"I really like your daughter. I would like to get to know her more. Would it be okay if I took her for a picnic today at the National Arboretum on the Mall?"

And that was it. My parents were under Rafael's spell.

"Of course," my dad said. "We don't mind."

I jumped up from my seat on the couch. "Okay! Great. Nobody objects to lunch. Let's go. Mom, Dad, Michael. It's been great."

Everyone else slowly stood up.

My dad leaned over to Raf. "You know she gets like this?"

"Dad!" I said.

"Yeah. I can handle it." He looked earnest.

I rolled my eyes and took Raf's hand and pulled him out of my house and to the black sedan with the Spanish flags that was parked outside.

When we got in, Raf put his arm around my shoulder. "I think that went well."

I used my hand to motion up and down Raf, from his face to his feet. "Look at you. How could you *not* impress parents?"

"Oh, you'd be surprised. You should've seen it when I met the Czech ambassador. I was dating his daughter—"

I held up my hand. "I don't want to hear it. Besides, can it be worse than the time I met your mother?"

I held my breath. Maybe it was too soon. But he smiled. "I know what you mean, right?" he said. "Awkward." He tightened his hold on me and smiled and kissed me just above my ear. "Okay. Why don't you tell me about your past relationships?"

"Ha!" I laughed before I realized that the fact that I'd had no past relationships might not be very attractive. "I mean, you know, there was this one guy . . ."

"Really? What was this one guy's name?"

"Jacob."

"Ah. Tell me about him."

"Well, he liked the color red, and sometimes he ate chalk. And one day, just before the last recess bell rang, he kissed me."

"Please tell me you were in grade school," Raf said.

"Kindergarten."

We were quiet for a while as Fritz signaled to turn onto the George Washington Memorial Parkway.

I wondered what was going through Raf's head. I kept watching his face, looking for clues. Fritz turned at the Jefferson

Memorial and then made a right and followed the Mall up to the arboretum.

"Anyone else?" Raf whispered in my hair.

I decided those were my favorite kinds of questions. The kinds that were filtered as a whisper through the strands of my hair.

"Freshman year, I had a crush on a boy named Fynn."

"Did you ever tell him?"

"No. Because haven't you ever noticed how safe anonymous love is?"

Raf nodded. "Oh, yeah. You get the high of being in love without the pain of losing that love. As long as the person you love doesn't officially know you're in love with him, there's always the possibility that he loves you back. It's like Schrödinger's cat."

"Huh?"

"Schrödinger's cat. It's a cat locked in a box with a vial of poison. As long as you don't open the box, you don't know if the cat is alive or dead. Either outcome is possible."

"What?" I pushed away from Raf so I could face him. "Why would someone do that to a cat? I mean, I'm personally a dog person, but that doesn't mean I don't have feelings for a cat in a box with poison."

He pulled me into him and held me tight. "Shhh. It's not a real cat."

"Then what's the point?"

He laughed. "It's a thought experiment. Devised by physicists.

I was only using it to illustrate the point that as long as the person you love doesn't know you love him, you don't know if that love would be requited or not."

I sighed and shook my head. "You Spaniards are weird."

"The physicist was Austrian, but that's neither here nor there."

We rode in silence for a little bit as Fritz made several turns to figure out the best parking place for us.

"So, who came before me?" I asked. I'd thought about asking the question for a while, and every time I imagined it, I pictured myself as this awesome Amazon woman who shoved her spear into the ground and bellowed, *Who came before me?*

But as it was, I sounded as weak as a kitten.

"No one I introduced to my dad."

"Anyone you admit exists to your dad?"

He shook his head. "No."

Fritz pulled up in front of the arboretum. Raf grabbed the basket at his feet and we got out.

As we were walking in, I got a text from Charlotte.

Charlotte: Did you check your email??

I turned to Raf. "It's my friend Charlotte. She says she has an early birthday present for me. Do you mind if . . . ?"

"Of course."

I held on to Raf's arm so he could lead me as I texted back.

Me: I thought you said it was at one?

Charlotte: It's past one!

Me: Oh! I'll check now.

I opened up the email in my phone, and as it was loading, I said to Raf, "Sorry. If she wasn't so excited about it . . ."

"No worries, Pip. I'll set up over here."

He gestured to a bench among the flowers, and I slowed to a halt as my emails downloaded. And then there was Charlotte's email.

I read the subject.

And I realized that my minutes with Rafael were no longer infinite. They were limited. And they were very few.

34

The subject of Charlotte's email read:

In the Next Issue of People: Drugs, Bribes, Statutory Rape, and
Get-Out-of-Jail-Free Cards: Why We Need to Rethink the US
Policy toward Diplomatic Immunity.

And I realized what I had said earlier to my mom—about
breathing in and out for the rest of my life—was wrong, because
my breathing totally stopped.

I accidentally crushed the arboretum handout the guy at the
front door had handed to us.

Headlines flooded my head.

Drugs.

Bribes.

Affairs.

Fights.

Once I clicked on the link, I quickly moved from not breathing to breathing too much.

There, in all its pixelated glory, was the blurry picture I'd taken of Raf and Alejandro, and it was obvious Raf was holding his brother up.

Shit.

I scrolled down past the other incendiary pictures I'd taken to read who the article was written by.

The byline read: "Edited by Carl Wittburgh from an Anonymous but Verified Insider."

Verified? Verified by who? I quickly scanned the first few paragraphs, and my sinking feeling was confirmed. It was my story.

Oh God. Oh God oh God oh God.

I closed my eyes.

What would this do to Raf?

I texted Charlotte.

Me: Please tell me you put this together as a joke.

Charlotte: No joke! I sent it to my uncle, the one who works for People, and we spent the week verifying it. Going over the photos making sure they weren't doctored. Interviewing servants in the embassy. Faculty at the school. It's your story!

I was literally panting at this point.

"Pip? You okay?"

I nodded and turned toward Raf, who looked at me with concern. I smiled and the tension in his face quickly eased.

How long before this article rocked his world? His safe, padded life inside the lines of diplomatic immunity was about to explode. Suddenly I had just this small pile of minutes with him, and I wouldn't be getting any more, and so I clung to them with the tenacity of a miser in his study clinging to his last sack of gold.

Maybe I should've warned him. But what would warning him accomplish?

I put my phone away. There would be time for texting Charlotte later.

Raf had a blanket spread out and the picnic of cold fried chicken and potato salad waiting.

"It's an American-themed picnic," he said.

I took his hand in mine and started tracing lines over the palm. I even wrote the words *I'm sorry* in cursive, but Raf didn't notice.

Another minute gone, and in its place, I took a mental snapshot of his face and tucked it away.

He sighed and lay back on the blanket. "Tell me something you've never told anyone, Pip."

I glanced around and then lay down next to him. "It's hard now."

"Why?"

Because I've ruined your life, and you don't know it. "It's early afternoon. And we're not alone. And we've had nothing to drink." I leaned my head toward him as I whispered, "And I'm not resting the side of my face on your belly."

He placed his lips lightly on my hair and whispered, "If you need incentive . . ." He pulled up his shirt. "My belly is available, yes?"

He had no concern about the stares we were getting. He only had eyes for me.

"Yes. And oh my God," I said, covering my hands with my eyes, unable to wipe the smile from my face. And that was how another minute slipped away, replaced by the image of Raf doing something that looked like it could be in a jeans commercial, provided, of course, he wasn't speaking in the commercial, because he just kept saying, "My belly is yours, Piper Baird. My. Belly. Is. Yours."

When someone treats you like that, you tell them the truth immediately. You tell them how you didn't mean for it to happen, but you accidentally did something that will probably lead to their deportation and his father losing the ambassadorship, as soon as possible so they will have as much time as they can to do something.

What if his father could pull something like he did with the paparazzi? Wouldn't that be worth an early warning?

I shook my head and told myself no. Raf's dad had been able to quash a story about an underage kid who made a bad decision one night because it was in a cheap tabloid magazine. Not *People*.

Maybe Raf would never find out I was the one who wrote it. Sure, things would change because he would probably be sent back to Spain very soon, but at least he wouldn't be out there in the world hating me.

I was on my side, my head propped up by my hand, facing Raf, who was doing the same.

How did we get here?

I never intended to hurt him. I just wanted an article that could get me into Columbia. Maybe I'd never wanted it to be published ever.

Who was I kidding? I'd imagined it in a paper, above the fold. Hell, I'd imagined it in the *Washington Post*.

"Pip? You look confused."

At least I could tell him the truth right now.

"I'm just struggling with the feelings, my feelings, about you, which are of the strong variety, and I'm bottling up our minutes together in my head so I can pull them out whenever I am missing you."

We stared at each other for a few minutes.

I waved good-bye to those used-up minutes, and glanced up and noticed how the sun was streaming through the skylights overhead and hitting Raf's brown hair perfectly, and I filed the image away in the little cabinet for "Things Too Painful to Think about Now, or Ever." Which was smaller than it used to be, but I had a feeling it would soon be filled with pictures of this boy.

And that was when his phone rang, and Fritz came over to us in a rush. Moments later, my dad texted me.

I want you home. Now.

"I'm sorry, Pip, we have to go," Raf said, helping me to my feet and quickly gathering up the picnic materials. "Something's happening at my home."

"What is it?" I said, sounding so fake and stupid to my own ears.

"I'm not sure. Everyone's fine; no one's hurt. But apparently there's a story coming out, and my dad wants us all together so he can figure out what to do."

I couldn't help but wince. Raf noticed.

"Hey, it'll be okay. This happens. Not all the time, and not lately, but it's happened before and it will all be okay."

I couldn't believe the irony. The executioner being comforted by the . . . executionee.

He held my hand and stroked his thumb over my knuckles.

I brought his hand up to my lips, kissed his knuckles and his thumb, and said, "Rafael Amador, I . . . really like you."

He smiled.

"Pipper Baird, you send me to the moon."

When his car pulled up to my house, I had the hardest time letting go of his hand.

"It's just a hand," Raf said.

"Huh?"

He smiled gently. "You were looking like you were trying to remember the name of said appendage. It's a hand."

My dad was standing at the door, his arms folded, a frown on his face.

"Good luck with your family stuff," I said.

Raf put his hands on either side of my cheek and pulled me in for a kiss. "You are not to worry about my family stuff. It will be resolved."

I got out of the car and rushed inside and my dad followed me in, closing the door behind us. He didn't wave at Raf.

"Piper, I don't want you hanging out with that boy right now."

I was sitting on the couch, my parents on the two chairs opposite.

"Why?" I said.

"The neighbors—you know, the Phillipses—showed us a story on the *People* magazine website. They knew you went to the same school, and they wanted to warn us. Did you know he has fake IDs? And regularly goes to bars and gets so drunk he has to be helped out? And he runs underground fighting rings?"

Oh my God, I was so stupid.

I quietly agreed not to see him anymore, mostly because I was sure there was no way he'd want to see *me*, and excused myself to my bedroom, feigning a stomachache.

It was actually a very real stomachache that reached northward to my heart.

I crawled into bed and pulled the covers over my head and put my earbuds in and turned up the music and started to think of the logistics of changing my name to Phyllis Muffler and leaving the country.

I wasn't sure how much time passed. Maybe a couple of hours. I'd dozed on and off, amazed that sleep was even an option, but then I remembered how when Michael was a baby and the doctors would give him a shot, the stress of it would put him to sleep.

Maybe this was one of those times.

A spinning hanger in the corner of my room caught my eye. Michael had wandered in.

"Hey, bud," I said.

Michael was looking at a picture on my desk of me and him from years ago. It had been taken just before he'd won the third-grade Scrabble competition.

"Rafael is downstairs."

I shot upright. "What?"

"Rafael is downstairs. He's at the door."

"What? Where are Mom and Dad?"

"They're out."

I took several deep breaths. "Michael, can you go downstairs and tell him I'll be right down?"

He looked at me and as he walked out of the room, he casually said, "No."

Argh.

Okay, Raf was here. Raf was here. And I looked like crap. There were so many things to fix: my hair. My smeared mascara. I was pretty sure I smelled. But there was no time because Raf was here and waiting for me, and he probably knew everything by now, so I wasn't sure he would wait for me to freshen up, and I wasn't sure if I wanted him to wait or I wanted him to give up.

Teeth. I could at least brush my teeth.

I did that in a flash, but I was really thorough, and then I raced downstairs and reached for the door . . . and froze.

It was like Schrödinger's cat. If I didn't open the door, maybe Raf still loved me. If I never opened the door, maybe Raf would love me forever.

No. That was crazy. If you put a cat in a box with a vial of poison, the cat is going to be dead, whether you open the door or not.

"I heard you run down the stairs." Raf's muffled voice came through the door. "Are you going to open?"

And still I couldn't move. For this one last minute, I could convince myself that Raf was my boyfriend, and he liked me.

I tucked that minute away and sealed the jar in my brain.

And opened the door.

Raf was waiting there. His hair was slightly messier than usual, and sticking out on the sides as if he'd been pulling at it. "It was you, wasn't it?"

My shoulders sagged and I walked past him and sank to the top step of my porch. It wasn't that long ago that my knee had kissed his head on this same porch. "How long did it take you?"

"Seconds," he said, sitting next to me. "I remember that one picture. From the party. You were taking it, and I wasn't looking at the lens. I was looking at you."

I tensed.

"And in that picture, you can tell my eyes are looking infinitesimally to the side. Where your eyes were."

I nodded. Slowly. And then put my face in my hands.

"Will you at least look at me?"

I stayed still. How could he think I could face him ever again? I was pretty sure if I looked at him, his eyes would bore holes right through my heart and I would bleed out on the porch.

It'd be a good death, though.

"Piper, this afternoon I offered you my belly in front of the world. The least you can do is face me right now."

There was no arguing with him. He was right. And he'd used my correct name.

I turned slowly, aware of each degree of the turn, and dropped my hands. Once I was facing him, the most I could do was look at his chin.

"Hey, my eyes are up here, you know," he said with a smile in his voice. How could he still have a smile in his voice? But then I realized it didn't sound like a very strong smile. It sounded fragile. "I'm so tired of girls always staring at my chin. They think I don't notice, but I do."

I squeezed my eyes shut, straightened my spine as much as I

could, and then looked him in the eye.

And his eyes did that melty thing to my heart, and I wanted nothing more than to collapse in his arms.

But his arms stayed down at his sides.

I didn't have a place to melt anymore. I didn't have a soft spot to land. I broke my soft spot.

"Why did you do it?" Raf said. "Is that what this was all about? Getting a story?"

I glanced up and down the street, looking for another soft spot to land, but everything was hard, and there were only sharp edges and pointy objects and shards of glass and one wrong move would cut me.

Who was I kidding? I was already cut.

I could make up a story. I was good at writing. Maybe there was a guy with a gun to my head, demanding the *True Hollywood Story* of the Amadors. Maybe there was a drug that makes a person tell the truth, like that sodium pentothal, only this particular drug makes the person *type* the truth.

And then, further, it makes the person email the truth. To her best friend. Whose uncle works for *People* magazine. And then, magically, the drug makes the receiving reporter post the story.

"Sift through all those stories in your head, and pick the truth," he said. This time, there was no smile in his voice.

I could tell the truth. I *would* tell the truth. But if I omitted a couple of key things, maybe I could salvage this.

"That story wasn't supposed to go anywhere. I started it as

an experiment to see what was possible. And then I sort of kept going, for fun." I could taste the lie. "But then my friend Charlotte sent it to her uncle who works at *People*, and he printed it without my knowledge. I had no idea." I leaned toward him and put my hand on his chest, but the way his eyes cut to the hand on his chest made me remove it as quickly as I'd placed it there. "I didn't even know it was going to be out there until Charlotte emailed it to me today during our picnic. And I don't have your father's clout to quash a story."

He raised an eyebrow. "Did you really just use this opportunity to insult my father?"

"No! No. Well, yes, I guess, but I didn't mean it. I only meant . . ." What did I mean?

"You meant to excuse what happened by saying you couldn't do anything about it. But my question, Piper, is this." He moved closer and I was reminded how much taller he was than me. "Why did you write the story in the first place? I mean, you did write it, yes?"

"Yes."

"So you listened to me tell you the things that were most private to my soul, and you kissed me and told me everything was going to be okay, and then you went and wrote a story."

"At the time, it was before we kissed, and I thought they were only words on a screen," I said, and the second the words hit the air I wished them back. Why couldn't I get them back?

"Only words on a screen?" He shook his head in disbelief.

"You took my secrets, all my weaknesses, all my mistakes, and you turned them into a knife. You gutted me, Piper Baird."

Fritz stepped forward, appearing as if he'd stepped out the air. "Your father needs you back home. Now."

Raf kept his eyes on mine. "Do you have anything else to say to me?"

There had to be words out there that would give him comfort. That would make everything okay. That would bring the smile back to Raf's voice.

I was an expert with words. I used them all the time. Why couldn't I find the magic ones that would fix this?

Raf closed his eyes in a long blink. There were none. The ones to make everything better didn't exist.

"I'm sorry," I said, feeling the complete and spectacular inadequacy of those two little words. They felt as useless as trying to slay a dragon with a toothpick.

So I did the thing I always did in situations such as these (of which I'd been in one).

I ran inside, locked the door, and vowed never to leave again.

35

Seriously, I'm Not Leaving My House. Not Ever Again.

I made a list.

<u>WAYS TO MAKE IT BETTER</u>

Call the editor of *People* magazine and demand a
     retraction. . . .

Storm the Spanish embassy and demand forgiveness. . . .

Get Mack to hack into *People*'s website and remove every
     shred of evidence of the story. . . .

The next day, I faked sick and skipped school. Instead, I
called *People*. They refused to retract the story. As for storming
the embassy, I wasn't quite ready to be shot. Then I called Mack.

She said she wasn't smart enough to hack into *People*'s website, but maybe after four years at MIT she'd be able to do it. So in four years, it would be like it had never existed at all.

So then I crawled into bed and pulled my quilt up over my head. My mother got me out from under the covers that afternoon and said she had two cups of coffee waiting for us downstairs.

"I'm sick," I said."

"I don't think so," she replied.

I sighed and rolled out of bed. Trudged down the stairs and to the kitchen.

"I thought you were going out," I said.

She took a deep breath in. "I was, but then I read that article. Sit down, Pipe."

My chest contracted a bit. She pushed a mug of coffee toward me.

"What's up?" I said.

"Piper, you wrote it, didn't you?"

I hung my head.

My mom held out her hand to me, and I grabbed it. "Oh, Mom. I'm so screwed up. The Amadors are a good family. And yes, Raf sort of goes looking for trouble. And he finds it. But I think he has good reasons. And don't even get me started on his mom. . . ." The word vomit stopped for a moment.

My mom squeezed my hand. "You screwed up. You're not screwed up."

I couldn't help but smile.

"I'm assuming you didn't mean for the story to be published?"

I shook my head. "Never." That wasn't true. The lies needed to stop. "Well, at one time I did."

"Pipe, I've never totally understood your obsession with journalism, but how could you have ever thought this story was a good idea? Sure, maybe when you're working for a paper and the people you are covering are strangers. But these are your classmates. Your friends."

I lowered my head. "I thought . . . I thought the only thing I cared about was finding a way to pay for college."

My mom reached for the coffeepot and topped off my mug. "That's important. It is. I feel bad that we can't afford to take away that worry for you. But that can't be the *only* thing you ever think about."

"I know. I think I realized that."

"Then can I ask why you kept writing the story? And why you let Charlotte believe you still intended to publish it?"

"I didn't want Charlotte to know I was . . ." *Falling for the subject. Just say it. Falling for Raf.* "I didn't want her to know I was falling for . . . the guy. The story. It was unprofessional."

My mom sighed. "So you continued investigating the kids with diplomatic immunity and writing an article and interviewing sources and taking pictures and adding to the exposé, all because you didn't want to admit to your best friend that you had a crush?"

"Well, when you put it that way, it sounds a little ridiculous. But I was trying to be professional."

My mom put her hand up. "You're a teenager. You're not a professional, and you're not supposed to be. Let's stop the excuses. The fact of the matter is, you wrote this article. And because of that, you've given up your right to excuses. Now what are you going to do about it?"

I put my forehead on top of our joined hands. "I'm going to change my name to Phyllis Muffler and run away to Tahiti."

"What will you live on?"

"Lost potential and broken dreams and whatever I can get for the Toyota."

My mom tugged on the top of my head, urging me to look up. "I think your friends deserve more than that."

"There's nothing I can do. Besides, they're not my friends."

"Aren't they?"

I nodded. "Not anymore." I stifled a sob, feeling a full-on waterfall of tears coming my way.

"Oh, Pipe." She rubbed her thumb softly across my knuckles.

"Mom?"

"Yeah?"

"I just want to go to hide out at Gramma Weeza's. And I want to go back to Clarendon."

My mom let out a long breath. "Should I call you Phyllis from now on?"

"This isn't me running away. This is me going home. I tried Chiswick, and it didn't work out. I can go to Clarendon and take back my co–editor in chief job and hope for a scholarship to the community college."

"Going back to Clarendon sounds a bit rash. It also sounds like running away."

"It's not! Don't you think I'll still have to go through all this pain and humiliation at Clarendon? Changing locations doesn't mean I'm avoiding the problem. It just means I'm going to face this problem from home. That's all this is. It's time to go home."

My mom ran her fingers over my hair the way she used to when I was little and I would lay my head in her lap while we watched a movie. I put my head on the table.

"You'll get through this, sweetie."

"When? Tomorrow?"

"No."

"Next week?"

She paused stroking my hair. "No."

"I can't go to school tomorrow."

"You're going to school tomorrow."

Some reporter I'd turned out to be. Yes, I'd made it to *People* magazine, but I was pretty sure successful reporters weren't supposed to lose every single friend afterward. And run to their grandma's house so no one could find them.

Well, maybe they did. Not the running-to-Gramma's part but the losing their contacts when the story was an exposé. It was called an exposé for a reason. It exposed weaknesses and secrets and underbellies.

But probably professional reporters didn't fall in love with the subjects of their stories. I decided to make a list of things professional reporters didn't do.

PROFESSIONAL REPORTERS DON'T:

1. Interview someone and come away with only the fact that the interviewee's eyes twinkled in the porch light.
2. Notice twinkling eyes.
3. Christiane Amanpour never obsessed over the fact that a knee touched a head.
4. Ann Curry never got the dictator of Zimbabwe to talk by putting her head on his belly.
5. Raf will probably never speak to me again.
6. I'll never see him again.
7. Because maybe he's being sent back to Spain.
8. Because I ruined his life.
9. And exposed his deepest, darkest secrets.
10. What happened to my list? It didn't feel like a list anymore so much as an inventory of my broken heart.
11 . . .
11 . . .

I put my pencil down and kept packing. No point in dwelling on things I couldn't change. What was it that twelve-step programs taught?

God grant me the ability to accept the things I cannot change, change the things I want, and then disappear.

Okay, maybe I was remembering it wrong.

Another step was making amends. I knew this. At Clarendon I'd done a story on children of parents who were in the twelve-step program.

Making amends.

How does one make amends for ruining a life?

I pulled myself together, showered, and drove to Gramma Weeza's house.

When I stepped through the door, she was waiting for me. She wore black skinny jeans, had a T-shirt with a black leather jacket over it, and then, oddly enough, had finished the outfit with a 1950s apron around her waist.

Her arms were wide open, and when I reached her, I fell into them. And my seventy-eight-year-old grandma held me up.

She was a soft spot on which to land. Thank God for more than one soft spot in this world.

She didn't mention the "incident" until after we'd had coffee with a lot of sugar, and even then it was only in a very general manner.

"So, your mom filled me in on a bit of the kerfuffle."

I snorted. "'Kerfuffle.' That makes it sound almost fluffy and nice." I swigged a gulp of coffee and let it burn my tongue. "See, Gramma? This is what happens when you get detention. This is what happens when I live outside my"—air quotes—"'well-placed lines.'"

She didn't try to correct me or convince me otherwise. She didn't ask me why I would do such a thing. She just loved me unconditionally. And that's when the snot works started.

"Oh, dear. It's getting ugly," Gramma Weeza said. She handed me a box of tissues. "Start from the bottom of your face and work your way up."

I did as instructed, mopping up the tear/snot concoction at my chin and mouth and then focusing on my nose for a bit.

"I can't . . . I can't . . ." *I can't do it.*

"I know, dear. But you can."

"I'm not . . . . I'm not . . ." *I'm not going to survive.*

"I know, sweetie. But you will." Gramma kissed her fingertip and then pressed it against my forehead like someone affixing a gold-star sticker. "The human body is amazing in what it can withstand. Tomorrow you'll feel a little bit better. And then the next day you'll feel a little bit better. The third day, you'll feel worse, because people always feel worse on the third day, but then the fourth day, you'll feel a little bit better."

I shook my head, and the tear factory overwhelmed that ill-equipped box of tissues.

"Maybe we should call Dr. What's-His-Face," I said, referring to the one time I'd seen a therapist when my parents were worried about my obsessive attention to detail back in grade school. "This can't be normal. This can't be healthy. What if my body runs out of water because it cries it all out?"

Gramma Weeza left the room and returned with a towel, which she used to replace the wadded-up tissue in my hand.

"On the contrary, Piper. I think this is the healthiest thing you've ever done."

For the next few hours, I swam in a sea of tears, snot, tea, coffee, and sugar.

"Give yourself time to grieve," Gramma Weeza said as she brought me a fresh cup of coffee.

"I'm not grieving," I insisted. "I didn't care about them."

She nodded. "You just keep crying until your mouth figures out what your heart already knows," she said.

Fresh sobs rose in my chest. "I don't have a heart."

Gramma Weeza looked pointedly at the sea of used tissues surrounding the kitchen table. "All evidence to the contrary."

I went to her bedroom and rolled myself up in the blankets like a giant burrito and imagined myself disappearing, but I didn't. The tears momentarily dried up and the sugar kept flowing and for the first time in a long time I smiled and I said, from under the blanket, "There's this boy named Rafael Amador."

"Go on," Gramma said. She'd been hovering.

"And this one night he whisked me away on a motorcycle and we broke through closed national park gates and ditched his security detail and broke some laws and then . . . he showed me the back side of water. I showed him the bottoms of planes."

"It sounds beautiful."

"It was."

"Tell me more."

Before I could, the doorbell rang. It was Charlotte. Gramma Weeza let her in and warned her to have a life jacket handy, and then she left us alone.

Charlotte sat down in a chair next to me. "I'm so sorry, Pipe. I never meant . . . I thought you were asking for my help. I didn't know it would hurt you so much. I thought you were too scared and you needed me."

"It's okay," I said. "I understand. I did everything in my power to make you think that publishing it was what I wanted. And it was. Until it wasn't. But I didn't tell you that. And I can be very convincing. I am a very, very good liar."

Charlotte squinted at me. "You seem different."

I felt my face and my cheeks and the puffy bags as big as mattresses under my eyes. "Yeah, I'm a mess."

"That's not what I mean by 'different,'" Charlotte said. "I just mean, yes, you're a mess. But I've never seen you in this much of a mess without some sort of plan."

"Welcome to the new me. I'm a mess and I don't have a plan. I don't even have a list. Or a subject heading for a list. Or a starting point."

Charlotte had this soft sort of reminiscent smile going on. "Remember when we were eight? And there was that one gully with all the fall leaves, like twelve feet deep? You suggested we try to see if we could actually swim in the leaves. We had leaves stuck in our hair for days."

I smiled. I remembered it not in the way where you replay a movie in your head, but in the way where the memory throws bits and pieces against your brain. The smell of the leaves. The sound of them crunching all around our flailing bodies. The feel of my mom scrubbing my head, cursing the nest of dirt and leaves that had made a permanent home there. The sight of Michael standing at the top of the ravine, looking at me like I was crazy.

"My mom finally gave up and had to cut my hair to within an inch of my scalp," I said.

"And you thought you looked like a boy, so you asked us all to call you 'Peter' until your hair was long enough to tuck behind your ears."

I did this sigh-mixed-with-laugh thing. "Where did those girls go?"

"We didn't go anywhere. We're the same people. When you convinced me to swim in leaves, you didn't have a plan. But it was the best day I'd had in years. I loved you. Plan or no plan."

The tears started again.

"Life jacket, Charlotte!" my grandma called from the other room. What, did she have a cup against the wall?

She hustled into the room with another towel. I buried my face in it and heaved giant sobs.

"This is what happens when you cork it up for years," Gramma

Weeza said. "At first I told her to let it all out. The problem is, this corked well runs deep."

Charlotte put her hand on my back and rubbed softly.

"What am I going to do, Charlotte?"

"I don't know. Have you talked to Rafael?"

"Not since he told me I ruined his life."

She sighed. "You'll get through this."

"How do you know?"

"Because it's either that or you die trying. And I don't think this is going to kill you."

I grimaced. "I think you're speaking too soon."

That night, I couldn't help but stalk the internet looking for news of Raf in the aftermath of the article. But there was nothing.

I went to Post-Anon. Maybe other people's misery would make me feel better. There was another entry of the poem about lost love.

> *Even though I'm out of chances*
> *You might notice in all my glances*
> *That I still love you, and my broken heart dances*
> *Just knowing that I had it good that one time*
> *Now all I've got is one last rhyme*

I shut my computer and hid under the covers and wondered how in the world I would make it to school in the morning.

36

As much as I tried to shut it out, Tuesday morning came. It sneaked through the crack at the bottom of my bedroom door and infiltrated the space between my window and the sill, and once it was inside, it bonked me on the head as if to say, *Wake up, world's biggest asshat.*

I checked my phone for any messages from Raf, but there was only one from Charlotte.

Charlotte: Thinking of you.

A knock came from my door, followed by Gramma Weeza's voice.

"Breakfast, Pipe."

"I'm not hungry," I mumbled.

"You need your energy," she said.

"I don't deserve energy," I said.

I heard her footsteps as she walked back down the hall. Usually she insisted on breakfast. It was always the biggest meal she prepared, and it sometimes resembled a dinner more than a breakfast. For my sixteenth birthday, she'd made me pork chops and rice. For breakfast.

But today she didn't pressure me. My situation must have been really pathetic if she was letting me off the hook so easily.

When I got to school, it was bad. Really bad. Like teen-movie bad, complete with fake coughs that sounded like "narc" and "bitch." My locker had a website scrawled across it in black permanent marker: "www.hopb.com."

Knowing it couldn't be anything good, I resisted checking it out for a full thirty seconds. When I gave in and looked it up on my phone, I gasped. A literal bottom-of-the-lungs gasp.

At the top of the page was a banner with a picture of me licking my hand. I recognized it as one night when I'd learned how to do a tequila shot one night at the embassy, but the angle and the way my eyes were closed made it look like I was passionately making out with my own hand.

The banner read: "Hate on Piper Baird."

Below it was some sort of mission statement.

Do you hate Piper Baird? So do we! Feel free to share your pictures or stories with us here. And since Piper values anonymity, don't bother leaving your name.

So many entries. So many unflattering pictures. Stupid cell phones with their cameras.

One anonymous poster even wrote a short story to go along with the hand-licking picture. The story was told from the perspective of my tongue, which I guess was creative.

Shutting off my phone, I straightened my spine and walked down the hallway, ignoring the glares and trying to ignore the tears streaming down my face, and hoping and not hoping for a glance of Raf.

When I got to chemistry, Raf's usual seat was empty.

At lunch, Mack and Faroush were sitting at their usual table; and when I got my tray of food, I started toward a different direction—because who would want Benedict Arnold at their table?—but Mack motioned me over.

"You sure know how to cause quite the fracas," she said once I'd sat down. "I knew what you were doing, but I didn't realize how ruthless it was going to be."

I put my head down and knocked it against the table. "I know. I'm a horrible person."

"You're not horrible," she said. She didn't elaborate.

A loud crack of plastic hit the table and made me jump. Giselle had thrown her tray next to us and sat down.

She stared at me with seething in her eyes. "What. The. Hell."

"I'm sorry," I said. "I didn't mean for it to be published."

"Don't hide behind that bullshit. You meant it all along. You are a narcissistic psychopath."

I put my head back down on the table. "I think you mean 'sociopath.'"

"What's the difference?"

"A sociopath feels remorse."

She sighed. "I don't care." Her French accent was coming out more than I'd ever heard it before. "You broke my best friend."

"I know," I said.

"Why did you do it?"

I shook my head. "I was trying to pay for college."

She glared at me for a few long moments. "That's all you have to say?"

"I'm sorry," I said.

"That doesn't fix anything."

She grabbed her tray and stood up.

"Wait," I said.

"What?"

"Where is he?"

She closed her eyes and shook her head. "I'm not telling you shit."

She stalked away.

"Well, that was exciting," Faroush said.

"Ow," I answered.

They were silent for the rest of lunch, and for that, I was grateful.

In journalism, Jesse went through the rundown and assigned me a story on the controversy over the school's expansion project, and the property's neighbors who were signing petitions to thwart the move. It was a good story, the top one, so I was pretty sure Jesse felt bad for me. After the meeting, Professor Ferguson called me over to his desk.

"We need to talk," he said.

"I already know it was a bad story," I said, staring at my feet.

"Not a bad story," the professor said. "Not badly written. Actually quite compelling."

I looked up. "Then why are you frowning?"

He leaned back in his chair. "I think you have a hit-and-run approach to journalism."

"What's that supposed to mean?"

"It means you went from textbook journalism to suicide bomber. You go for the most damage, but at your own expense. I saw it in the story about the communications system changeover, which, as it turns out, was not instigated by a stalking situation. It was a technical malfunction. But the point is, you crossed bridges and then you burned them, leaving nowhere for you to go. Journalism is a game with rules. You have to learn how to play without blowing stuff up."

The pit in my stomach radiated throughout my entire body. "I think I understand," I said.

"One more thing," he said. "If I were you, I would make sure you have another option for college besides the Bennington."

My heart turned into an anvil as I nodded.

I dived into my assigned story, first interviewing angry neighbors and then trying to get a comment from Principal Wallace, who was making it very difficult for me to see him. Then I took a camera out to get some B-roll of the grounds and the houses nearby. Jesse texted me to see if I needed any help, but I told him I could do it on my own. Following the story was the only time I was, for just a moment, able to think about something other than how I'd messed everything up.

After school, Mack helped me put together the video footage of my story. We worked in silence mostly, but she spent extra time adding special effects to the video clips and sound engineering it so that my voice sounded a little less nasal.

Right as I was finished, I got a text message from Charlotte.

Charlotte: Meet me outside.

I put the finishing touches on the package and sent it off to Jesse and then gathered my things and went out to the roundabout in front of the school. Charlotte was there in her silver Prius.

She rolled down the window. "Get in," she said.

I obeyed.

She took off down the road and in the direction of Embassy Row.

"Where are we going?" I said, suspiciously.

"Number two on your list. We're going to storm the embassy and demand forgiveness," she said, turning on her windshield wipers. It had begun to snow, which meant all of DC would soon be shutting down.

"We're not even going to be able to get past the gate."

"We're going to try."

"And what would I say to him if we did get in?"

"You could start with 'I'm sorry' and go from there."

There was no use arguing anymore, and I didn't feel like trying. Instead, I pulled my knees into my chest and rested my chin on top and tried to take deep breaths.

Sooner than I wanted, Charlotte made a turn and the Spanish embassy came into view, with its red-and-yellow flags and ornate iron gate that seemed twice as tall as the last time I'd seen it.

Charlotte drove right up to the guard's gate and rolled down her window.

"Pipper Baird, here to see Rafael Amador."

"I'm sorry," the guard said. "He is unavailable."

"Could you just please use your little radio thing and let him know that she's here? And very contrite?"

"It is impossible."

"No, it's not," she said. "I can see the radio thing, and the button you would need to press."

"Charlotte," I started, but she shushed me.

"You just press that green button on top of your walkie-talkie and tell him."

I began to hope.

The guard shifted his weight from one foot to the other, and for a moment I thought he might be about to send his attack dogs at us. "Miss, it's not possible because Rafael is out of the country."

"What?" I blurted out. "Where?"

"I'm not allowed to say."

I practically crawled over Charlotte. "Is he back in Spain?"

"I'm not allowed to say. Please circle around and remove your car from the premises."

Charlotte frowned and did as she was told, and on the way back to Chiswick, she said, "Well, at least you can say you tried."

When I was a little girl, my mom used to buy this really expensive Irish butter from the specialty store. It was rich and creamy and it made her fresh bread taste better than any cake. And if I ever felt sad, or I was having a bad day, I used to sneak into the kitchen and use my finger to shovel small bites of cold butter into my mouth and it would make me feel better.

So today, I went home and tried the same thing with the cheap stuff we had now. And I gagged.

Rafael was out of the country. Probably back in Spain. I Googled his name, but no new stories came up. No explanations of where he was. No hints as to whether he would ever forgive me.

Not even butter could assuage the pain.

So to cope, I did the only thing I really knew how to do. I opened my laptop and started typing.

I had him here. His hand in mine. His fingers laced with my fingers.

I let go first.

And then I closed my laptop.

Sometimes writing was a release.

Sometimes it was an ascent up the face of a mountain, with no harness and no safety line.

Sometimes it was a leap off a cliff attached to a hang glider.

Sometimes it was a leap off a cliff attached to nothing.

Sometimes each word filled my soul.

And sometimes each word ripped a piece of it out. This was one of those times.

37

Over the next month, I dived into the school paper, sang extra loud for tips, and at night worked on my computer as much as my heart would let me.

My fingers were strong enough to hold him, and my will was strong enough to hold him, but the thing you don't understand, the thing you don't see coming, is that point when it's too late for your strength and your will to keep someone.

I finally stopped looking for Rafael. I didn't think even any of the DIs knew where he was, except maybe Giselle, and she would never tell me. In fact I was pretty sure she would never talk to me again. Which wasn't that hard because she had never talked that much to me in the first place.

Eventually, the nasty glares subsided, and the snickers in the hallways stopped, and one day, when I got to my locker, I saw that there was no fresh permanent marker on it. I considered that a good day.

I gave up on the living-on-tips story. Bottom line was, I couldn't.

So I was left grasping at air. At empty chairs. At water that could be caught only for a moment before it seeped between my fingers, or dried up. Gone.

I failed you.

I stuck with the stories that Jesse assigned or that I discussed with the department before I actually started writing them. By the time March was over, I was back in my form and was consistently scoring some of the top stories.

The only thing I had was that moment I would never get back. That great and terrible what-if.

What if I hadn't let go of his hand?

And when the deep freeze of winter was gone for good, I found a story. A big one. One that had all the elements of a Bennington winner.

Children in the community were losing teeth at a higher rate than in any other area in Fairfax County. I first discovered it when I heard my neighbor, who was a dentist, remark upon it to my dad.

I started to dig. And dig. First I made a list of things that could cause tooth loss and narrowed it to three factors: diet, tooth-care routines, and environment. The easiest way to check was to interview parents about tooth-care routines.

I didn't find anything, so I moved on to diet. Again, nothing that stuck out as different from any community in the country.

The third was environment. I began looking up stories of environmental oddities and found one about a local factory that had developed a leak in their waste process, allowing several toxins into the water supply.

There it was. It didn't take long to draw lines connecting the toxins and early tooth loss.

Professor Ferguson told me that the story was a contender. It would go up against Jesse's story, where he followed a marijuana plant from its growth to harvest to transportation to preparation to rolled-up joint.

It would be a tough competition, but at least I was a contender. More important, I'd found my passion for reporting again.

Then you came along. And you said those three words.

Not "I love you." But, "I've got you."

And you had me. And I had you.

The story got me attention, first from the local papers and then from the regional ones and then the news stations and then the national news.

Maybe I hadn't saved the world, but I'd saved a lot of teeth.

But I let go first. I let go and watched you fall to the ground. And then you let go and watched the ground swallow me up.

And for the second time in my life, I'm left with a haunting what-if.

What if I hadn't written the story that destroyed you?

By mid-April, the Bennington committee held the vote to determine the winner of the Bennington Scholarship.

Professor Ferguson told me it was the closest vote they'd ever seen.

Jesse won.

My savings account was empty and I had no Bennington and no Rafael.

But it didn't destroy you. At least, I don't think it did. If I know you, you're out there in the world scaling national treasures and ignoring fences and showing someone else the back side of water. But I hope you're not out there in the world hating me.

Because I love you.

There was nowhere to send my words. It wasn't newsworthy. It had no hook. No scandal. None of the hallmarks that make a good story.

I couldn't help thinking that Raf would want to see it, but if I was being honest, it was me who wanted him to see it. I didn't deserve that. He didn't deserve that. So I did the equivalent of sending it up in a balloon. I submitted it to the Post-Anon website. Three days later, it appeared on the site.

I read it one more time and said good-bye to Rafael Amador.

38

I didn't get the Bennington.

But I did get a scholarship to the University of Maryland, College Park, thanks in part to the letter of recommendation Professor Ferguson sent.

> . . . *Piper Baird was one of the brightest and most difficult students I've ever had, but what she lacks in manageability she makes up for in resourcefulness. You'd be a fool not to pay for her to come to your school.* . . .

The scholarship paid for everything including room and board. And the best part about it was that Charlotte would be going there too. She didn't have a scholarship, but it was a top-ten program and her parents could afford to help her. They even talked about renting a room for her near campus.

Late April brought the annual National Cherry Blossom Festival. The tradition commemorates the gift of three thousand cherry trees from Japan to Washington, DC. When they bloom, they blanket the perimeter of the tidal basin next to the Jefferson Memorial in a layer of pink. It was late this year, due to an unseasonably cold winter that seemed interminable.

On the morning of the middle Saturday of the festival, Charlotte texted me.

Charlotte: Hey! Want to meet at the Jefferson Memorial at noon?

The memorial was at the center of the cherry blossoms.

Me: Sure! Want to ride together? We can save on gas.

Charlotte: I can't. I'm going to be in DC beforehand.

Me: Why?

It took a few moments longer than usual to get a response.

Charlotte: Shopping. For college stuff. Lamps.

The answer seemed too detailed, but I shrugged it off.

Me: Okay. See you at noon.

Before I left, I opened my laptop and put together a little postcard collage made of various pictures of the Spanish flag, and I typed the words I'M SORRY over the top. Then I sent it in to Post-Anon.

It was the thirty-fifth *I'm Sorry* I had sent since my first message. Only two had been published on the site. The rest ignored. The people at Post-Anon were probably tired of receiving them.

I didn't know why I was doing it anymore. I guess I hoped that one day my apology would reach him.

Michael popped into my room as I was shutting my laptop.

"What are you doing?" he asked.

"An exercise in futility," I replied.

"I hate exercise."

I chuckled.

I took the metro to the Smithsonian station, the closest to the Jefferson Memorial but still a fifteen-minute walk. It was actually a gorgeous day to walk and contemplate the meaning of life and how I'd already screwed something up so bad. Did other people my age have this much regret?

Maybe. But right now, I felt alone in the weight of it.

The wind picked up, and pink cherry blossom leaves floated and danced above my head. One of the things that make cherry blossoms so beautiful is the fact that they're so ephemoral. They bloom all at once, and then just when you're growing accustomed to the Tidal Basin being blanketed in brilliant pink, they're gone.

I was not about to make it a metaphor for life, or disappointment, or missing someone. That would be such a cliché, and reporters . . .

Who was I kidding? I wasn't a reporter. Yet.

I got to the steps at 12:05, but there was no Charlotte.

Just as I sat down, my phone rang. The number was one I didn't recognize. I swiped it open.

"Hello?" I said.

There was a pause.

"Hello?" I said again.

"Did you mean it?"

It was Raf's voice. His smooth rich voice. I'd know it anywhere. I bit my lip and put my hand over my heart to keep it from bursting through my lungs.

"Did I mean what?"

"What you wrote."

I shook my head even though I knew he couldn't see me. "No. I didn't mean it. I should never have written it. I am so sorry. I thought about all the things I would say to you if I ever got to speak to you again, but now they just all seem so trite and inadequate. I was stupid. So stupid. Seriously, dumb as dirt. And . . . did I say stupid?" My voice trailed off.

"Keep going," he said.

"So so stupid. I just . . . Ever since I was twelve I've been obsessed with how to pay for college, and I got it in my head that this was the only way. The tips I make at the Yogurt Shop are nothing. I was desperate."

He was quiet on the other end for a few long moments.

"Okay, maybe that sounds like too much of an excuse. I'm sorry."

Quiet again.

"I wish you were here," I said.

"Why?"

"Because I'm looking at the prettiest cherry blossoms we've had in years. Seriously, they look like a nuclear bomb went off, only instead of fire and destruction, there . . . are . . . blossoms."

"Yeah, not the best analogy, is it?"

"No, it isn't."

He was quiet again, and I wanted to reach through the phone and touch his face.

"Where are you?" I said.

"I can't tell you."

"Oh," I said. He still didn't trust me. And rightly so.

"I miss you, Pip."

The words. The words. I'd let myself go so long without hoping I would ever hear them.

"Does that mean . . . you forgive me?"

He didn't answer for a long time. Hours.

"Yes," he said.

I blinked and a tiny tear fell down my cheek. "A fat lot of good that does, now that you're half a world away."

"At least you know I'm not out there somewhere in the world hating you."

My breath caught. "What?"

"I'm not out there in the world hating you."

Not out there in the world hating me. I'd written those words in my Post-Anon essay.

"So, did you mean what you wrote?" he said.

"You're not talking about the *People* article, are you?"

"No."

A couple more tears followed that first one, and I wiped my cheek with the palm of my hand.

"Don't cry, Pip."

"What? How do you know . . . ?" I looked left and right but didn't see anything.

"Your friend Charlotte sent me to the Post-Anon site. My dad filtered emails from you, but not from her."

I started down the stairs, desperately searching the throngs of people for that face. His face. Where was he?

"You said you loved me," he said. "Is that true?"

I fought my way through the crowd, going against traffic toward the cherry blossoms.

"Warmer," he said.

I smiled and scanned the crowds.

"Warmer," he said.

I was about ready to grab people and turn them around and then I saw him leaning against a tree, his phone up to his ear and a huge smile on his face.

I ran to him and he picked me up and kissed my face all over and I kissed his face off. Clean off.

* * *

"So you stayed with your uncle and finished your credits in Spain." We were lying on the grass, looking up at the blossoms that seemed to outnumber the stars in the sky, my head on Raf's belly. Where it belonged. Though not all the time, because that would be weird.

But it was where it belonged at this moment.

"Yep," Raf said. "And I learned to make the family sangria."

Fritz stood nearby, pretending not to notice our flagrant display of affection.

Raf told me that after the article came out, it was the last straw for his father, and he sent him to Andalusia immediately to live with his uncle and be homeschooled for the rest of the year. He took away his phone and restricted his internet access.

"But you must've been able to get on a computer somehow," I said.

His chest rose and fell. "Yes. But I couldn't bring myself to contact you."

I nodded. "I understand."

"But then last week, I got an email from your friend Charlotte, and she told me everything that had happened and then she sent me to the Post-Anon site."

"I didn't even know she'd seen the post," I said. "I didn't tell her about it."

"Well, your friend seems to know you very well." A soft breeze shook some blossoms loose, and they fell around us like falling stars. "Anyway, I read it, and I knew it was you, and afterward all I could think about was getting to you. Taking away at least one of your what-ifs."

I took his hand and put it on my stomach and felt his fingers and his knuckles and compared their lines with the ones in my memory. It all fit.

"What did your dad say?"

"Oh, he forbade me to come back."

"It's because I'm poor, right?"

He nodded. "Absolutely."

"So how did you get back?"

"Plane. And a cashier's check with my trust fund."

I shoved him softly and nestled closer. "Your parents disapprove because I'm poor. My parents will most likely disapprove because they read my article about you and all your shenanigans. And in the fall, I'll be going to the University of Maryland, and who knows where you'll be?"

"The University of Maryland."

"What?" I sat up and looked at him. His arms were bent, his hands under his head. He had this smile, and he was beautiful.

"They have a great chemistry department," he said.

"No! You're kidding me, right? Wait. Is that too sudden?"

"It's a college choice. Not a marriage proposal."

"So, you want the milk for free without buying the cow?"

He turned toward me and raised an eyebrow.

"It's an expression. A stupid . . . anyway, if we're on the same campus and this ends disastrously, and one of us has to dump me, or you, it will be very awkward—"

He stopped me with his lips. I didn't object.

ACKNOWLEDGMENTS

So many people to thank. So so many.

First off, to my amazing editor, Kristin Daly Rens. We sure went through the wringer on this one, didn't we? Or is it "ringer"? Was that question mark supposed to go inside or outside the quotation mark? ~~Does this acknowledgment feel flat? Could cut?~~ Yes, but what are your FEELINGS??

To Kristin's assistant, Kelsey Murphy, and to the amazing copyediting team. So many comments to input. So many discrepancies to correct. I don't know the color of my characters' clothes, but you do! And how on earth did you calculate the passage of days to figure out when Thanksgiving was?

To Alessandra Balzer and Donna Bray, for making me feel so at home.

To my agent, Michael Bourret. Seriously, did you think I'd ever be done with this &$%^$%$#ing book? Say yes. Because I need you to say yes. But I don't want to be needy. Because I'm not one of *those* authors who call their agents and dump all their emotional baggage. *Pulls up couch* But I remember it like it was yesterday, and I was all, "How about a book about diplomatic immunity? That should be easy. . . . And I'd especially like it if you could read my mind, and know what I'm thinking so I don't have to communicate. Got it?"

And to Lauren and Erin and the rest of the team at DGLM: high fives! *slaps on the bums*

To my poker group, all of whom have names in this book: I'm going to take your money. So, thank you.

To my family, especially my mom, who never wavers in her love and support, and my boys who can't seem to find the toilet with a map, thank you thank you thank you for being the best parts of my life. And to Sam, the best coparent a gal could ask for. And to Michael, who is my mom's new boyfriend. I'm so sure things will work out that I'm putting his name in a book. No pressure.

And to Mark Pett, who one day said to me, "I have this idea for a book about kids with diplomatic immunity who get away with everything." And then the next day, I took that idea and sold that book. Thank you for the inspiration and help, but I will never publicly admit the idea was yours in the first place. Taking that secret to the grave.

BRODI ASHTON

is also the author of *Everneath*, a *VOYA* Perfect 10 for 2011; *Everbound*; and *Evertrue*; and she is the author, with Cynthia Hand and Jodi Meadows, of *My Lady Jane*. She received a bachelor's degree in journalism from the University of Utah and a master's degree in international relations from the London School of Economics. Brodi lives in Utah with her family. You can visit her online at www.brodiashton.blogspot.com.

FOLLOW BRODI ASHTON ON